Easter Stories

EASTER STORIES

Classic Tales for the Holy Season

Compiled by Miriam LeBlanc
Woodcuts by Lisa Toth

PLOUGH PUBLISHING HOUSE

Published by Plough Publishing House
Walden, New York
Robertsbridge, England
Elsmore, Australia
www.plough.com

Copyright © 2015 by Plough Publishing House
All rights reserved.

ISBN: 978-0-87486-598-1
25 24 23 22 21 20   10 9 8 7 6 5 4

Illustrations by Lisa Toth.
Cover image by Rebecca Vincent, © Rebecca Vincent. Used by permission.

A catalog record for this book is available from the British Library.
Library of Congress Cataloging-in-Publication Data

Easter stories : classic tales for the holy season / compiled by Miriam
LeBlanc ; woodcuts by Lisa Toth.
     pages cm
  ISBN 978-0-87486-598-1 (pbk.)
  1. Easter--Literary collections I. LeBlanc, Miriam, compiler. II. Toth,
Lisa illustrator.
  PN6071.E2E3 2015
  808.8'0334--dc 3
                        2014040600

Printed in the United States of America

Carol of Hope

Jane Tyson Clement

The lambs leap in the meadow,
The larks leap in the sky,
and all the bells of heaven ring
because our Lord rides by.

The sun lies golden on the bank,
warmth wakens in the deepest root;
like golden stars the celandine
now opens to the day;
the sherds of winter blow away
and buds break unconfined.

Stars of the heart, now open wide!
All frozen roots that once had died,
rise again, oh rise!

The lambs leap in the meadow,
The larks leap in the sky,
and all the bells of heaven ring
because our Lord rides by.

Contents

The White Lily

Jane Tyson Clement

Adapted from Frances Jenkins Olcott

ONCE LONG AGO, near a village far away, there lived an old peasant known as Ivan. He had a little hut, a small garden, a dog named Rubles, and a six-year-old nephew, Peter, who was an orphan. Ivan was not a bad man, as he did not murder, did not steal, told no lies, and did not meddle in other people's business. But on the other hand he couldn't be called a good man either. He was cross and dirty. He seldom spoke, and then only grudgingly and unpleasantly. He paid no attention to his neighbors, never showed them kindness, and refused any small courtesy or friendliness they offered him. Eventually they paid no attention to him either and let him go his own way. As for Rubles the dog, he was afraid of his master and never went near him. He would follow him at a distance to the village and back, would bark at all strangers as watchdogs should do, and he would drive off the foxes that tried to molest the hens. So Ivan kept the dog and left scraps for him, but never stroked or praised him.

Peter was a silent little boy, since he was never spoken to except in anger. He had no friends, for the village children feared his uncle too much to come near him, and Peter was too shy to speak to anyone. So he ran wild in the woods and made up his own lonely games. He feared his uncle Ivan, who had never beaten him hard but had laid a stick to him now and then, and who spoke to him so fiercely that Peter was quite cowed and frightened.

All this was bad enough, but added to it was filth and ugliness. The little cottage was brown and bleak, the windows (there were two quite nice ones) grimy and stained, the wooden rafters sooty, and all the walls and corners full of cobwebs. On the floor were the scraps and leavings of many meals, and the mud dragged in from many rainy months. The hearth was black, the pots and kettles dingy, the big bed for Ivan and the trundle bed for Peter tumbled and unmade, the table littered and smeared, and the chairs half-broken. It was all a sorry sight, and no better outdoors, for the doorsill was tumble-down, weeds grew everywhere, the vegetables came up as best they might, and not a flower was to be seen.

The living things themselves were even worse. Rubles was thin and dirty and full of burrs. Poor Peter wore rags, his hair grew long and was tangled with straw from his bed, and he was so filthy one could scarcely see the boy beneath. As for Ivan, he was huge. His black hair and beard were unkempt, and he looked quite terrifying. His clothes were as black with age and no washings as his hair. He was so unpleasant to look at that all he met turned their heads away, wrinkled their noses, and passed him as quickly as possible.

One bleak March day, when it seemed as if all had been waiting for spring for many weeks, Ivan had to go to the village to fetch some beans. As he trudged along the road, homeward bound again, in the distance he saw a man coming toward him. Ivan was ready as usual to pass him by without a glance, but when he drew nearer, out of the tail of his eye Ivan noticed he was a stranger, and in spite of himself Ivan looked full at him. Then he could not look away. The stranger was young, tall and spare, in rough peasant dress, with a shepherd's staff. On one arm he carried a sheaf of white lilies, like the day lilies that grew wild in the fields, only so fair and glowing that they dazzled the eye. Ivan stopped in his tracks, and with a smile the stranger stopped also. While Ivan stared, the stranger looked him over slowly, from his broken boots to his lined and dirty face. Then he spoke:

"Good day, friend."

When there was only silence, with Ivan staring, the stranger spoke again.

"What is it you see?"

Ivan lifted his eyes then to the man's face. The light there was like the lilies, and he looked at them again.

"Those flowers . . . I never saw any so fair."

"One of them is yours," said the stranger.

"Mine?" said Ivan.

The stranger took one of them and offered it to Ivan, who with astonishment and unbelief exclaimed, "What do you want for it? I am a poor man."

"I want nothing in return, only that you should keep the flower clean and pure."

Ivan wiped his dirty hands on his coat and reached for the lily. His fingers closed around the stem, and he stood in the road staring at it for a long while, not knowing what to do with the precious thing now that he had it. When he looked up at last, the stranger had passed into the distance again. Carefully Ivan carried the lily home.

Once inside the door he stood doubtfully in the middle of the floor, looking all around at the filth and disorder and not knowing where to put the white shining lily. Peter had been sitting dejectedly by the dead fire, but now he stood up slowly, gazing at his uncle in amazement. At last he found his voice and said to him, "Where did you find it?"

And in a hushed tone Ivan answered, "A stranger gave it to me, for nothing, and told me only to keep it clean and pure. . . . What am I to do with it?"

In an eager voice Peter answered, "We must find something to hold it! On that high shelf you put an empty wine bottle last Easter. That would do."

"Then you must hold it while I fetch the bottle down. But your hands are too dirty! Draw water from the well and wash first!"

This Peter rushed to do, coming back at last with clean hands. Ivan carefully gave him the flower, but cried out when Peter put it to his face to smell it. "Wait! Your face is too dirty!" Ivan seized a rag and rushed outside to the well, where he drew a bucket of water and washed the rag first, and then came in and awkwardly scrubbed Peter's face. When he was through he stepped back, unbelieving, as the boy with care smelled the white flower. He thought he had never seen that boy before. Then he remembered the bottle and clambered up to get it. But it was dirty, too, and clogged with cobwebs. So out to the well it went, and came in clean and shining, filled with clear water. He set the lily in it and placed it on the windowsill. Then they both looked at it. Its glow lit the dim and dingy room, and as they looked at it a wonder rose in Ivan at all the filth around him. "This fair lily cannot live in such a place!" he said aloud. "I must clean it."

"Can I help?" asked Peter.

It was a hard task and took more than one day. Windows were washed, walls and floors swept and scrubbed, pots and kettles scoured, and chairs mended. The table was washed, the beds aired and beaten and put in order, and the hearth polished till the long-neglected tiles gleamed in the firelight and the pots and kettles winked back. The unaccustomed daylight flooded in the windows and the dark rafters shone in the shadows. All the while the lily glowed on the windowsill. When they were done, they looked about them in wonder and pleasure that the little house could be so fair. And then they saw each other.

"We don't belong in a house like this!" said Ivan. "Next we scrub ourselves."

By now he and the boy were friends, having worked so well together. So they scrubbed themselves, and Ivan went to the village to buy decent clothes for them both. He noticed Rubles following him at a distance. When he came home he thought to himself, "That dog is a sight, dirty and full of burrs. He doesn't belong to this house. He must be cleaned." But when he went to get him, the dog slunk away out of reach and feared to come to him. Ivan put gentleness into his tone, but it took nearly a day to win the dog, until with Peter's help he could brush him and wash him. After soft words and a good supper, Rubles no longer cowered and whined, but gazed at Ivan with a wondering love in his eyes, and beat his tail on the floor, and licked Ivan's hand. And Ivan felt a strange glow in his heart.

So all was well within. But without? What of the broken sill and the brown tumbled garden thick with last year's weeds? "A house like this cannot live in a garden like that," said Ivan in a cheerful voice. "We must clean it up." So they went to work, while Rubles sat on his haunches to look at them. And a neighbor passing by stopped to watch, perplexed and astounded and scarcely recognizing the two who worked.

"What are you staring at, neighbor?" called Ivan. "Come in to see our lily. But first go fetch your good wife."

And this the neighbor did, in haste and astonishment, eager to be friendly at last to the old man and his little boy.

For seven days the lily glowed and gleamed on the windowsill, and all the life around it was transformed. Then on the seventh day it vanished. There was no trace of it to be found, though Ivan and Peter searched for it everywhere. But when Ivan looked at Peter's face he thought, "The lily glows there still." When they saw the clean pure house, and spoke with love to each other, and greeted their neighbors, and tended the growing things in the new garden, each thought to himself, "The lily still lives, though we see it no longer."

The Coming of the King

Laura E. Richards

SOME CHILDREN were at play in their playground one day, when a herald rode through the town, blowing a trumpet and crying aloud, "The king! The king passes by this road today. Make ready for the king!"

The children stopped their play and looked at one another. "Did you hear that?" they said. "The king is coming. He may look over the wall and see our playground; who knows? We must put it in order."

The playground was sadly dirty, and in the corners were scraps of paper and broken toys, for these were careless children. But now, one brought a hoe, and another a rake, and a third ran to fetch the wheelbarrow from behind the garden gate. They labored hard till at length all was clean and tidy.

"Now it is clean!" they said. "But we must make it pretty, too, for kings are used to fine things; maybe he would not notice mere cleanness, for he may have it all the time."

Then one brought sweet rushes and strewed them on the ground; others made garlands of oak leaves and pine tassels and hung them on the walls; and the littlest one pulled marigold buds and threw them all about the playground, "to look like gold," he said.

When all was done, the playground was so beautiful that the children stood and looked at it and clapped their hands with pleasure.

"Let us keep it always like this!" said the littlest one; and the others cried, "Yes! Yes! That is what we will do."

They waited all day for the coming of the king, but he never came; only towards sunset a man, with travel-worn clothes and a kind, tired face, passed along the road and stopped to look over the wall.

"What a pleasant place!" said the man. "May I come in and rest, dear children?"

The children brought him in gladly and set him on the seat that they had made out of an old cask. They had covered it with the old red cloak to make it look like a throne, and it made a very good one.

"It is our playground!" they said. "We made it pretty for the king, but he did not come, and now we mean to keep it so for ourselves."

"That is good!" said the man.

"Because we think pretty and clean is nicer than ugly and dirty!" said another.

"That is better!" said the man.

"And for tired people to rest in!" said the littlest one.

"That is best of all!" said the man.

He sat and rested, and looked at the children with such kind eyes that they came about him and told him all they knew – about the five puppies in the barn, and the thrush's nest with four blue eggs, and the shore where the gold shells grew; and the man nodded and understood all about it.

By and by he asked for a cup of water, and they brought it to him in the best cup, with the gold sprigs on it. Then he thanked the children and rose and went on his way; but before he went he laid his hand on their heads for a moment, and the touch went warm to their hearts.

The children stood by the wall and watched the man as he went slowly along. The sun was setting, and the light fell in long slanting rays across the road.

"He looks so tired!" said one of the children.

"But he was so kind!" said another.

"See!" said the littlest one. "How the sun shines on his hair! It looks like a crown of gold."

How Donkeys Got
the Spirit of Contradiction

André Trocmé

Translated by Nellie Trocmé Hewett

On a Christmas Day during World War II in Nazi-occupied France, Pastor André Trocmé gathered his congregation together in the Protestant church in the small mountain village of Le Chambon. The people of the area had formed an underground network for saving refugees, many of them Jewish children. Fear kept them from talking much to each other – none of them knew which of their neighbors might betray them to the German occupiers. The rescuers of Le Chambon knew that they might face concentration camp or worse if found out.

Wishing to strengthen his congregation in their resolve to do what is right, Pastor Trocmé told them stories about Jesus' life. Later collected into a book, these original, child-like stories testify to the power of faith to enable ordinary people to risk their lives for strangers.

A Story about Saving Children, and the Courage It Takes to Go against Social Conventions and Expectations

UNTIL THE BIRTH OF JESUS, donkeys were like anyone else; that is, just like human beings. I mean just like grown-up human beings, not like children. Children have always had the Spirit of Contradiction. But donkeys used to be docile, just like grown-ups today.

Here is how things changed.

In Bethlehem at the entrance of the town lived a Samaritan. He was a good man. He tried as much as possible to help people forget he was a Samaritan. He thought, spoke, and dressed just like anyone else. He was a conformist.

Everyone respects social conventions. Each of us likes to welcome our guests into clean, well decorated homes. Our Samaritan, who was single and whose house was in disarray, preferred to receive no one. There was one exception – if his best friend warned him way ahead of time, he would allow him to come into his house.

Everyone belongs to a clique. We trust the members of our families and our intimate friends. We like to do them favors. But of strangers, everyone has distrust. We don't know whom we are dealing with.

So thought our Samaritan also.

Everyone is scared of traveling alone in deserted areas in the evening, when roads are especially dangerous. One hears so many terrible reports, so many stories about bandits! Our Samaritan, who was a peddler by trade, was always on the road. But just like everyone, he had common sense and managed not to be delayed.

So, our Samaritan was almost like everyone. He did own a donkey, and not everyone could boast about owning such a donkey.

Why the big fuss, you will say, about owning a donkey? Well, first of all, this donkey was indispensable. It was used as a truck, since in those days trucks had four legs instead of four wheels as they do today. The donkey carried heavy merchandise for the Samaritan. It carried the Samaritan's whole wealth.

Second, this donkey was a female, a very important fact for the rest of the story.

Third, one reason the Samaritan was so original was that his donkey was not like everyone. It had the Spirit of Contradiction.

Was the donkey, this female donkey, a descendant of Balaam's female donkey in the Old Testament? (Read the Book of Numbers, chapter 22, in the Bible.) Maybe. In any case, while other donkeys obeyed, this donkey was a thinking donkey, and its thoughts resulted in the most unexpected, the strangest, consequences.

Sometimes in the middle of the road the donkey came to a dead stop, smelling something with its grey muzzle. It resisted so firmly that neither blows nor shouts could force it to walk any further.

Oftentimes the donkey did just the opposite. It took off at a trot, its nostrils open to the wind, and nothing could stop it, neither the calls nor the angry objections of its master. Had a special smell or a light on the horizon attracted it? Then the donkey would come back much later, having satisfied its taste for adventure.

Everyone felt sorry for the poor Samaritan for owning such a donkey. He who wanted desperately to look like everyone else, suffered severely to stand out so noticeably.

Ridiculous confrontations occurred so often between him and his donkey that in faraway villages he was simply known as "the man with the donkey." People talked endlessly about his adventures.

But the most humiliating factor was that when the donkey opposed him and everyone else, the stupid animal ended up being right.

How the Donkey Revolted against the Rules of Social Conventions

VERY LATE ONE EVENING, a man and a woman came to the door of the Samaritan. It was on the eve of the census ordered by the Governor Quirinius.

"Can't you take us in?" they asked. "We come from far away and are very tired."

"Impossible," growled the Samaritan, thinking of his messy room. "Go elsewhere. There are hotels, and there are rich people with better lodging than I have."

"We just came from the village," answered the travelers, "and we knocked on every door. Everything is full. Wouldn't you have a place in your barn? We could sleep on the hay."

"I don't have a barn. I keep my hay in haystacks. I have only a stable."

"Oh! Put us in the stable," begged the woman. "I can't take one more step!"

"It is too little. Both of you would not fit in it," mumbled the peddler, lighting a torch to prove his point.

The stable was indeed very small and quite miserable. There was just enough room for the donkey that turned its head and stared at the flickering light of the torch with its big eyeballs.

"You see," said the owner, "it's impossible."

"If you only put a bale of straw under the manger, we could manage," suggested the woman.

Giving in to her persistence rather than to pity, the Samaritan accepted her idea. He untied the donkey to make it go out. For once, it would spend the night under the stars.

But the animal decided otherwise and launched a most ridiculous scene of stubbornness. Well-planted on its four legs, eyes protruding, nostrils dilated, it refused to move.

The Samaritan was furious. One really shouldn't let people sleep under the muzzle of an animal. It is not correct! He kept jerking hard on the halter, swearing at the stupid animal. But knowing its habits, he knew ahead of time that he would not make the donkey budge.

"Nothing doing," he said after a while, shrugging his shoulders.

"Leave it there," said Mary with a smile. "We'll get along fine with it."

They got along so well, in fact, that the donkey became the quiet and patient witness of the birth of Jesus.

Joseph put the newborn child in the manger, above Mary. This way the breath of the dozing animal kept the child warm. Its big body also kept the stable warm, so that the child and its mother didn't suffer anymore from the cold.

When he opened the door the next morning, the bewildered Samaritan discovered that the two travelers of the previous evening had become three.

"It is lucky my donkey refused to get out," said he to Joseph. "The frost was so deep last night that without her in the stable, the newborn child would certainly have died from the cold!"

"Once more," he murmured on his way home, "it is the donkey who was right and not me."

How the Donkey Taught Its Master about Helping Strangers

TEN DAYS LATER, Mary was up and nearly back to her normal health. Joseph was thinking about returning to Nazareth when, during the night, he was divinely warned of the threat hanging over the child's head. They must flee, he was told, before morning came; they must go to Egypt.

He woke Mary, but soon realized that she wasn't yet strong enough to take such a long trip on foot.

Joseph knocked on the door of the Samaritan.

"Lend me your donkey for one month," said he, "or for six weeks at the most. We must flee to Egypt and my wife is still weary."

"Don't even dream of it," answered the Samaritan. "I need my donkey to make a living, and also – I don't know you. How do I know you would bring it back?"

"I promise," said Joseph. "You can count on me."

"No way," cut in the Samaritan. "Can I trust the word of a stranger? The answer is no!"

Very worried, the new parents and their baby started out before dawn. Joseph walked ahead, making the trail. Mary followed, stumbling sometimes as she carried the child. But what was the galloping sound they heard from far away? Were Herod's soldiers pursuing them? Already?

No, it was the donkey, who soon caught up with them, sniffing them in the night with its wet muzzle. Possessed by one of its wild whims, the donkey had gnawed at its tie, escaped from the stable, and left on its night adventure.

Awakened by the noise, the Samaritan went out, calling his animal back but without success. "It followed those strangers," he exclaimed furiously. "Well, I have to resign myself to the loss. Ah, cursed be that animal! What will become of me without it to work?"

Six weeks later Herod had died, and the Samaritan looked up to see Joseph walking toward him. Mary sat on the donkey, holding the child.

"Your animal saved us," said Joseph. "Without it, my wife could not have gone very far. The king's soldiers would have discovered us and killed the child."

"I was wrong again," said the peddler to himself, full of gratefulness. "There are some honest people, even among strangers! One must learn to trust them. It is God's way."

How the Donkey Taught Its Master Courage

S EVERAL YEARS WENT BY. Conflicts between the donkey and its master became less frequent. Not that the animal had become more reasonable; instead, its master had, little by little, fallen into the habit of obeying the donkey. Its lunacy seemed wiser than the man's good sense.

One evening, and contrary to his habit, the Samaritan was delayed between Jerusalem and Jericho. His trip almost turned into tragedy.

He had heard about a band of robbers operating in that area, demanding money from travelers – that is, if they didn't kill them outright.

It was nightfall. The Samaritan spurred his animal on, exciting it as much as possible. Often he thought he heard soft steps behind him.

Suddenly the animal started one of its caprices and refused to advance any further. First the peddler pulled on the bridle. Then, overtaken by fear, he turned nasty. He tore the flesh in the donkey's mouth by jerking the bit roughly. Nothing changed the donkey's mind.

Discouraged, he stopped and started thinking. He was thinking of fleeing, of abandoning the animal and its precious cargo, when in the silence he heard a moan. He was not superstitious, but the noise in the darkness filled him with terror. Once more he tried to drag the animal along, but with its muzzle on the ground it arched its back and obstinately dug its hooves into the ground.

The moaning became a long wail. The Samaritan thought he detected a call coming from a ravine below the road. He thought to himself, "What if the donkey is right once more?" Mastering his fear, he walked down among the boulders and found an injured man who would die if he got no help. Using oil and wine, he dressed the wounds of this unfortunate man, hoisted him up on his donkey, and immediately took him to the nearest inn. He watched over him through the night. Whenever he saw him weaken, he poured a cordial between his clenched teeth to give him strength.

The next morning the wounded man felt better. Convinced that the donkey had shown him what God wanted, the Samaritan pulled out nearly all the cash he had, gave it to the innkeeper, and said, "Take care of him. If you spend more than that, I'll pay you on my way back."

Although the innkeeper had no donkey to advise him, he trusted the Samaritan.

How the Donkey
Found What It Was Looking For

THIRTY YEARS WENT BY. The Samaritan had left Bethlehem and moved to Bethphage by the gates of Jerusalem. It was a better location for his business.

The donkey was still alive. Donkeys live long, sometimes for thirty-five years. But this one's legs had become shaky, and its flanks had lost their luster and their fullness. Yet it was still the same courageous animal, only a little less original. In its mysterious animal consciousness, it had always looked for something, expected something. That's why it had not been like everyone, docile like those who do not look for anything.

Now death was approaching and the donkey had not found what it was looking for, neither in the tufts of grass nor on the distant horizon.

The donkey found some compensation, however. She had given birth to a little donkey, a shaggy and petulant foal, of which she was most proud. The foal was already strong and would soon be ready to work. The mother donkey had begun dreaming something like this: "He'll be the one to find what I always looked for."

Old people console themselves with comforting thoughts, hoping their children will someday accomplish what they haven't done themselves. And those children, when they grow old, will nurture the same dream. So it is with each generation.

One day, the donkey and its foal were tethered in front of their master's dwelling in Bethphage. Two men appeared, put their hands on the bridles, and appeared to be about to take the animals away.

The Samaritan made a big racket. Flying out of his room, he yelled to the passersby, "Thief! Thief!"

"The Lord needs them," the two strangers kept repeating.

"The Lord? The Lord? And who is the Lord?" shouted the indignant peddler. "These animals are mine. And, who are you? I don't know you."

"We'll return them to you," said the two men, who did look honest. "You can count on us."

The Samaritan was about ready to end the discussion with his usual answer – "No, the answer is no!" – when a faint memory came back to him, of a man and woman and his refusal to lend them his donkey long ago. They were strangers, and everyone would have done the same. You can't trust anybody. But then the donkey had run away, and it had been right in the end.

"Pull the old donkey by the bridle," he told the men. "It doesn't know you. If it obeys you, well, then we'll see!"

The man who held the donkey pulled, and the docile animal followed him, while its little foal trotted alongside.

When they were a short distance away, the peddler shouted to the disciples, "Take it to your Lord! This animal is always right!"

And without worrying anymore, he went into his house.

As the prophet predicted, it was at the Bethphage gate that Jesus saw the donkey and its foal coming toward him. (The story is in Matthew 21:1–9.) Along the roadside, he picked a bunch of fragrant grass and offered it to the old donkey.

The donkey smelled it longingly with its grey muzzle. This was exactly what it had always looked for. A hundred times through the years it had trotted on this very same path and had hastily grazed this kind of grass. But today the grass held a new fragrance and flavor.

In their confused minds, as you know, animals see God less clearly than we do. They see God through their masters. This time, from the hand of the true Master, the donkey received the nourishment it had always hoped to find.

Jesus straddled the young donkey "which had never before been ridden." The crowd spread clothing under its steps, and the old donkey followed behind, trampling it with its hooves.

A multitude of disciples waved palm branches, crying out, "Blessed be the kingdom which is coming, the kingdom of David, our father!"

When the procession reached the slope of the Mount of Olives, the old donkey noticed the white wall of Jerusalem. Through the years the donkey had traveled this path countless times, setting its eyes on the spectacle with the indifference common to animals. But today, these brilliant walls shining on the horizon seemed to be the sides of a Stable which it had always dreamed about and looked for.

The donkey raised its head and walked ahead more bravely.

Yet there was even more for the animal than the satisfaction carried by the fragrant grass and the vision of the Stable. On that morning, the old donkey also experienced the noblest of joys. It found itself in the middle of a large crowd acclaiming a King. And it had become the servant of this Prince who, it believed, was truly noble and truly good.

The old donkey's soul felt overwhelmed with joy. True, the Creator had assigned the animal to the humblest of duties; but it saw its little donkey assigned to a place of honor. Until death came, the old donkey would happily remain in last place, following the steps of its own offspring.

So why do you think donkeys have the Spirit of Contradiction? Because the young donkey inherited his mother's temperament. Later on, he married and had lots of children.

The Church of the Washing of the Feet

Alan Paton

This story of reconciliation in apartheid-era South Africa, told by Alan Paton, author of Cry the Beloved Country, *takes place in an area called Bochabela. Karel Bosman, the superintendent of Bochabela, was a white man who had been much loved by all the people in the district because of his compassion and fairness. When he died, shortly before Holy Week, his funeral was to be held in a white Presbyterian church, and many black residents came to pay their respects. But when the pastor saw the mixed congregation sitting together in the church, he cancelled the service before it had begun. To the black people of Bochabela, this insult was intolerable; the young people were especially angry, and there was talk of retaliation. One local black pastor decided he needed to take action.*

THE REVEREND ISAIAH BUTI, pastor of the Holy Church of Zion in Bochabela, entered the room of the acting chief justice, if not with awe, then certainly with deference. And certainly with respect too, for not only did Judge Olivier occupy one of the highest seats in the land, but he was held in high esteem by the black people of Bloemfontein. Was he not the man who had tried to prevent Parliament from removing colored voters from the common roll?

The room was the biggest Mr. Buti had seen in his life. The table was also the biggest he had seen, and behind it was a grand carved chair, and behind the chair, portraits of those who had been chief justices of the Union of South Africa. And now from the chair rose the impressive figure of Acting Chief Justice Olivier, with his hand held out to his visitor.

—Welcome, Mr. Buti. I got your letter, and now you are here. Sit down and tell me all about it.

—Thank you, judge. I must first collect myself. I must get used to this room.

—Take your time. It's a very big room.

—There's much power in this room, judge.

The judge laughed.

—Not so much as people think, Mr. Buti.

—Judge, I wrote to you because I am anxious. I have lived in the Orange Free State all my life. Of course, we are a conquered people, but we have lived in peace with the white rulers. But things are changing, judge, and I am anxious that they should not change in the way they are changing now.

—What are you referring to, Mr. Buti? The killing of the police?

—Certainly that, judge. But not only that. I am referring to the feeling against whites. It is the worst I have known it to be.

—And the causes?

Mr. Buti gave a humble and apologetic smile.

—You know them as well as I do, judge.

—And what is the biggest?

—The pass laws, judge, perhaps most of all. You have heard those words, "temporary sojourner"?

—Indeed.

—That's what we are, judge, temporary sojourners. Do you know the prayer of Chief Hosea Kutako?

—I have read it. But I do not remember it. What did he say?

—His prayer ended thus: O Lord, help us who roam about. Help us who have been placed in Africa and have no dwelling place. Give us back a dwelling place. O God, all power is yours in Heaven and Earth. Amen.

—Yes, I remember.

—That's what we are, judge. We have no dwelling place. The Government says I have a dwelling place in Thaba Nchu. They say my dwelling place is not here in Bochabela, where I live and work and have my wife and my children, and my church, the Holy Church of Zion. I am lucky, judge, because I am a minister. But most of the people of my church are workers. They work in white factories and white shops, they work for white builders and white carpenters. Our girls, and often our women too, work in white houses. Sometimes we feel, judge, that we have no meaning for white people except our work. My son works in a white factory and my two daughters work in white houses. But if I were to die, they would all be sent to Thaba Nchu. My wife is not allowed to rent a house, and my son is too young to rent one. Judge, you are a very busy man. Do you want to hear any more causes?

—No, Mr. Buti. The one you mention is cause enough.

—You see, judge, I am a minister. I am not likely to lose my job. But the men of my church often lose their jobs. Sometimes it is their fault, but sometimes it is not. The factory closes down, the white employer dies. The employer of Mr. Philemon Moroka died, and he could not get a job. So they told him he would have to give up his house and go back to Thaba Nchu with his wife and four children. Once you lose a house, judge, it is very hard to get another. If Mr. Moroka is offered another job in Bloemfontein, he will have to leave his wife and children and come to a single men's hostel in Bochabela. Then perhaps after a year he will get another house, and he will be able to bring his wife and children back. And sometimes it happens that, just after a man gets another house, he loses his job again, or he dies. The Moroka family are luckier than most, because his mother has a nice house in Thaba Nchu. But sometimes widows and their children are sent back and there is no house, and no work either. There is not much work in such places. That's the way we live, judge. We have been placed in Africa, and we have no dwelling place of our own.

Judge Olivier listened to Mr. Buti with much pain, not only pain for the people that Mr. Buti was talking about, but pain for his own impotence. How can the judge invoke the majestic power of the law when it is the law itself that is the cause of the injustice? What had Mr. Buti come to ask him? To do something that he had no power to do? He thought wryly of Mr. Buti's words that there was much power in this room.

It was almost as though the black man knew the white man was suffering, for his next words were meant to comfort.

—Judge, we have had more luck in Bochabela than in many other places. The laws have not been applied so harshly. Sometimes they have not been applied at all. You will find widows still living in Bochabela. That was the work of Mr. Karel Bosman. No one shouted at you in his offices. No one called you boy, no one called your wife Jane. They called us Bantu, of course, which is a word we do not like, but we never heard the word kaffir.

Then Mr. Buti was silent for a long time.

—The funeral service was very painful, judge. We wanted the people of Bloemfontein to see that we loved this man. We went there to show our love. But it wasn't wanted. I haven't come here to attack the church, my lord. I have come to ask you to do a work of reconciliation.

—Me?

—Yes, you, my lord.

—What can I do, Mr. Buti?

—Judge, every year on the Thursday before Good Friday we have in the Holy Church of Zion the service of the Washing of the Feet. Many people from other churches come to see it, and they are satisfied. This year the minister, that is myself, is going to wash the feet of Mrs. Hannah Mofokeng, who is the oldest woman in Bochabela. And my daughter is going to wash the feet of Esther Moloi, who is a crippled child. And I am asking you, Judge Olivier, to wash the feet of Martha Fortuin.

—Martha?

—Yes, judge.

—She has washed the feet of all my children. Why should I hesitate to wash her feet?

Mr. Buti's face was filled with joy. He stood up and opened wide his arms.

—Do you understand, judge, I want our people to see that their love is not rejected. Do you see that?

—Yes, I can see that.

—It will be simple, judge. I shall call out the name of Martha Fortuin, and she will come up and take a seat at the front of the altar. Then I shall call out the name of Jan Christiaan Olivier – you will not mind, judge, if I do not call you a judge?

—No.

—Then you come up to the altar, and I shall give you a towel to put round yourself, and then a basin of water. I shall take off her shoes, and you will wash her feet and dry them, and go back to your seat. Then I shall put on her shoes, and she will go back to her seat.

—Does she know that I am to wash her feet?

—She knows that her feet are to be washed, but she does not know who is going to wash them.

—Will she be embarrassed?

—I do not think so, judge. She is a holy woman. She knows the meaning of it. After all, the disciples' feet were washed by the Lord, and no one was embarrassed but Peter, and he was rebuked for it.

—There's one more thing, Mr. Buti.

—Yes, judge.

—She does not know. Then who does know?

—Only myself and my elders. And of course you, judge.

—Well, that is proper. You see, Mr. Buti, a judge can do this kind of thing privately. He is as free to do it as anyone

else. But a judge must not parade himself – you understand? – he must not . . .

—I understand, judge. Judge, you have made my heart
glad. For me, and for many of my people, this will be a
work of healing. I hope for our young people, too. You
know, judge, some of them think that white people do not
know how to love, so why should they love them? I told
them that Jesus said we must love our enemies, and one
bright boy said to me that Jesus never lived in Bochabela.

ON THE EVENING of the day before Good Friday, Judge
Olivier set out privately for the Holy Church of Zion in
Bochabela. He parked his car near the church and set out
to walk the short distance. As he passed under one of the
dim street lamps, he was recognized by a young reporter
by the name of David McGillivray, who was in Bochabela
following up a story, but who decided that it might be
better to follow the acting chief justice.

The judge was welcomed at the door by Mr. Buti and
was taken to a seat at the back of the church.

—I am sorry to put you at the back, judge, but I do not
want Martha to see you.

So it was that David McGillivray saw the washing of
the feet:

—Brothers and sisters, this is the night of the Last
Supper. And when supper was over, Jesus rose from the
table, and he put a towel round himself, as I do now in
remembrance of him. Then he took a dish and poured
water into it, and began to wash the feet of his disciples,
and to wipe them with the towel. And when he came to
Peter, Peter said to him, Lord, are you going to wash my

feet? And Jesus said, What I do now you do not understand, but you will understand it later. Peter said, You will
never wash my feet. Jesus said, If I do not wash your feet,
you will have no part in me. And Peter said, Lord, not only
my feet, but also my hands and my head. Jesus said, If I
wash your feet, you are clean altogether.

—Hannah Mofokeng, I ask you to come forward.

The old woman was brought forward by her son
Jonathan, a white-haired man of seventy. Mr. Buti washed
her feet and dried them, and told her to go in peace. Then
he called for Esther Moloi, the crippled child, who was
brought forward in her chair, and for Maria Buti, his own
daughter, who washed and dried Esther's feet. Then both
girls were told to go in peace.

—Martha Fortuin, I ask you to come forward.

So Martha Fortuin, who thirty years earlier had gone to
work in the home of the newly married Advocate Olivier
of Bloemfontein, and had gone with him to Cape Town
and Pretoria when he became a judge, and had returned
with him to Bloemfontein when he became a justice of
the Appellate Court, now left her seat to walk to the chair
before the altar. She walked with head downcast as becomes
a modest and devout woman, conscious of the honor that
had been done her by the Reverend Isaiah Buti. Then she
heard him call out the name of Jan Christiaan Olivier and,
though she was herself silent, she heard the gasp of the
congregation as the great judge of Bloemfontein walked
up to the altar to wash her feet.

Then Mr. Buti gave the towel to the judge, and the
judge, as the Word says, girded himself with it, and took
the dish of water and knelt at the feet of Martha Fortuin.

He took her right foot in his hands and washed it and dried it with the towel. Then he took her other foot in his hands and washed it and dried it with the towel. And as he was doing this, he thought how far these feet had walked for his family. And suddenly he saw Martha and his own daughter when she was a child, and he remembered clearly how Martha would kiss her feet. So he thought to himself, if she can kiss my daughter's feet, why can I not kiss her feet? Then he took both her feet in his hands with gentleness, for they were no doubt tired with much serving, and he kissed them both. Then Martha Fortuin, and many others in the Holy Church of Zion, fell a-weeping in that holy place.

Then the judge gave the towel and the dish to Mr. Buti, who said to him, Go in peace. Mr. Buti put the shoes back on the woman's feet and said to her also, Go in peace. And she returned to her place, in a church silent except for those who wept. Then Mr. Buti read again.

—So after he had washed their feet and had sat down, Jesus said to them, Do you understand what I have done? If I, your Lord and Master, have washed your feet, you ought also to wash one another's feet. For I have given you an example, that you should do as I have done to you.

But young David McGillivray does not hear these words. He has left the Holy Church of Zion, and has gone to find his editor at all costs.

YOUNG MCGILLIVRAY HAS got the story of the year, there can't be any doubt about that. In the whole of South Africa, his paper alone carried the great story, and it enjoyed pride of place for twenty-four hours because the afternoon papers don't publish on Good Friday. It was the front-page story, with great black headlines like those that tell of war, or the eruption of Krakatoa, or a rugby victory over New Zealand. Even on Saturday morning it was still the big story: "Acting Chief Justice Kisses Black Woman's Feet." No fewer than three papers had those identical words, and that's not surprising, for how else can you tell that story?

Well, for better or for worse, the story has gone round the nation. It's the kind of story that hardly any South African could be indifferent to. You either like it or you don't like it. They don't like it at all in the Palace of Justice or the Union Buildings. As for the judges in Bloemfontein, most of them don't like it. Such things are not done and, if they are done, they should not be seen to be done. Some people think that Judge Olivier did it on purpose, but those who know him well don't believe that at all. In fact most judges don't believe it. Probably no one reads a news item with greater clarity than a judge, and young McGillivray's story makes it quite clear that he was in Bochabela for quite another purpose.

Perhaps it's wrong to say that the story has gone right round the nation. *Die Stem* of Pretoria has not mentioned the strange happening in Bloemfontein and, as far as the South African Broadcasting Corporation is concerned, it didn't happen at all. The English press – ah well, of course, of course, but they do blow things up, don't they?

And on Saturday two of the great papers of the world, *The Times* of London and *The New York Times,* told the story. Stories like that place the South African ambassador in Washington in a most unsatisfactory position. In the

White House such an event is regarded as a redeeming act in the history of a wayward nation, but in the embassy it is regarded as an act destructive to the tireless propaganda that goes out in praise of separate coexistence and separate education and separate worship and separate lavatorial accommodation.

     —Judge.

     —Yes, Mr. Buti.

     —I am ashamed to look at you, judge. I didn't know that that young man was from the newspaper. You asked for it to be private, but now everybody knows it.

     —That's not your fault, Mr. Buti.

     —So you forgive me?

     —There is nothing to forgive. But if you wish me to forgive you for nothing, I do so.

     —That makes me feel better, judge. But apart from that, you did a great work. You helped to heal the pain of the Bosman funeral. There's nothing else that could have done it. I could preach a thousand sermons and I couldn't do it. I told you about the boy who said that Jesus taught that we should love our enemies because he did not have to live in Bochabela. He told me on Friday that he was sorry. And, judge, the people want to give a new name to the church. It will still be the Holy Church of Zion, because all our churches are called that, but they want to call the church in Bochabela the Church of the Washing of the Feet. Some wanted to call it the Church of the Kissing of the Feet, but most of them thought we must keep to the Bible.

     —Very sensible.

     —And I want to ask you one more thing, judge.

—Ask it then.

—It's not an easy question, judge. But people are saying the government will be angry with what you have done, and that you will not become the Chief Judge of South Africa. Is that so?

—I do not know, Mr. Buti. It may be so, and it may not. But taking part in your service on Thursday is to me more important than the chief-justiceship. Think no more about it. Think no more about it.

Stories from the Cotton Patch Gospel

Clarence Jordan

Based on Luke 22–24

Born out of the Civil Rights struggle, Clarence Jordan's classic rendering of the New Testament in the idiom of the American South brings the faraway places of scripture closer to home – the events of Jesus' life and death play out in Gainesville, Selma, Birmingham, Atlanta, and Washington, DC.

NOW THE ANNUAL MEETING, which is called the Convention, was drawing near. And the denominational executives and secretaries were trying to find a way to get rid of Jesus, for they didn't trust the people. Then the devil got into Judas Iscariot, who was one of the inner circle of twelve, and he went and discussed with the executives and detectives as to how he might turn Jesus over to them. They were real happy, and offered to pay him money. He agreed, and started looking for an opportunity to turn him over to them apart from the crowd.

Then the time came for what the program called "Alumni Banquets and Communion." So Jesus sent Rock and Jack with these instructions: "Go and make arrangements for us to have a banquet." They asked, "Where do you suggest we have it?" He replied, "Well, as you enter the city you'll meet a man carrying a pitcher of ice water. Follow him into the hotel that he enters and tell the hotel manager, 'The Professor says to ask you, "Where is the dining room where I'm to hold a banquet with my students?"' He'll show you a large room on the mezzanine. Get it in shape."

They went and found it exactly as he had said, and they got everything ready for the banquet.

When the hour arrived, he and the twelve sat down, and he said to them, "With a deep longing I've wanted to eat this annual fellowship meal with you before I suffer. For I'm telling you that I'll not eat it again until it has become a symbol of the God Movement."

And he took a cup, and having given thanks, he said, "Take this and share it among you. I tell you, from now on I'm not drinking 'fruit of the vine' until the God Movement has come."

And he took a loaf, and having given thanks, he broke it and gave it to them, saying, "This is my body.

"But even so, the man who'll turn me in is eating my food. Indeed, the Son of Man is going his predetermined way, but it will be hell for that fellow who turns him in."

And they began questioning among themselves as to which one of them might do such a thing.

Later they got into an argument over who was the most important. He said to them, "Big business men hold the reins over their subordinates, and those invested with authority are called 'executives.' But don't you all act that way. Instead, let the oldest among you be the same as the youngest, and the boss the same as the janitor. Now look, who's the greater, the one eating at the table or the one serving the table? The one eating, of course. But I'm taking the position of your servant. And you, you're the ones who have shared so deeply with me in my struggles. Now I'm outlining the Movement for you just as my Father outlined it for me, so that you can be my intimate associates in my Movement. And you'll be the twelve pillars of a new 'Reformation.'

"Simon! Simon! Look here! Satan begged to run all of you through the combine like heads of wheat. But I prayed over you particularly, that your faith might not cave in. And you, when you have got on your feet, help your brothers to stand up."

"Master," he replied, "I am ready to go with you to jail or death."

Jesus said to him, "Rock, I tell you that before the rooster crows at dawn, you'll have denied three times that you ever knew me."

He turned to them all. "When I sent you out without a wallet or a suitcase or walking shoes, did you lack for anything?"

They said, "Not a thing."

He said, "Okay, but now if you've got a wallet, go get it; and do the same if you have a suitcase. If you don't have either, sell your shirt and buy a switchblade. The fact is that it's going to happen to me just as this scripture says: 'And he was lumped with the lawless.' And it's just about here."

"Master, look here," they said. "We got two switchblades."

He said, "Forget it."

So he left, and as he had been in the habit of doing, he went out to Peach Orchard Hill. His students, too, went along. When they got there, he said, "Pray hard that you don't get in a bind."

He withdrew from them about a stone's throw and got down on his knees and prayed, "O Father, if you please, relieve me of this agony. But let your wish, rather than mine, be carried out."

(It seemed that an angel from heaven was strengthening him. And being in agony, he prayed the more fervently, and the sweat was pouring from him and onto the ground like blood from a fresh cut.)

And he got up from praying and came to his students, only to find them sleeping from their grief. He said to them, "Why are you sleeping? Get up and start praying so that you might not get in a bind."

Even as he was speaking, here comes a crowd, and the fellow named Judas, one of the twelve, was leading them. And he came up to Jesus to kiss him. Jesus said to him, "Judas, are you kissing the Son of Man goodbye?"

When those around him caught on to what would follow, they asked, "Master, shall we slash 'em with the switchblade?" And one of them slashed the bishop's lackey and chopped off his right ear.

"Stop it!" shouted Jesus, and he touched the ear and healed it.

He then said to the executives and church workers and officers who had come out to get him, "So you've come out with guns and clubs as though you were after a traitor? Every day I was at the church with you, and you didn't lay hands on me. But this hour, when darkness rules, suits you."

They grabbed him, took him away, and brought him into the archbishop's house.

Now Rock was trailing a good way behind. When they got a fire going in the backyard and had gathered around it, Rock sidled up, too. A teenage girl, catching a glimpse of his face in the light, started at him and said, "Hey, this fellow was with him."

But he denied it and said, "No, I don't know him, miss."

A little while later someone else saw him and said, "You over there, you were one of them."

Rock said, "Not me, mister."

About another hour passed and a man really jumped him and said, "I know positively this guy was with him, because he sounds like a Yankee."

Rock said to him, "Listen here, man, I don't know what you're talking about."

Right away, while he was saying it, the rooster crowed.

The Master turned and looked at Rock, and Rock recalled the Master's word when he told him, "Before the rooster crows at dawn, you will have denied me three times." And he walked away and cried like a baby.

And the men were shoving Jesus around and poking fun at him and slapping him. They blindfolded him and jeeringly asked, "Guess who socked you?" And many other insults they heaped upon him.

When day came, a "peoples' presbytery," composed of executives and professors, met and had him brought into the meeting room. They said, "If you are the Leader, tell us."

"When I tell you something," he answered, "you don't accept it, and when I ask you a question, you don't answer. From here on out, the Son of Man will be backed up by God's power."

They all said, "Well, then, does that mean you are God's Son?"

He replied, "It does indeed."

They said, "Do we need any further evidence? We ourselves have heard it straight from his own mouth."

Then the whole crowd of them got up and took him to Governor Pilate. They began by leveling these charges against him:

1. We have caught this fellow agitating our people.
2. He advocates the refusal to pay Federal taxes.
3. He claims to be the Leader of a Movement.

Pilate then asked him, "You are the Head of the Church?"

He answered him, "Yes, I am."

Pilate said to both the church executives and the people, "I don't find this man guilty of anything."

But they kept shouting and yelling, "He's agitating the people, spreading his ideas through the whole state of Georgia, all the way from Alabama to here."

When Pilate heard this, he asked if the man had ever lived in Alabama. On learning that he had been in Governor Herod's state, he sent him to Herod, who happened to be in Atlanta on that very day. When Governor Herod saw Jesus he was quite happy, because he had been hearing about him for a long time and had been wanting to see him. He thought he could get him to perform some miracle. He asked Jesus a lot of questions, but he never would answer him. The executives and leading ministers tore into him with all kinds of accusations. Governor Herod and his henchmen made wisecracks and poked fun at him, and finally dressed him up like a big politician and sent him back to Pilate. (From that day on, Herod and Pilate became friends with one another, although previously they had been at each other's throats.)

Then Pilate called together the executives and the leaders of the people, and said to them, "You brought this man before me as a rabble-rouser. Now look, I've heard the case publicly, and haven't found this man guilty of a thing that you're accusing him of. Nor did Herod, for he sent him back to us. Clearly he has done nothing to deserve death. So I'm going to whip him and let him go."

Howling like a mob, they said, "Do away with this guy! We want 'Daddy-boy'!" (This was a fellow who had been put in jail for inciting to riot in the city and for murder.)

Again Pilate addressed them, wanting to release Jesus. But they yelled back, "Kill him. Kill him."

The third time he said to them, "Why? What's his crime? I've found no reason to give him the death penalty. So I'm going to whip him and let him go."

But they screamed at the top of their voices, demanding that he be killed.

And their voices won.

Pilate decided to grant their request.

He released the one who had been put in jail for riot and murder, just as they asked, and he let them have Jesus to do to him as they pleased.

And so they led him away.

Along the road they grabbed Simon "the New Yorker" as he was coming in from the field. They made him walk behind Jesus and bear his cross.

There was a big crowd of people following him. There were some women who were sobbing and crying their hearts out over him. Jesus turned and said to them, "Dear sisters of the South, you need not cry over me. Rather, you should cry for yourselves and for your children. Because the time is surely coming when women will say, 'We wish we had been barren and never had a baby or ever nursed a child.' People will then begin to cry out to the mountains, 'Fall on us,' and to the hills, 'Cover us.' Because if they do things like this with green wood, what will they do with dry?"

The two other criminals were taken out with him to be killed. And when they came to a place called "Skull," there they killed him and the criminals, the one on his right and the other on his left.

Jesus said, "Father, forgive them, for they don't know what they're up to."

They rolled dice to see who would get his clothes.

The crowd stood around staring.

The leaders thumbed their noses at him. They said, "He saved others; let him save himself, if he is really God's special Leader."

The policemen, too, made fun of him. They offered him a drink of whiskey. They said, "Since you are the Head of the Church, save yourself."

One of the criminals hanging beside him railed at him, "Hey, you, ain't you the Leader? Save yourself and us."

But the other one rebuked him. He said, "Ain't you got no fear of God, seeing as how you're accused of the same thing he is? And we had it comin' to us, and got just what we deserved for what we done. But him, he ain't broke no law."

And he said, "Please, Jesus, remember me when you git your Movement goin'."

He said to him, "I tell you straight, today you'll be with me in highest Heaven."

It was already about noon. The sun's light went out and darkness settled over the land until three o'clock.

The big curtain in the sanctuary was split in two.

And calling out with a loud cry, Jesus said, "O Father, I'm placing my spirit in your hands." He said this and he died.

Now the police captain, when he saw how it had happened, praised God and said, "Surely this was a good man!"

The whole crowd, who had come along for the sight, when they saw how it all turned out, went home heaving great sobs.

And the people who had known him, with the women who had followed him all the way from Alabama, stood off in the distance to see what was going on.

And now, there was a man by the name of Joseph from the white suburb of Sylvan Hills. He was a member of the denominational board, and a good and honest man. (He himself had not voted for their plan of action. In fact, he was a God Movement sympathizer.) This man went to Governor Pilate and requested the body of Jesus. It was granted, and he took down the body and wrapped it in a sheer. Then he put it in a burial vault carved from the rock and in which no one had ever been buried.

It was late Friday afternoon. In just a little while it would be the Sabbath.

The women who had come along with Jesus from Alabama went with Joseph and saw the vault and how the body was placed in it. Then they went home and fixed some wreaths and potted plants.

They kept quiet on the Sabbath, like the Bible said they should.

But real early on the first day of the week, they came to the vault, bringing the flowers which they had fixed. They found the entrance stone rolled away from the vault, and when they entered they didn't find the body of the Lord Jesus. While they were wondering about this, two men in sparkling clothes stood before them. The women were very much frightened and turned their faces toward the ground. The men said to them, "Why are you looking for a live person among dead ones? Remember how he told you while he was still with you in Alabama that it would be necessary for the Son of Man to be abandoned into the hands of unsympathetic people, and to be lynched, and on the third day to rise?"

They did remember his words. They returned from the vault and told the whole story to the eleven and the rest. The women who were telling the apostles these things were Maria, "the Magdala girl," and Jo Ann and Maria James, and others with them. But it all seemed to the men like so much female chatter, and they wouldn't believe it.

But then on that same day, two of them were walking along the road toward a town named Austell, which is seventeen miles from Atlanta. They were talking with one another about all these recent events. While they were talking and raising questions, Jesus himself drew near and joined them. They didn't notice him closely and didn't recognize him. He said to them, "What's all this you're discussing as you walk?"

They just stood there with tears in their eyes. One of them named Clifford said to him, "Are you the only fellow from Atlanta who doesn't know the things that have happened there in these days?"

He said, "What things?"

They said, "Why, about Jesus the Valdostan, a powerful preacher both in his messages from God and in his public actions; how our leading ministers and officials got him a death sentence and killed him. And we were hoping all along he'd be the one who would get the church out of its mess. It has now been three days since he was killed.

"But you know, some of our women amazed us. Early this morning they went to the burial vault and didn't find his body. They came back and said they'd had a vision – had seen some angels who told them he was alive! Some of the rest of us went with them to the vault and found it just as the women had said, but we didn't see him."

He said to them: "Oh, how dense you are, and how sluggish your minds are in catching on to all that the prophets spoke! Can't you see how necessary it was for the Leader to suffer like this in order to be inaugurated Head?"

Then, beginning with Genesis and continuing on through the prophets, he explained to them various scriptures referring to himself.

They arrived at the town where they were going, and he kept walking as though he would continue on through. They warmly invited him in, saying, "Please stay with us, because it's late and the day is already over." So he went in to stay with them.

At supper time he took the bread and blessed it. Then he broke it and passed it to them. At that it dawned on them, and they recognized him!

And he became invisible.

They said to one another, "Weren't our hearts on fire inside of us while he was talking to us along the way and explaining the scriptures to us?" So they got right up, late as it was, and went back to Atlanta. There they found the eleven and some others gathered with them who were saying, "The Master has really and truly risen! Simon saw him!"

Then they began rehearsing all that had occurred along the road, and how they had recognized him when he broke the bread.

Even as they were discussing these things, Jesus himself stood in their midst. They were scared out of their wits and almost took off, because they thought they were seeing a ghost.

He said, "Why are you shaking so? And why are your minds so filled with doubts? Take a look at my hands. And my feet. See, it's me. Feel me. And keep looking. A ghost doesn't have flesh and bones, as you can clearly see that I have."

And while they were busting out all over with joy, and wondering if they could believe their own eyes, he asked, "Have you got anything around here to eat?"

Somebody brought him a piece of fried fish. He took it and ate it right there in front of them.

He said to them, "All this is what I was talking about while I was still with you – how everything written about me in the law of Moses and in the Prophets and Psalms had to take place."

Then he gave them the insight to understand the scriptures.

And he said to them, "The scriptures said that the Leader would suffer and be raised from the dead on the third day, and that there would be proclaimed in his name a change of attitude based on the giving up of sins against all races. Beginning in Atlanta, you all are the ones who'll make these things real. And listen, I myself am calling forth my Father's blessing on you. You all just stay right here in the city until you are charged with power from above."

He led them out toward College Park, and put his arms around them and blessed them. As he blessed them, he withdrew from them.

They went back into Atlanta with bounding joy. And they were continually in the church, praising God.

Saint Veronica's Kerchief

Selma Lagerlöf

Translated by Velma Swanston Howard

I

DURING ONE OF THE LATTER YEARS of Emperor Tiberius's reign, a poor vinedresser and his wife came and settled in a solitary hut among the Sabine mountains. They were strangers and lived in absolute solitude, without ever receiving a visit from a human being. But one morning when the laborer opened his door, he found, to his astonishment, that an old woman sat huddled up on the threshold. She was wrapped in a plain gray mantle and looked very poor. Nevertheless, she impressed him as compelling so much respect, as she rose and came to meet him, that it made him think of what the legends had to say about goddesses who, in the form of old women, had visited mortals.

"My friend," said the old woman to the vinedresser, "you must not wonder that I have slept this night on your threshold. My parents lived in this hut, and here I was born nearly ninety years ago. I expected to find it empty and deserted. I did not know that people still occupied it."

"I do not wonder that you thought a hut which lies so high up among these desolate hills should stand empty and deserted," said the vinedresser. "But my wife and I come from a foreign land, and as poor strangers we have not been able to find a better dwelling place. But to you, who must be tired and hungry after the long journey which you at your extreme age have undertaken, it is perhaps more welcome that the hut is occupied by people than by Sabine mountain wolves. You will at least find a bed within to rest on, and a bowl of goats' milk, and a bread-cake, if you will accept them."

The old woman smiled a little, but this smile was so fleeting that it could not dispel the expression of deep sorrow which rested upon her countenance.

"I spent my entire youth up here among these mountains," she said. "I have not yet forgotten the trick of driving a wolf from his lair."

And she actually looked so strong and vigorous that the laborer didn't doubt that she still possessed strength enough, despite her great age, to fight with the wild beasts of the forest.

He repeated his invitation, and the old woman stepped into the cottage. She sat down to the frugal meal and partook of it without hesitancy. Although she seemed to be well satisfied with the fare of coarse bread soaked in goats' milk, both the man and his wife thought: "Where can this old wanderer come from? She has certainly eaten pheasants served on silver plates oftener than she has drunk goats' milk from earthen bowls."

Now and then she raised her eyes from the food and looked around – as if attempting to realize that she was back in the hut. The poor old home with its bare clay walls and its earth floor was certainly not much changed. She pointed out to her hosts that on the walls there were still visible some traces of dogs and deer which her father had sketched there to amuse his little children. And on a shelf, high up, she thought she saw fragments of an earthen dish which she herself had used to measure milk in.

The man and his wife thought to themselves, "It must be true that she was born in this hut, but she has surely had much more to attend to in this life than milking goats and making butter and cheese."

They observed also that her thoughts were often far away, and that she sighed heavily and anxiously every time she came back to herself.

Finally she rose from the table. She thanked them graciously for the hospitality she had enjoyed, and walked toward the door.

But then it seemed to the vinedresser that she was pitifully poor and lonely, and he exclaimed, "If I am not mistaken, it was not your intention, when you dragged yourself up here last night, to leave this hut so soon. If you are actually as poor as you seem, it must have been your intention to remain here for the rest of your life. But now you wish to leave because my wife and I have taken possession of the hut."

The old woman did not deny that he had guessed rightly. "But this hut, which for many years has been deserted, belongs to you as much as to me," she said. "I have no right to drive you from it."

"It is still your parents' hut," said the laborer, "and you surely have a better right to it than we have. Besides, we are young and you are old; therefore, you shall remain and we will go."

When the old woman heard this, she was greatly astonished. She turned around on the threshold and stared at the man, as though she had not understood what he meant by his words.

But now the young wife joined in the conversation.

"If I might suggest," said she to her husband, "I should beg you to ask this old woman if she won't look upon us as her own children, and permit us to stay with her and take care of her. What service would we render her if we gave her this miserable hut and then left her? It would be terrible for her to live here in this wilderness alone! And what would she live on? It would be just like letting her starve to death."

The old woman went up to the man and his wife and regarded them carefully. "Why do you speak thus?" she asked. "Why are you so merciful to me? You are strangers."

Then the young wife answered: "It is because we ourselves once met with great mercy."

II

THIS IS HOW the old woman came to live in the vinedresser's hut. And she conceived a great friendship for the young people. But, for all that, she never told them whence she had come or who she was, and they understood that she would not have taken it in good part had they questioned her.

But one evening when the day's work was done and all three sat on the big, flat rock which lay before the entrance, and partook of their evening meal, they saw an old man coming up the path.

He was a tall and powerfully built man, with shoulders as broad as a gladiator's. His face wore a cheerless and stern expression. The brows jutted far out over the deep-set eyes, and the lines around the mouth expressed bitterness and contempt. He walked with erect bearing and quick movements.

The man wore a simple dress, and the instant the vine-dresser saw him he said, "He is an old soldier, one who has been discharged from service and is now on his way home."

When the stranger came directly before them he paused, as if in doubt. The laborer, who knew that the road terminated a short distance beyond the hut, laid down his spoon and called out to him, "Have you gone astray, stranger, since you come hither? Usually, no one takes the trouble to climb up here unless he has an errand to one of us who live here."

When he questioned in this manner, the stranger came nearer. "It is as you say," said he. "I have taken the wrong road, and now I know not whither I shall direct my steps. If you will let me rest here a while, and then tell me which path I shall follow to get to some farm, I shall be grateful to you."

As he spoke he sat down upon one of the stones which lay before the hut. The young woman asked him if he wouldn't share their supper, but this he declined with a smile. On the other hand, it was very evident that he was inclined to talk with them while they ate. He asked the young folks about their manner of living, and their work, and they answered him frankly and cheerfully.

Suddenly the laborer turned toward the stranger and began to question him. "You see in what a lonely and isolated way we live," said he. "It must be a year at least since I have talked with anyone except shepherds and vineyard laborers. Cannot you, who must come from some camp, tell us something about Rome and the emperor?"

Hardly had the man said this than the young wife noticed that the old woman gave him a warning glance, and made with her hand the sign which means, Have a care what you say.

The stranger, meanwhile, answered very affably, "I understand that you take me for a soldier, which is not incorrect, although I have long since left the service. During Tiberius's reign there has not been much work for us soldiers. Yet he was once a great commander. Those were the days of his good fortune. Now he thinks of nothing except to guard himself against conspiracies. In Rome, everyone is talking about how, last week, he let Senator Titius be seized and executed on the merest suspicion."

"The poor emperor no longer knows what he does!" exclaimed the young woman; and shook her head in pity and surprise.

"You are perfectly right," said the stranger, as an expression of the deepest melancholy crossed his countenance. "Tiberius knows that everyone hates him, and this is driving him insane."

"What say you?" the woman retorted. "Why should we hate him? We only deplore the fact that he is no longer the great emperor he was in the beginning of his reign."

"You are mistaken," said the stranger. "Everyone hates and detests Tiberius. Why should they do otherwise? He is nothing but a cruel and merciless tyrant. In Rome they think that from now on he will become even more unreasonable than he has been."

"Has anything happened, then, which will turn him into a worse beast than he is already?" queried the vinedresser.

When he said this, the wife noticed that the old woman gave him a new warning signal, but so stealthily that he could not see it.

The stranger answered him in a kindly manner, but at the same time a singular smile played about his lips.

"You have heard, perhaps, that until now Tiberius has had a friend in his household on whom he could rely, and who has always told him the truth. All the rest who live in his palace are fortune-hunters and hypocrites, who praise the emperor's wicked and cunning acts just as much as his good and admirable ones. But there was, as we have said, one alone who never feared to let him know how his conduct was actually regarded. This person, who was more courageous than senators and generals, was the emperor's old nurse, Faustina."

"I have heard of her," said the laborer. "I've been told that the emperor has always shown her great friendship."

"Yes, Tiberius knew how to prize her affection and loyalty. He treated this poor peasant woman, who came from a miserable hut in the Sabine Mountains, as his second mother. As long as he stayed in Rome, he let her live in a mansion on the Palatine, that he might always have her near him. None of Rome's noble matrons has fared better than she. She was borne through the streets in a litter, and her dress was that of an empress. When the emperor moved to Capri, she had to accompany him, and he bought a country estate for her there and filled it with slaves and costly furnishings."

"She has certainly fared well," said the husband.

Now it was he who kept up the conversation with the stranger. The wife sat silent and observed with surprise the change which had come over the old woman. Since the stranger arrived, she had not spoken a word. She had lost her mild and friendly expression. She had pushed her food aside and sat erect and rigid against the doorpost, and stared straight ahead with a severe and stony countenance.

"It was the emperor's intention that she should have a happy life," said the stranger. "But despite all his kindly acts, she too has deserted him."

The old woman gave a start at these words, but the young one laid her hand on her arm to quiet her. Then she began to speak in her soft, sympathetic voice. "I cannot believe that Faustina has been as happy at court as you say," she said as she turned toward the stranger. "I am sure that she has loved Tiberius as if he had been her own son. I can understand how proud she has been of his noble youth, and I can even understand how it must have grieved her to see him abandon himself in his old age to suspicion and cruelty. She has certainly warned and admonished him every day. It has been terrible for her always to plead in vain. At last she could no longer bear to see him sink lower and lower."

The stranger, astonished, leaned forward a bit when he heard this; but the young woman did not glance up at him. She kept her eyes lowered and spoke very calmly and gently.

"Perhaps you are right in what you say of the old woman," he replied. "Faustina has really not been happy at court. It seems strange, nevertheless, that she has left the emperor in his old age, when she had endured him the span of a lifetime."

"What are you saying?" asked the husband. "Has old Faustina left the emperor?"

"She has stolen away from Capri without anyone's knowledge," said the stranger. "She left just as poor as she came. She has not taken one of her treasures with her."

"And does the emperor really not know where she has gone?" asked the wife.

"No! No one knows for certain what road the old woman has taken. Still, one takes it for granted that she has sought refuge among her native mountains."

"And the emperor does not know, either, why she has gone away?" asked the young woman.

"No, the emperor knows nothing of this. He cannot believe she left him because he once told her that she served him for money and gifts only, like all the rest. She knows, however, that he has never doubted her unselfishness. He has hoped all along that she would return to him voluntarily, for no one knows better than she that he is absolutely without friends."

"I do not know her," said the young woman, "but I think I can tell you why she has left the emperor. The old woman was brought up among these mountains in simplicity and piety, and she has always longed to come back here again. Surely she never would have abandoned the emperor if he had not insulted her. But I understand that, after this, she feels she has the right to think of herself, since her days are numbered. If I were a poor woman of the mountains, I certainly would have acted as she did. I would have thought that I had done enough when I had served my master for a whole lifetime. I would at last have abandoned luxury and royal favors to give my soul a taste of honor and integrity before it left me for the long journey."

The stranger glanced with a deep and tender sadness at the young woman. "You do not consider that the emperor's propensities will become worse than ever. Now there is no one who can calm him when suspicion and misanthropy take possession of him. Think of this," he continued, as his melancholy gaze penetrated deeply into the eyes of the young woman, "in all the world there is no one now whom he does not hate; no one whom he does not despise – no one!"

As he uttered these words of bitter despair, the old woman made a sudden movement and turned toward him, but the young woman looked him straight in the eyes and answered, "Tiberius knows that Faustina will come back to him whenever he wishes it. But first she must know that her old eyes need never more behold vice and infamy at his court."

They had all risen during this speech; but the vinedresser and his wife placed themselves in front of the old woman as if to shield her.

The stranger did not utter another syllable, but regarded the old woman with a questioning glance. Is this *your* last word also? he seemed to want to say. The old woman's lips quivered, but words would not pass them.

"If the emperor has loved his old servant, then he can also let her live her last days in peace," said the young woman.

The stranger hesitated still, but suddenly his dark countenance brightened. "My friends," said he, "whatever one may say of Tiberius, there is one thing which he has learned better than others, and that is renunciation. I have only one thing more to say to you: If this old woman of whom we have spoken should come to this hut, receive her well! The emperor's favor rests upon anyone who succors her."

He wrapped his mantle about him and departed the same way that he had come.

III

AFTER THIS, the vinedresser and his wife never again spoke to the old woman about the emperor. Between themselves they marveled that she at her great age had had the strength to renounce all the wealth and power to which she had become accustomed. "I wonder if she will not soon go back to Tiberius?" they asked themselves. "It is certain that she still loves him. It is in the hope that it will awaken him to reason and enable him to repent of his low conduct, that she has left him."

"A man as old as the emperor will never begin a new life," said the laborer. "How are you going to rid him of his great contempt for mankind? Who could go to him and teach him to love his fellow man? Until this happens, he cannot be cured of suspicion and cruelty."

"You know that there is one who could actually do it," said the wife. "I often think of how it would turn out if the two should meet. But God's ways are not our ways."

The old woman did not seem to miss her former life at all. After a time the young wife gave birth to a child. The old woman had the care of it; she seemed so content in consequence that one could have thought she had forgotten all her sorrows.

Once every half-year she used to wrap her long, gray mantle around her and wander down to Rome. There she did not seek a soul but went straight to the Forum. Here she stopped outside a little temple which was erected on one side of the superbly decorated square.

All there was of this temple was an uncommonly large altar, which stood in a marble-paved court under the open sky. On the top of the altar, Fortuna, the goddess of happiness, was enthroned, and at its foot was a statue of Tiberius. Encircling the court were buildings for the priests, storerooms for fuel, and stalls for the beasts of sacrifice.

Old Faustina's journeys never extended beyond this temple where those who would pray for the welfare of Tiberius were wont to come. When she cast a glance in there and saw that both the goddess's and the emperor's statue were wreathed in flowers; that the sacrificial fire burned; that throngs of reverent worshipers were assembled before the altar; and when she heard the priests' low chants sounding thereabouts, she turned around and went back to the mountains.

In this way she learned, without having to question a human being, that Tiberius was still among the living, and that all was well with him.

The third time she undertook this journey, she met with a surprise. When she reached the little temple, she found it empty and deserted. No fire burned before the statue, and not a worshiper was seen. A couple of dried garlands still hung on one side of the altar, but this was all that testified to its former glory. The priests were gone and the emperor's statue, which stood there unguarded, was damaged and mud-bespattered.

The old woman turned to the first passerby. "What does this mean?" she asked. "Is Tiberius dead? Have we another emperor?"

"No," replied the Roman, "Tiberius is still emperor, but we have ceased to pray for him. Our prayers can no longer benefit him."

"My friend," said the old woman, "I live far away among the mountains, where one learns nothing of what happens out in the world. Won't you tell me what dreadful misfortune has overtaken the emperor?"

"The most dreadful of all misfortunes! He has been stricken with a disease which has never before been known in Italy, but which seems to be common in the Orient. Since this evil has befallen the emperor, his features are changed, his voice has become like an animal's grunt, and his toes and fingers are rotting away. And for this illness there appears to be no remedy. They believe that he will die within a few weeks. But if he does not die he will be dethroned, for such an ill and wretched man can no longer conduct the affairs of state. You understand, of course, that his fate is a foregone conclusion. It is useless to invoke the gods for his success, and it is not worthwhile," he added with a faint smile. "No one has anything more either to fear or hope from him. Why, then, should we trouble ourselves on his account?"

He nodded and walked away; but the old woman stood there as if stunned. For the first time in her life, old age seemed to have got the better of her. She stood with bent back and trembling head, and with hands that groped feebly in the air. She longed to get away from the place, but she moved her feet slowly. She looked around to find something which she could use as a staff. But after a few moments, by a tremendous effort of the will, she succeeded in conquering the faintness.

IV

A WEEK LATER, old Faustina wandered up the steep inclines on the Island of Capri. It was a warm day, and the dread consciousness of old age and feebleness came over her as she labored up the winding roads and the hewn-out steps in the mountain, which led to Tiberius's villa.

This feeling increased when she observed how changed everything had become during the time she had been away. In truth, on and alongside these steps there had always before been throngs of people. Here it used to fairly swarm with senators borne by giant Libyans; with messengers from the provinces attended by long processions of slaves; with office-seekers; with noblemen invited to participate in the emperor's feasts.

But today the steps and passages were entirely deserted. Gray-greenish lizards were the only living things which the old woman saw in her path.

She was amazed to see that already everything appeared to be going to ruin. At most the emperor's illness could not have progressed more than two months, and yet the grass had already taken root in the cracks between the marble stones. Rare growths planted in beautiful vases were already withered, and here and there mischievous spoilers whom no one had taken the trouble to stop had broken down the balustrade.

But to her the most singular thing of all was the entire absence of people. Even if strangers were forbidden to appear on the island, attendants at least should still be found there: the endless crowds of soldiers and slaves; of dancers and musicians; of cooks and stewards; of palace-sentinels and gardeners, who belonged to the emperor's household.

When Faustina reached the upper terrace, she caught sight of two slaves who sat on the steps in front of the villa. As she approached, they rose and bowed to her.

"Be greeted, Faustina!" said one of them. "It is a god who sends thee to lighten our sorrows."

"What does this mean, Milo?" asked Faustina. "Why is it so deserted here? Yet they have told me that Tiberius still lives at Capri."

"The emperor has driven away all his slaves because he suspects that one of us has given him poisoned wine to drink and that this has brought on the illness. He would have driven even Tito and myself away, if we had not refused to obey him; yet as you know, we have served the emperor and his mother all our lives."

"I do not ask after slaves only," said Faustina. "Where are the senators and field marshals? Where are the emperor's intimate friends, and all the fawning fortune-hunters?"

"Tiberius does not wish to show himself before strangers," said the slave. "Senator Lucius and Marco, commander of the Life Guard, come here every day and receive orders. No one else may approach him."

Faustina had gone up the steps to enter the villa. The slave went before her, and on the way she asked, "What say the physicians of Tiberius's illness?"

"None of them understands how to treat this illness. They do not even know if it kills quickly or slowly. But this I can tell you, Faustina, Tiberius must die if he continues to refuse all food for fear it may be poisoned. And I know that a sick man cannot stay awake night and day, as the emperor does for fear he may be murdered in his sleep. If he will trust you as in former days, you might succeed in making him eat and sleep. Thereby you can prolong his life for many days."

The slave conducted Faustina through several passages and courts to a terrace which Tiberius used to frequent to enjoy the view of the beautiful bays and proud Vesuvius.

When Faustina stepped out upon the terrace, she saw a hideous creature with a swollen face and animal-like features. His hands and feet were swathed in white bandages, but through the bandages protruded half-rotted fingers and toes. And this being's clothes were soiled and dusty. It was evident he could not walk erect, but had been obliged to crawl out upon the terrace. He lay with closed eyes near the balustrade at the farthest end, and did not move when the slave and Faustina came.

Faustina whispered to the slave who walked before her: "But Milo, how can such a creature be found here on the emperor's private terrace? Make haste and take him away!"

But she had scarcely said this when she saw the slave bow to the ground before the miserable creature who lay there.

"Caesar Tiberius," said he, "at last I have glad tidings to bring thee."

At the same time the slave turned toward Faustina, but he shrank back aghast and could not speak another word.

He did not behold the proud matron who had looked so strong that one might have expected that she would live to the age of a sibyl. For at that moment she had drooped into impotent age, and the slave saw before him a bent old woman with misty eyes and fumbling hands.

Faustina had certainly heard that the emperor was terribly changed, yet never for a moment had she ceased to think of him as the strong man he was when she last saw him. She had also heard someone say that this illness progressed slowly and that it took years to transform a human being. But here it had advanced with such virulence that it had made the emperor unrecognizable in just two months.

She tottered up to the emperor. She could not speak, but stood silent beside him and wept.

"Are you come now, Faustina?" he said without opening his eyes. "I lay and fancied that you stood here and wept over me. I dare not look up for fear I will find that it was only an illusion."

Then the old woman sat down beside him. She raised his head and placed it on her knee.

But Tiberius lay still, without looking at her. A sense of sweet repose enfolded him, and the next moment he sank into a peaceful slumber.

V

A FEW WEEKS LATER, one of the emperor's slaves came to the lonely hut in the Sabine mountains. It drew on toward evening, and the vinedresser and his wife stood in the doorway, watching the sun set in the distant west. The slave turned out of the path and came up and greeted them.

Thereupon he took a heavy purse which he carried in his girdle and laid it in the husband's hands.

"This, Faustina, the old woman to whom you have shown compassion, sends you," said the slave. "She begs that with this money you will purchase a vineyard of your own, and build you a house that does not lie as high in the air as the eagles' nests."

"Old Faustina still lives, then?" asked the husband. "We have searched for her in cleft and morass. When she did not come back to us, I thought that she had met her death in these wretched mountains."

"Don't you remember," the wife interposed, "that I would not believe that she was dead? Did I not say to you that she had gone back to the emperor?"

This the husband admitted. "And I am glad," he added, "that you were right, not only because Faustina has become rich enough to help us out of our poverty, but also on the poor emperor's account."

The slave wanted to say farewell at once in order to reach densely settled quarters before dark, but this the couple would not permit. "You must stop with us until morning," said they. "We cannot let you go before you have told us all that has happened to Faustina. Why has she returned to the emperor? What was their meeting like? Are they glad to be together again?"

The slave yielded to these solicitations. He followed them into the hut, and during the evening meal he told them all about the emperor's illness and Faustina's return.

When the slave had finished his narrative, he saw that both the man and the woman sat motionless, dumb with amazement. Their gaze was fixed on the ground as though not to betray the emotion which affected them.

Finally the man looked up and said to his wife, "Don't you believe God has decreed this?"

"Yes," said the wife, "surely it was for this that our Lord sent us across the sea to this lonely hut. Surely this was his purpose when he sent the old woman to our door."

As soon as the wife had spoken these words, the vinedresser turned again to the slave. "Friend!" he said to him, "you shall carry a message from me to Faustina. Tell her this word for word! Thus your friend the vineyard laborer from the Sabine mountains greets you. You have seen the young woman, my wife. Did she not appear fair to you, and blooming with health? And yet this young woman once suffered from the same disease which now has stricken Tiberius."

The slave made a gesture of surprise, but the vinedresser continued with greater emphasis on his words.

"If Faustina refuses to believe my word, tell her that my wife and I came from Palestine, in Asia, a land where this disease is common. There the law is such that the lepers are driven from the cities and towns and must live in tombs and mountain grottoes. Tell Faustina that my wife was born of diseased parents in a mountain grotto. As long as she was a child she was healthy, but when she grew up into young maidenhood she was stricken with the disease."

The slave bowed, smiled pleasantly, and said, "How can you expect that Faustina will believe this? She has seen your wife in her beauty and health. And she must know that there is no remedy for this illness."

The man replied, "It were best for her that she believed me. But I am not without witnesses. She can send inquiries over to Nazareth, in Galilee. There everyone will confirm my statement."

"Is it perchance through a miracle of some god that your wife has been cured?" asked the slave.

"Yes, it is as you say," answered the laborer, and then launched into this story:

One day a rumor reached the sick who lived in the wilderness: "Behold, a great prophet has arisen in Nazareth of Galilee. He is filled with the power of God's spirit, and he can cure your illness just by laying his hand upon your forehead!" But the sick, who lay in their misery, would not believe that this rumor was the truth. "No one can heal us," they said. "Since the days of the great prophets no one has been able to save one of us from this misfortune."

But there was one amongst them who believed, and that was a young maiden. She left the others to seek her way to the city of Nazareth, where the prophet lived. One day, when she wandered over wide plains, she met a man tall of stature, with a pale face and hair which lay in even, black curls. His dark eyes shone like stars and drew her toward him. But before they met, she called out to him, "Come not near me, for I am unclean, but tell me where I can find the prophet from Nazareth!" But the man continued to walk towards her, and when he stood directly in front of her, he said, "Why do you seek the prophet of Nazareth?"

"I seek him that he may lay his hand on my forehead and heal me of my illness." Then the man went up and laid his hand upon her brow. But she said to him, "What does it avail me that you lay your hand upon my forehead? You surely are no prophet?" Then he smiled on her and said, "Go now into the city which lies yonder at the foot of the mountain, and show yourself before the priests!"

The sick maiden thought to herself, "He mocks me because I believe I can be healed. From him I cannot learn what I would know." And she went farther. Soon after she saw a man who was going out to hunt, riding across the wide field. When he came so near that he could hear her, she called to him, "Come not close to me, I am unclean! But tell me where I can find the prophet of Nazareth!"

"What do you want of the prophet?" asked the man, riding slowly toward her.

"I wish only that he might lay his hand on my forehead and heal me of my illness."

The man rode still nearer. "Of what illness do you wish to be healed?" said he. "Surely you need no physician!"

"Can't you see that I am a leper?" she asked. "I was born of diseased parents in a mountain grotto."

But the man continued to approach, for she was beautiful and fair like a new-blown rose. "You are the most beautiful maiden in Judea!" he exclaimed.

"Oh, please, don't you too taunt me!" she replied. "I know that my features are destroyed and that my voice is like a wild beast's growl."

He looked deep into her eyes and said to her, "Your voice is as resonant as the spring brook's when it ripples over pebbles, and your face is as smooth as a coverlet of soft satin."

That moment he rode so close to her that she could see her face in the shining mountings which decorated his saddle. "You shall look at yourself here," he said to her.

She did so, and saw a face smooth and soft as a newly-formed butterfly wing. "What is this that I see?" she said. "This is not my face!"

"Yes, it is your face," said the rider.

"But my voice, isn't it rough? Doesn't it sound like wagons being drawn over a stony road?"

"No! It sounds like a zither player's sweetest songs," said the rider.

She turned and pointed toward the road. "Do you know who that man is, just disappearing behind the two oaks?" she asked.

"It is he whom you lately asked after; it is the prophet from Nazareth," said the man.

Then she clasped her hands in astonishment, and tears filled her eyes. "Oh, you Holy One! Oh, you messenger of God's power!" she cried. "You have healed me!"

Then the rider lifted her into the saddle and bore her to the city at the foot of the mountain and went with her to the priests and elders, and told them how he had found her. They questioned her carefully; but when they heard that the maiden was born in the wilderness of diseased parents, they would not believe that she was healed. "Go back from where you came!" they said. "If you have been ill, you must remain so as long as you live. You must not come here to the city to infect the rest of us with your disease."

She said to them, "I know that I am well, for the prophet from Nazareth laid his hand upon my forehead."

When they heard this they exclaimed, "Who is he, that he should be able to make clean the unclean? All this is but a delusion of the evil spirits. Go back to your own, that you may not bring destruction upon all of us!"

They would not declare her healed, and they forbade her to remain in the city. They decreed that each and every one who gave her shelter should also be adjudged unclean.

When the priests had pronounced this judgment, the young maiden turned to the man who had found her in the field. "Where shall I go now? Must I go back again to the lepers in the wilderness?"

But the man lifted her once more upon his horse, and said to her, "No, under no condition shall you go out to the lepers in their mountain caves, but we two shall travel across the sea to another land, where there are no laws for clean and unclean." And they –

But when the vineyard laborer had got thus far in his narrative, the slave arose and interrupted him. "You need not tell any more," said he. "Rather, stand up and follow me on the way, you who know the mountains, so that I can begin my home journey tonight and not wait until morning. The emperor and Faustina cannot hear your tidings a moment too soon."

When the vinedresser had accompanied the slave and come home again to the hut, he found his wife still awake.

"I cannot sleep," said she. "I am thinking that these two will meet: he who loves all mankind, and he who hates it. Such a meeting would be enough to sweep the earth out of existence!"

VI

OLD FAUSTINA was in distant Palestine, on her way to Jerusalem. She had not desired that the mission to seek the prophet and bring him to the emperor should be entrusted to anyone but herself. She said to herself, "That which we demand of this stranger is something which we cannot coax from him either by force or bribes. But perhaps he will grant it to us if someone falls at his feet and tells him in what dire need the emperor is. Who can make an honest plea for Tiberius, but the one who suffers from his misfortune as much as he does?"

The hope of possibly saving Tiberius had renewed the old woman's youth. She withstood without difficulty the long sea trip to Joppa, and on the journey to Jerusalem she made no use of a litter but rode a horse. She appeared to stand the difficult ride as easily as the Roman nobles, the soldiers, and the slaves who made up her retinue.

The journey from Joppa to Jerusalem filled the old woman's heart with joy and bright hopes. It was spring-time, and Sharon's plain, over which they had ridden during the first day's travel, had been a brilliant carpet of flowers. Even during the second day's journey, when they came to the hills of Judea, they were not abandoned by the flowers. All the multi-formed hills between which the road wound were planted with fruit trees which stood in full bloom. And when the travelers wearied of looking at the white and red blossoms of the apricots and persimmons, they could rest their eyes by observing the young vine-leaves, which pushed their way through the dark brown branches, and their growth was so rapid that one could almost follow it with the eye.

It was not only flowers and spring green that made the journey pleasant, but the pleasure was enhanced by watching the throngs of people who were on their way to Jerusalem this morning. From all the roads and bypaths, from lonely heights, and from the most remote corners of the plain came travelers. When they had reached the road to Jerusalem, those who traveled alone formed themselves into companies and marched forward with glad shouts. Around an elderly man, who rode on a jogging camel, walked his sons and daughters, his sons-in-law and daughters-in-law, and all his grandchildren. It was such a large family that it made up an entire little village. An old grandmother who was too feeble to walk, her sons had taken in their arms, and with pride she let herself be borne among the crowds, who respectfully stepped aside.

Truly, it was a morning to inspire joy even in the most disconsolate. To be sure, the sky was not clear but was overcast with a thin grayish-white mist, but none of the wayfarers thought of grumbling because the sun's piercing brilliancy was dampened. Under this veiled sky the perfume of the budding leaves and blossoms did not penetrate the air as usual, but lingered over roads and fields. And this beautiful day, with its faint mist and hushed winds which reminded one of night's rest and calm, seemed to communicate to the hastening crowds somewhat of itself, so that they went forward happy yet with solemnity, singing in subdued voices ancient hymns, or playing upon peculiar old-fashioned instruments, from which came tones like the buzzing of gnats or grasshoppers' piping.

When old Faustina rode forward among all the people, she became infected with their joy and excitement. She prodded her horse to quicker speed, as she said to a young Roman who rode beside her, "I dreamt last night that I saw Tiberius, and he implored me not to postpone the journey, but to ride to Jerusalem today. It appears as if the gods had wished to send me a warning not to neglect to go there this beautiful morning."

Just as she said this she came to the top of a long mountain ridge, and there she was obliged to halt. Before her lay a large, deep valley-basin surrounded by pretty hills, and from the dark, shadowy depths of the vale rose the massive mountain which held on its head the city of Jerusalem.

But the narrow mountain city, with its walls and towers, which lay like a jeweled coronet upon the cliff's smooth height, was this day magnified a thousandfold. All the hills which encircled the valley were bedecked with colorful tents and with a swarm of human beings.

It was evident to Faustina that all the inhabitants were on their way to Jerusalem to celebrate some great holiday. Those from a distance had already come and had managed to put their tents in order. On the other hand, those who lived near the city were still on their way. Along all the shining rock-heights one saw them come streaming in like an unbroken sea of white robes, of songs, of holiday cheer.

For some time the old woman surveyed these seething throngs of people and the long rows of tent-poles. Then she said to the young Roman who rode beside her, "Truly, Sulpicius, the whole nation must have come to Jerusalem."

"It really appears that way," replied the Roman, who had been chosen by Tiberius to accompany Faustina because he had for a number of years lived in Judea. "They celebrate now the great Spring Festival, and at this time all the people, both old and young, come to Jerusalem."

Faustina reflected a moment. "I am glad that we came to this city on the day that the people celebrate their festival," said she. "It cannot signify anything else than that the gods protect our journey. Do you think it likely that he whom we seek, the prophet of Nazareth, has also come to Jerusalem to participate in the festivities?"

"You are surely right, Faustina," said the Roman. "He must be here in Jerusalem. This is indeed a decree of the gods. Strong and vigorous though you be, you may consider yourself fortunate if you escape making the long and troublesome journey up to Galilee."

At once he rode over to a couple of wayfarers and asked them if they thought the prophet of Nazareth was in Jerusalem.

"In former years we have seen him here every day at this season," answered one. "Surely he must be here also this year, for he is a holy and righteous man."

A woman stretched forth her hand and pointed towards a hill which lay east of the city. "Do you see the foot of that mountain which is covered with olive trees?" she said. "It is there that the Galileans usually raise their tents, and there you will get the most reliable information about him whom you seek." They journeyed farther and traveled on a winding path all the way down to the bottom of the valley, and then they began to ride up toward Zion's hill to reach the city on its heights. The woman who had spoken went along the same way.

The steep ascending road was encompassed here by low walls, and upon these countless beggars and cripples sat or lolled. "Look," said the woman who had spoken, pointing to one of the beggars who sat on the wall, "there is a Galilean! I recollect that I have seen him among the prophet's disciples. He can tell you where you will find him you seek."

Faustina and Sulpicius rode up to the man who had been pointed out to her. He was a poor old man with a heavy, iron-gray beard. His face was bronzed by heat and sunshine. He asked no alms; on the contrary, he was so engrossed in anxious thought that he did not even glance at the passersby. Nor did he hear that Sulpicius addressed him, and the latter had to repeat his question several times.

"My friend, I've been told that you are a Galilean. I beg you, therefore, to tell me where I shall find the prophet from Nazareth!"

The Galilean gave a sudden start and looked around him, confused. But when he finally comprehended what was wanted of him, he was seized with rage mixed with terror. "What are you talking about?" he burst out. "Why do you ask me about that man? I know nothing of him. I'm not a Galilean."

The Hebrew woman now joined in the conversation. "Still, I have seen you in his company," she protested. "Do not fear, but tell this noble Roman lady, who is the emperor's friend, where she is most likely to find him."

But the terrified disciple grew more and more irascible. "Have all the people gone mad today?" said he. "Are they possessed by an evil spirit, that they come again and again and ask me about that man? Why will no one believe me when I say that I do not know the prophet? I do not come from his country. I have never seen him."

His irritability attracted attention, and a couple of beggars who sat on the wall beside him also began to dispute his word. "Certainly you were among his disciples," said one. "We all know that you came with him from Galilee."

Then the man raised his arms toward heaven and cried, "I could not endure it in Jerusalem today on that man's account, and now they will not even leave me in peace out here among the beggars! Why don't you believe me when I say to you that I have never seen him?"

Faustina turned away with a shrug. "Let us go farther!" said she. "The man is mad. From him we will learn nothing."

They went farther up the mountain. Faustina was not more than two steps from the city gate, when the Hebrew woman who had wished to help her find the prophet called to her to be careful. She pulled in her reins and saw that a man lay in the road, just in front of the horse's feet where the crush was greatest. It was a miracle that he had not already been trampled to death by animals or people.

The man lay upon his back and stared upward with lusterless eyes. He did not move, although the camels placed their heavy feet close beside him. He was poorly clad, and besides he was covered with dust and dirt. In fact, he had thrown so much gravel over himself that it looked as if he tried to hide himself, to be more easily overridden and trampled down.

"What does this mean? Why does this man lie here on the road?" asked Faustina.

Instantly the man began shouting to the passersby: "In mercy, brothers and sisters, drive your horses and camels over me! Do not turn aside for me! Trample me to dust! I have betrayed innocent blood. Trample me to dust!"

Sulpicius caught Faustina's horse by the bridle and turned it to one side. "It is a sinner who wants to do penance," said he. "Do not let this delay your journey. These people are peculiar, and one must let them follow their own bent."

The man in the road continued to shout, "Set your heels on my heart! Let the camels crush my breast and the asses dig their hoofs into my eyes!"

But Faustina seemed loath to ride past the miserable man without trying to make him rise. She remained all the while beside him.

The Hebrew woman who had wished to serve her once before, pushed her way forward again. "This man also belonged to the prophet's disciples," said she. "Do you wish me to ask him about his master?"

Faustina nodded affirmatively, and the woman bent down over the man.

"What have you Galileans done this day with your master?" she asked. "I meet you scattered on highways and byways, but him I see nowhere."

But when she questioned in this manner, the man who lay in the dust rose to his knees. "What evil spirit hath possessed you to ask me about him?" he said in a voice that was filled with despair. "You see, surely, that I have lain down in the road to be trampled to death. Is not that enough for you? Shall you come also and ask me what I have done with him?"

When she repeated the question, the man staggered to his feet and put both hands to his ears. "Woe unto you, that you cannot let me die in peace!" he cried. He forced his way through the crowds that thronged in front of the gate, and rushed away shrieking with terror, while his torn robe fluttered around him like dark wings.

"It appears to me as though we had come to a nation of madmen," said Faustina when she saw the man flee. She had become depressed by seeing these disciples of the prophet. Could the man who numbered such fools among his followers do anything for the emperor?

Even the Hebrew woman looked distressed, and she said very earnestly to Faustina, "Mistress, don't delay in your search for him whom you would find! I fear some evil has befallen him, since his disciples are beside themselves and cannot bear to hear him spoken of."

Faustina and her retinue finally rode through the gate archway and came in on the narrow and dark streets, which were alive with people. It seemed well-nigh impossible to get through the city. The riders time and again had to stand still. Slaves and soldiers tried in vain to clear the way. The people continued to rush on in a compact, irresistible stream.

"Really," said the old woman, "the streets of Rome are peaceful pleasure gardens compared with these!"

Sulpicius soon saw that almost insurmountable difficulties awaited them.

"On these overcrowded streets it is easier to walk than to ride," said he. "If you are not too fatigued, I should advise you to walk to the governor's palace. It is a good distance away, but if we ride we certainly will not get there until after midnight."

Faustina accepted the suggestion at once. She dismounted and left her horse with one of the slaves. Thereupon the Roman travelers began to walk through the city.

This was much better. They pushed their way quickly toward the heart of the city, and Sulpicius showed Faustina a rather wide street which they were nearing.

"Look, Faustina," he said, "if we take this street we will soon be there. It leads directly down to our quarters."

But just as they were about to turn into the street, the worst obstacle met them.

It happened that the very moment when Faustina reached the street which extended from the governor's palace to Righteousness Gate and Golgotha, they brought through it a prisoner who was to be taken out and crucified. Before him ran a crowd of wild youths who wanted to witness the execution. They raced up the street, waved their arms in rapture towards the hill, and emitted unintelligible howls in their delight at being allowed to view something which they did not see every day.

Behind them came companies of men in silken robes, who appeared to belong to the city's elite and foremost. Then came women, many of whom had tear-stained faces. A gathering of poor and maimed staggered forward, uttering shrieks that pierced the ears.

"O God!" they cried, "save him! Send your angel and save him! Send a deliverer in his direst need!"

Finally there came a few Roman soldiers on great horses. They kept guard so that none of the people could dash up to the prisoner and try to rescue him.

Directly behind them followed the executioners, whose task it was to lead forward the man that was to be crucified. They had laid a heavy wooden cross over his shoulder, but he was too weak for this burden. It weighed him down so that his body was almost bent to the ground. He held his head down so far that no one could see his face.

Faustina stood at the opening of the little by-street and saw the doomed man's heavy tread. She noticed with surprise that he wore a purple mantle, and that a crown of thorns was pressed down upon his head.

"Who is this man?" she asked.

One of the bystanders answered her: "It is one who wished to make himself emperor."

"And must he suffer death for a thing which is scarcely worth striving after?" said the old woman sadly.

The doomed man staggered under the cross. He dragged himself forward more and more slowly. The executioners had tied a rope around his waist, and they began to pull on it to hasten the speed. But as they pulled the rope the man fell, and lay there with the cross over him.

There was a terrible uproar. The Roman soldiers had all they could do to hold the crowds back. They drew their swords on a couple of women who tried to rush forward to help the fallen man. The executioners attempted to force him up with cuffs and lashes, but he could not move because of the cross. Finally two of them took hold of the cross to remove it.

Then he raised his head, and old Faustina could see his face. The cheeks were streaked by lashes from a whip, and from his brow, which was wounded by the thorn-crown, trickled some drops of blood. His hair hung in knotted tangles, clotted with sweat and blood. His jaw was firmly set, but his lips trembled as if they struggled to suppress a cry. His eyes, tear-filled and almost blinded from torture and fatigue, stared straight ahead.

But back of this half-dead person's face, the old woman saw, as in a vision, a pale and beautiful one with glorious, majestic eyes and gentle features, and she was seized with sudden grief – touched by the unknown man's misfortune and degradation.

"Oh, what have they done with you, you poor soul!" she burst out, and moved a step nearer him, while her eyes filled with tears. She forgot her own sorrow and anxiety, for this tortured man's distress. She thought her heart would burst from pity. She, like the other women, wanted to rush forward and tear him away from the executioners!

The fallen man saw how she came toward him, and he crept closer to her. It was as though he had expected to find protection with her against all those who persecuted and tortured him. He embraced her knees. He pressed himself against her, like a child who clings close to his mother for safety.

The old woman bent over him, and as the tears streamed down her cheeks, she felt the most blissful joy because he had come and sought protection with her. She placed one arm around his neck, and as a mother first of all wipes away the tears from her child's eyes, she laid her kerchief of sheer fine linen over his face to wipe away the tears and the blood.

But now the executioners were ready with the cross. They came and snatched away the prisoner. Impatient over the delay, they dragged him off in wild haste. The condemned man uttered a groan when he was led away from the refuge he had found, but he made no resistance.

Faustina embraced him to hold him back, and when her feeble old hands were powerless and she saw him borne away, she felt as if someone had torn from her her own child, and she cried, "No, no! Do not take him from me! He must not die! He shall not die!"

She felt the most intense grief and indignation because he was being led away. She wanted to rush after him. She wanted to fight with the executioners and tear him from them.

But with the first step she took, she was seized with weakness and dizziness. Sulpicius made haste to place his arm around her to prevent her from falling.

On one side of the street he saw a little shop and carried her in. There was neither bench nor chair inside, but the shopkeeper was a kindly man. He helped her over to a rug and arranged a bed for her on the stone floor.

She was not unconscious, but such a great dizziness had seized her that she could not sit up, but was forced to lie down.

"She has made a long journey today, and the noise and crush in the city have been too much for her," said Sulpicius to the merchant. "She is very old, and no one is so strong as not to be conquered by age."

"This is a trying day, even for one who is not old," said the merchant. "The air is almost too heavy to breathe. It would not surprise me if a severe storm were in store for us."

Sulpicius bent over the old woman. She had fallen asleep, and she slept with calm, regular respirations after all the excitement and fatigue.

He walked over to the shop door, stood there, and looked at the crowds while he awaited her waking.

VII

THE ROMAN GOVERNOR at Jerusalem had a young wife, and she had had a dream during the night preceding the day when Faustina entered the city.

She dreamed that she stood on the roof of her house and looked down upon the beautiful court, which, according to the Oriental custom, was paved with marble and planted with rare growths.

But in the court she saw assembled all the sick and blind and halt there were in the world. She saw before her the pest-ridden, with bodies swollen with boils; lepers with disfigured faces; the paralytics, who could not move but lay helpless upon the ground, and all the wretched creatures who writhed in torment and pain.

They all crowded up towards the entrance to get into the house; and a number of those who walked foremost pounded on the palace door.

At last she saw that a slave opened the door and came out on the threshold, and she heard him ask what they wanted.

Then they answered him, saying, "We seek the great prophet whom God hath sent to the world. Where is the prophet of Nazareth, he who is master of all suffering? Where is he who can deliver us from all our torment?"

Then the slave answered them in an arrogant and indifferent tone – as palace servants do when they turn away the poor stranger: "It will profit you nothing to seek the great prophet. Pilate has killed him."

Then there arose among all the sick a grief and a moaning and a gnashing of teeth which she could not bear to hear. Her heart was wrung with compassion and tears streamed from her eyes. But when she had begun to weep, she awakened.

Again she fell asleep; and again she dreamed that she stood on the roof of her house and looked down upon the big court, which was as broad as a square.

And behold! the court was filled with all the insane and soul-sick and those possessed of evil spirits. And she saw those who were naked and those who were covered with their long hair, and those who had braided themselves crowns of straw and mantles of grass and believed they were kings, and those who crawled on the ground and thought themselves beasts, and those who came dragging heavy stones which they believed to be gold, and those who thought that the evil spirits spoke through their mouths.

She saw all these crowd up toward the palace gate. And the ones who stood nearest to it knocked and pounded to get in.

At last the door opened and a slave stepped out on the threshold and asked, "What do you want?"

Then all began to cry aloud, saying, "Where is the great prophet of Nazareth, he who was sent of God and who shall restore to us our souls and our wits?"

She heard the slave answer them in the most indifferent tone: "It is useless for you to seek the great prophet. Pilate has killed him."

When this was said, they uttered a shriek as wild as a beast's howl, and in their despair they began to lacerate themselves until the blood ran down on the stones. And when she that dreamed saw their distress, she wrung her hands and moaned. And her own moans awakened her.

But again she fell asleep, and again, in her dream, she was on the roof of her house. Round about her sat her slaves, who played for her upon cymbals and zithers, and the almond trees shook their white blossoms over her, and clambering rose-vines exhaled their perfume.

As she sat there, a voice spoke to her: "Go over to the balustrade which encloses the roof and see who they are that stand and wait in your court!"

But in the dream she declined and said, "I do not care to see any more of those who throng my court tonight."

Just then she heard a clanking of chains and a pounding of heavy hammers, and the pounding of wood against wood. Her slaves ceased their singing and playing and hurried over to the railing and looked down. Nor could she herself remain seated, but walked thither and looked down on the court.

Then she saw that the court was filled with all the poor prisoners in the world. She saw those who must lie in dark prison dungeons, fettered with heavy chains; she saw those who labored in the dark mines come dragging their heavy planks, and those who were rowers on war galleys come with their heavy iron-bound oars. And those who were condemned to be crucified came dragging their crosses, and those who were to be beheaded came with their broad-axes. She saw those who were sent into slavery to foreign lands and whose eyes burned with homesickness. She saw those who must serve as beasts of burden and whose backs were bleeding from lashes.

All these unfortunates cried as with one voice: "Open, open!"

Then the slave who guarded the entrance stepped to the door and asked: "What is it that you wish?"

And these answered like the others: "We seek the great prophet of Nazareth, who has come to the world to give the prisoners their freedom and the slaves their lost happiness."

The slave answered them in a tired and indifferent tone: "You cannot find him here. Pilate has killed him."

When this was said, she who dreamed thought that among all the unhappy there arose such an outburst of scorn and blasphemy that heaven and earth trembled. She was ice-cold with fright, and her body shook so that she awaked.

When she was thoroughly awake, she sat up in bed and thought to herself, "I would not dream more. Now I want to remain awake all night, that I may escape seeing more of this horror."

But almost the very moment she thought this, sleep had overtaken her anew, and she had laid her head on the pillow and fallen asleep.

Again she dreamed that she sat on the roof of her house, and her little son ran back and forth up there and played with a ball.

Then she heard a voice that said to her: "Go over to the balustrade which encloses the roof and see who they are that stand and wait in your court!" But she who dreamed said to herself, "I have seen enough misery this night. I cannot endure any more. I would remain where I am."

At that moment her son threw his ball so that it dropped outside the balustrade, and the child ran forward and clambered up on the railing. Then she was frightened. She rushed over and seized hold of the child.

But with that she happened to cast her eyes downward, and once more she saw that the court was full of people.

In the court were all the peoples of earth who had been wounded in battle. They came with severed bodies, with cut-off limbs, and with big open wounds from which the blood oozed so that the whole court was drenched with it.

And beside these, came all the people in the world who had lost their loved ones on the battlefield. They were the fatherless who mourned their protectors, and the young maidens who cried for their lovers, and the aged who sighed for their sons.

The foremost among them pushed against the door, and the watchman came out as before and opened it.

He asked all these who had been wounded in battles and skirmishes, "What do you seek in this house?"

And they answered: "We seek the great prophet of Nazareth, who shall prohibit wars and rumors of wars and bring peace to the earth. We seek him who shall convert spears into scythes and swords into pruning hooks."

Then answered the slave somewhat impatiently: "Let no more come to pester me! I have already said it often enough. The great prophet is not here. Pilate has killed him."

Thereupon he closed the gate. But she who dreamed thought of all the lamentation which would come now. "I do not wish to hear it," said she, and rushed away from the balustrade. That instant she awoke. Then she discovered that in her terror she had jumped out of her bed and down on the cold stone floor.

Again she thought she did not want to sleep more that night, and again sleep overpowered her, and she closed her eyes and began to dream. She sat once more on the roof of her house, and beside her stood her husband. She told him of her dreams, and he ridiculed her.

Again she heard a voice, which said to her, "Go see the people who wait in your court!"

But she thought, "I would not see them. I have seen enough misery tonight."

Just then she heard three loud raps on the gate, and her husband walked over to the balustrade to see who it was that asked admittance to his house.

But no sooner had he leaned over the railing, than he beckoned to his wife to come over to him.

"Know you not this man?" said he, and pointed down.

When she looked down on the court, she found that it was filled with horses and riders. Slaves were busy unloading asses and camels. It looked as though a distinguished traveler might have landed.

At the entrance gate stood the traveler. He was a large elderly man with broad shoulders and a heavy and gloomy appearance.

The dreamer recognized the stranger instantly, and whispered to her husband, "It is Caesar Tiberius, who is here in Jerusalem. It cannot be anyone else."

"I also seem to recognize him," said her husband; at the same time he placed his finger on his mouth, as a signal that they should be quiet and listen to what was said down in the court.

They saw that the doorkeeper came out and asked the stranger, "Whom do you seek?"

And the traveler answered, "I seek the great prophet of Nazareth, who is endowed with God's power to perform miracles. It is Emperor Tiberius who calls him, that he may liberate him from a terrible disease which no other physician can cure."

When he had spoken, the slave bowed very humbly and said, "My lord, don't be angry! But your wish cannot be fulfilled."

Then the emperor turned toward his slaves, who waited below in the court, and gave them a command. Then the slaves hastened forward – some with handfuls of ornaments, others carried goblets studded with pearls, others again dragged sacks filled with gold coins. The emperor turned to the slave who guarded the gate and said, "All this shall be his, if he helps Tiberius. With this he can give riches to all the world's poor."

But the doorkeeper bowed still lower and said, "Master, don't be angry with your servant, but your request cannot be fulfilled."

Then the emperor beckoned again to his slaves, and a pair of them hurried forward with a richly embroidered robe upon which glittered a breast-piece of jewels. And the emperor said to the slave, "See! This which I offer him is the power over Judea. He shall rule his people like the highest judge, if he will only come and heal Tiberius!"

The slave bowed still nearer the earth and said, "Master, it is not within my power to help you."

Then the emperor beckoned once again, and his slaves rushed up with a golden coronet and a purple mantle. "See," he said, "this is the emperor's will: he promises to appoint the prophet his successor and give him dominion over the world. He shall have power to rule the world according to his God's will, if he will only stretch forth his hand and heal Tiberius!"

Then the slave fell at the emperor's feet and said in an imploring tone, "Master, it does not lie in my power to attend to your command. He whom you seek is no longer here. Pilate has killed him."

VIII

WHEN THE YOUNG WOMAN AWOKE, it was already full, clear day, and her female slaves stood and waited that they might help her dress.

She was very silent while she dressed, but finally she asked the slave who arranged her hair, if her husband was up. She learned that he had been called out to pass judgment on a criminal. "I should have liked to talk with him," said the young woman.

"Mistress," said the slave, "it will be difficult to do so during the trial. We will let you know as soon as it is over."

She sat silent now until her toilet was completed. Then she asked, "Has any among you heard of the prophet of Nazareth?"

"The prophet of Nazareth is a Jewish miracle performer," answered one of the slaves instantly.

"It is strange, mistress, that you should ask after him today," said another slave. "It is just he whom the Jews have brought here to the palace, to let him be tried by the governor."

She bade them go at once and ascertain for what cause he was arraigned, and one of the slaves withdrew. When she returned she said, "They accuse him of wanting to make himself king over this land, and they entreat the governor to let him be crucified."

When the governor's wife heard this, she grew terrified and said, "I must speak with my husband, otherwise a terrible calamity will happen here this day."

When the slaves said once again that this was impossible, she began to weep and shudder. And one among them was touched, so she said, "If you will send a written message to the governor, I will try to take it to him."

Immediately she took a stylus and wrote a few words on a wax tablet, and this was given to Pilate. But him she did not meet alone the whole day; for when he had dismissed the Jews, and the condemned man was taken to the place of execution, the hour for repast had come, and to this Pilate had invited a few of the Romans who visited Jerusalem at this season. They were the commander of the troops and a young instructor in oratory, and several others besides. This repast was not very merry, for the governor's wife sat all the while silent and dejected and took no part in the conversation.

When the guests asked if she was ill or distraught, the governor laughingly related how she had sent him the message that morning. He chaffed her because she had believed that a Roman governor would let himself be guided in his judgments by a woman's dreams.

She answered gently and sadly, "In truth, it was no dream, but a warning sent by the gods. You should at least have let the man live through this one day." They saw that she was seriously distressed. She would not be comforted, no matter how much the guests exerted themselves by keeping up the conversation to make her forget these empty fancies.

But after a while one of them raised his head and exclaimed, "What is this? Have we sat so long at table that the day is already gone?"

All looked up now, and they observed that a dim twilight settled down over nature. Above all, it was remarkable to see how the whole variegated play of color which it spread over all creatures and objects, faded away slowly, so that all looked a uniform gray. Like everything else, even their own faces lost their color. "We actually look like the dead," said the young orator with a shudder. "Our cheeks are gray and our lips black."

As the darkness grew more intense, the woman's fear increased. "Oh, my friend!" she burst out at last. "Can't you perceive even now that the immortals would warn you? They are incensed because you condemned a holy and innocent man. I am thinking that although he may already be on the cross, he is surely not dead yet. Let him be taken down from the cross! I would with my own hands nurse his wounds. Only grant that he be called back to life!"

But Pilate answered laughingly, "You are surely right in that this is a sign from the gods. But they do not let the sun lose its luster because a Jewish heretic has been condemned to the cross. On the contrary, we may expect that important matters shall appear, which concern the whole kingdom. Who can tell how long old Tiberius –"

He did not finish the sentence, for the darkness had become so profound he could not see even the wine goblet standing in front of him. He broke off, therefore, to order the slaves to fetch some lamps instantly.

When it had become so light that he could see the faces of his guests, it was impossible for him not to notice the depression which had come over them. "Mark you!" he said half-angrily to his wife. "Now it is apparent to me that you have succeeded with your dreams in driving away the joys of the table. But if it must needs be that you cannot think of anything else today, then let us hear what you have dreamed. Tell us the dream and we will try to interpret its meaning!"

For this the young wife was ready at once. And while she related vision after vision, the guests grew more and more serious. They ceased emptying their goblets, and they sat with brows knit. The only one who continued to laugh and to call the whole thing madness was the governor himself.

When the narrative was ended, the young rhetorician said, "Truly, this is something more than a dream, for I have seen this day not the emperor, but his old friend Faustina, march into the city. Only it surprises me that she has not already appeared in the governor's palace."

"There is actually a rumor abroad to the effect that the emperor has been stricken with a terrible illness," observed the leader of the troops. "It also seems very possible to me that your wife's dream may be a god-sent warning."

"There's nothing incredible in this, that Tiberius has sent messengers after the prophet to summon him to his sick-bed," agreed the young rhetorician.

The commander turned with profound seriousness toward Pilate. "If the emperor has actually taken it into his head to let this miracle-worker be summoned, it were better for you and for all of us that he found him alive."

Pilate answered irritably: "Is it the darkness that has turned you into children? One would think that you had all been transformed into dream-interpreters and prophets."

But the courtier continued his argument: "It may not be impossible, perhaps, to save the man's life, if you sent a swift messenger."

"You want to make a laughing-stock of me," answered the governor. "Tell me, what would become of law and order in this land if they learned that the governor pardoned a criminal because his wife has dreamed a bad dream?"

"It is the truth, however, and not a dream, that I have seen Faustina in Jerusalem," said the young orator.

"I shall take the responsibility of defending my actions before the emperor," said Pilate. "He will understand that this visionary, who let himself be misused by my soldiers without resistance, would not have had the power to help him."

As he was speaking, the house was shaken by a noise like a powerful rolling thunder, and an earthquake shook the ground. The governor's palace stood intact, but during some minutes just after the earthquake, a terrific crash of crumbling houses and falling pillars was heard.

As soon as a human voice could make itself heard, the governor called a slave.

"Run out to the place of execution and command in my name that the prophet of Nazareth shall be taken down from the cross!"

The slave hurried away. The guests filed from the dining-hall out on the peristyle, to be under the open sky in case the earthquake should be repeated. No one dared to utter a word while they awaited the slave's return.

He came back very shortly. He stopped before the governor.

"You found him alive?" he asked.

"Master, he was dead, and on the very second that he gave up the ghost, the earthquake occurred." The words were hardly spoken when two loud knocks sounded against the outer gate. When these knocks were heard, they all staggered back and leaped up as though it had been a new earthquake.

Immediately afterwards a slave came up. "It is the noble Faustina and the emperor's kinsman Sulpicius. They are come to beg you help them find the prophet from Nazareth."

A low murmur passed through the peristyle, and soft footfalls were heard. When the governor looked around, he noticed that his friends had withdrawn from him, as from one upon whom misfortune has fallen.

IX

OLD FAUSTINA HAD RETURNED to Capri and had sought out the emperor. She told him her story, and while she spoke she hardly dared look at him. During her absence the illness had made frightful ravages, and she thought to herself, "If there had been any pity among the celestials, they would have let me die before being forced to tell this poor, tortured man that all hope is gone."

To her astonishment, Tiberius listened to her with the utmost indifference. When she related how the great miracle performer had been crucified the same day that she had arrived in Jerusalem, and how near she had been to saving him, she began to weep under the weight of her failure. But Tiberius only remarked, "You actually grieve over this? Ah, Faustina! A whole lifetime in Rome has not weaned you, then, of faith in sorcerers and miracle workers, which you imbibed during your childhood in the Sabine mountains!"

Then the old woman perceived that Tiberius had never expected any help from the prophet of Nazareth. "Why did you let me make the journey to that distant land, if you believed all the while that it was useless?"

"You are the only friend I have," said the emperor. "Why should I deny your prayer, so long as I still have the power to grant it?"

But the old woman did not like it that the emperor had taken her for a fool. "Ah! this is your usual cunning," she burst out. "This is just what I can tolerate least in you."

"You should not have come back to me," said Tiberius. "You should have remained in the mountains."

It looked for a moment as if these two, who had clashed so often, would again fall into a war of words, but the old woman's anger subsided immediately. The times were past when she could quarrel in earnest with the emperor. She lowered her voice again; but she could not altogether relinquish every effort to obtain justice.

"But this man was really a prophet," she said. "I have seen him. When his eyes met mine I thought he was a god. I was mad to allow him to go to his death."

"I am glad you let him die," said Tiberius. "He was a traitor and a dangerous agitator."

Faustina was about to burst into another passion – then checked herself. "I have spoken with many of his friends in Jerusalem about him," she said. "He had not committed the crimes for which he was arraigned."

"Even if he had not committed just these crimes, he was surely no better than anyone else," said the emperor wearily. "Where will you find the person who during his lifetime has not a thousand times deserved death?"

But these remarks of the emperor decided Faustina to undertake something which she had until now hesitated about. "I will show you a proof of his power," said she. "I said to you just now that I laid my kerchief over his face. It is the same kerchief which I hold in my hand. Will you look at it a moment?"

She spread the kerchief out before the emperor, and he saw delineated thereon the shadowy likeness of a human face.

The old woman's voice shook with emotion as she continued, "This man saw that I loved him. I know not by what power he was enabled to leave me his portrait. But mine eyes fill up with tears when I see it."

The emperor leaned forward and regarded the picture, which appeared to be made up of blood and tears and the dark shadows of grief. Gradually the whole face stood out before him, exactly as it had been imprinted upon the kerchief. He saw the blood-drops on the forehead, the piercing thorn-crown, the hair matted with blood, and the mouth, whose lips seemed to quiver with agony.

He bent down closer and closer to the picture. The face stood out clearer and clearer. From out the shadow-like outlines, all at once, he saw the eyes sparkle as with hidden life. And while they spoke to him of the most terrible suffering, they also revealed a purity and sublimity which he had never seen before.

He lay upon his couch and drank in the picture with his eyes. "Is this a mortal?" he said softly and slowly. "Is this a mortal?"

Again he lay still and regarded the picture. The tears began to stream down his cheeks. "I mourn over your death, you Unknown!" he whispered.

"Faustina!" he cried out at last. "Why did you let this man die? He would have healed me."

And again he was lost in the picture.

"O Man!" he said after a moment, "if I cannot gain my health from you, I can still avenge your murder. My hand shall rest heavily upon those who have robbed me of you!"

Again he lay still a long time; then he let himself glide down to the floor – and he knelt before the picture:

"You are Man!" said he. "You are that which I never dreamed I should see." And he pointed to his disfigured face and destroyed hands. "I and all others are wild beasts and monsters, but you are Man." He bowed his head so low before the picture that it touched the floor. "Have pity on me, you Unknown!" he sobbed, and his tears watered the stones. "If you had lived, your glance alone would have healed me."

The poor old woman was terror-stricken over what she had done. It would have been wiser not to show the emperor the picture, she thought. From the start she had been afraid that if he should see it his grief would be too overwhelming. And in her despair over the emperor's grief, she snatched the picture away, as if to remove it from his sight.

Then the emperor looked up. And lo! His features were transformed, and he was as he had been before the illness. It was as if the illness had had its root and sustenance in the contempt and hatred of mankind which had lived in his heart; and it had been forced to flee the very moment he had felt love and compassion.

The following day Tiberius dispatched three messengers.

The first messenger traveled to Rome with the command that the senate should institute investigations as to how the governor of Palestine administered his official duties and punish him, should it appear that he oppressed the people and condemned the innocent to death.

The second messenger went to the vineyard-laborer and his wife, to thank them and reward them for the counsel they had given the emperor, and also to tell them how everything had turned out. When they had heard all, they wept silently, and the man said, "I know that all my life I shall ponder what would have happened if these two had met." But the woman answered, "It could not happen in any other way. It was too great a thought that these two should meet. God knew that the world could not support it."

The third messenger traveled to Palestine and brought back with him to Capri some of Jesus' disciples, and these began to teach there the doctrine that had been preached by the crucified one.

When the disciples landed at Capri, old Faustina lay upon her deathbed. Still, they had time before her death to make of her a follower of the great prophet and to baptize her. And in the baptism she was called VERONICA, because to her it had been granted to give to mankind the true likeness of their Savior.

The Way to the Cross

Lew Wallace

In his much-loved novel Ben-Hur, *Lew Wallace tells the story of two boyhood friends who come of age during the Roman occupation of Judea: Messala and Ben-Hur. On reaching adulthood, the two men's ways diverge. Messala, a Roman, becomes one of the oppressors, while Ben-Hur, a Jew, joins the fight for independence from Rome.*

Betrayed and sent to the galleys by Messala, Ben-Hur vows revenge. Eventually regaining his freedom, he wounds and bankrupts Messala in a fateful chariot race. Not long after, the talk in Judea is of a new leader of the Jewish people, Jesus of Nazareth. Many believe the miracle worker will be their political savior, and Ben-Hur recruits freedom fighters to back him in an uprising against Caesar. But the destiny of this messiah is far different than the military triumph Ben-Hur imagines.

THE STREETS WERE FULL of people going and coming, or grouped about the fires roasting meat, and feasting and singing, and happy. The odor of scorching flesh, mixed with the odor of cedar-wood aflame and smoking, loaded the air; and as this was the occasion when every son of Israel was full brother to every other son of Israel, and hospitality was without bounds, Ben-Hur was saluted at every step, while the groups by the fires insisted, "Stay and partake with us. We are brethren in the love of the Lord." But with thanks to them he hurried on, intending to take horse at the khan and return to the tents on the Cedron.

To make the place, it was necessary for him to cross the thoroughfare so soon to receive sorrowful Christian perpetuation. There also the pious celebration was at its height. Looking up the street, he noticed the flames of torches in motion streaming out like pennons; then he observed that the singing ceased where the torches came. His wonder rose to its highest, however, when he became certain that amidst the smoke and dancing sparks he saw the keener sparkling of burnished spear-tips, arguing the presence of Roman soldiers. What were they, the scoffing legionaries, doing in a Jewish religious procession? The circumstance was unheard of, and he stayed to see the meaning of it.

The moon was shining its best; yet, as if the moon and the torches, and the fires in the street, and the rays streaming from windows and open doors, were not enough to make the way clear, some of the processionists carried lighted lanterns; and fancying he discovered a special purpose in the use of such equipments, Ben-Hur stepped into the street so close to the line of march as to bring every one of the company under view while passing. The torches and the lanterns were being borne by servants, each of whom was armed with a bludgeon or a sharpened stave. Their present duty seemed to be to pick out the smoothest places among the rocks in the street for certain dignitaries among them – elders and priests; rabbis with long beards, heavy brows, and beaked noses; men of the class potential in the councils of Caiaphas and Hannas. Where could they be going? Not to the temple, certainly, for the route to the sacred house from Zion, whence these appeared to be coming, was by the Zystus. And their business – if peaceful, why the soldiers?

As the procession began to go by Ben-Hur, his attention was particularly called to three persons walking together. They were well towards the front, and the servants who went before them with lanterns appeared unusually careful in the service. In the person moving on the left of this group he recognized a chief policeman of the temple; the one on the right was a priest; the middle man was not at first so easily placed, as he walked leaning heavily upon the arms of the others and carried his head so low upon his breast as to hide his face. With great assurance, Ben-Hur fell in on the right of the priest and walked along with him. Now if the man would lift his head! And presently he did so, letting the light of the lanterns strike full in his face, pale, dazed, pinched with dread; the beard roughed; the eyes filmy, sunken, and despairing. In much going about following the Nazarene, Ben-Hur had come to know his disciples as well as the Master; and now, at sight of the dismal countenance, he cried out, "The 'Scariot!"

Slowly the head of the man turned until his eyes settled upon Ben-Hur, and his lips moved as if he were about to speak; but the priest interfered.

"Who are you? Begone!" he said to Ben-Hur, pushing him away.

The young man took the push good-naturedly and, waiting an opportunity, fell into the procession again. Thus he was carried passively along down the street, through the crowded lowlands between the hill Bezetha and the Castle of Antonia, and on by the Bethesda reservoir to the Sheep Gate. There were people everywhere, and everywhere the people were engaged in sacred observances.

It being Passover night, the valves of the Gate stood open. The keepers were off somewhere feasting. In front of the procession as it passed out unchallenged was the deep gorge of the Cedron, with Olivet beyond, its dressing of cedar and olive trees made darker by the moonlight silvering all the heavens. Two roads met and merged into the street at the gate – one from the northeast, the other from Bethany. Ere Ben-Hur could finish wondering whether he were to go farther, and if so which road was to be taken, he was led off down into the gorge. And still no hint of the purpose of the midnight march.

Down the gorge and over the bridge at the bottom of it. There was a clatter on the floor as the crowd, now a straggling rabble, passed over, beating and pounding with their clubs and staves. A little farther and they turned off to the left in the direction of an olive orchard enclosed by a stone wall in view from the road. Ben-Hur knew there was nothing in the place but old gnarled trees, the grass, and a trough hewn out of a rock for the treading of oil after the fashion of the country. While, yet more wonder-struck, he was thinking what could bring such a company at such an hour to a quarter so lonesome, they were all brought to a standstill. Voices called out excitedly in front; a chill sensation ran from man to man; there was a rapid fall-back, and a blind stumbling over each other. The soldiers alone kept their order.

It took Ben-Hur but a moment to disengage himself from the mob and run forward. There he found a gateway without a gate admitting to the orchard, and he halted to take in the scene.

A man in white clothes, and bareheaded, was standing outside the entrance, his hands crossed before him – a slender, stooping figure, with long hair and thin face – in an attitude of resignation and waiting.

It was the Nazarene!

Behind him, next to the gateway, were the disciples in a group; they were excited, but no man was ever calmer than he. The torchlight beat redly upon him, giving his hair a tint ruddier than was natural to it; yet the expression of the countenance was as usual all gentleness and pity.

Opposite this most unmartial figure stood the rabble, gaping, silent, awed, cowering – ready at a sign of anger from him to break and run. And from him to them – then at Judas, conspicuous in their midst – Ben-Hur looked – one quick glance, and the object of the visit lay open to his understanding. Here was the betrayer, there the betrayed; and these with the clubs and staves, and the legionaries, were brought to take him.

A man may not always tell what he will do until the trial is upon him. This was the emergency for which Ben-Hur had been for years preparing. The man to whose security he had devoted himself, and upon whose life he had been building so largely, was in personal peril; yet he stood still. Such contradictions are there in human nature! To say truth, the very calmness with which the mysterious person confronted the mob held him in restraint, by suggesting the possession of a power more than sufficient for the peril. Peace and goodwill, love and nonresistance, had been the burden of the Nazarene's teaching; would he put his preaching into practice? He was master of life; he could restore it when lost; he could take it at pleasure. What use would he make of the power now? Defend himself? And how? A word – a breath – a thought would be sufficient. That there would be some signal exhibition of astonishing force beyond the natural, Ben-Hur believed, and in that faith waited. And in all this he was still measuring the Nazarene by himself – by the human standard.

Presently the clear voice of the Christ arose.

"Whom do you seek?"

"Jesus of Nazareth," the priest replied.

"I am he."

At these simplest of words, spoken without passion or alarm, the assailants fell back several steps, the timid among them cowering to the ground; and they might have let him alone and gone away had not Judas walked over to him.

"Hail, master!"

With this friendly speech, he kissed him.

"Judas," said the Nazarene mildly, "do you betray the Son of Man with a kiss? Wherefore have you come?"

Receiving no reply, the Master spoke to the crowd again.

"Whom do you seek?"

"Jesus of Nazareth."

"I have told you that I am he. If, therefore, you seek me, let these go their way."

At these words of entreaty the rabbis advanced upon him; and, seeing their intent, some of the disciples for whom he interceded drew nearer; one of them cut off a man's ear, but without saving the Master from being taken. And yet Ben-Hur stood still! While the officers were making ready with their ropes, the Nazarene was doing his greatest charity.

"Suffer you thus far," he said, and healed the wounded man with a touch.

Both friends and enemies were confounded – one side that he could do such a thing, the other that he would do it under the circumstances.

"Surely he will not allow them to bind him!"

Thus thought Ben-Hur.

"Put up your sword into its sheath; the cup which my Father has given me, shall I not drink it?" From the offending follower, the Nazarene turned to his captors. "Are you come out as against a thief, with swords and staves to take me? I was daily with you in the temple, and you did not take me; but this is your hour, when darkness reigns."

The posse plucked up courage and closed about him; and when Ben-Hur looked for the faithful they were gone – not one of them remained.

The crowd about the deserted man seemed very busy, with tongue, hand, and foot. Over their heads, between the torch-sticks, through the smoke, sometimes in openings between the restless men, Ben-Hur caught momentary glimpses of the prisoner. Never had anything struck him as so piteous, so unfriended, so forsaken! Yet, he thought, the man could have defended himself – he could have slain his enemies with a breath – but he would not. What was the cup his father had given him to drink? And who was the father to be so obeyed? Mystery upon mystery!

Directly the mob started to return to the city, the soldiers in the lead. Ben-Hur became anxious; he was not satisfied with himself. Where the torches were in the midst of the rabble he knew the Nazarene was to be found. Suddenly he resolved to see him again. He would ask him one question.

Taking off his long outer garment and the handkerchief from his head, he threw them upon the orchard wall and started after the posse, which he boldly joined. Through the stragglers he made way, and at length reached the man who carried the ends of the rope with which the prisoner was bound.

The Nazarene was walking slowly, his head down, his hands bound behind him; the hair fell thickly over his face, and he stooped more than usual; apparently he was oblivious to all going on around him. In advance a few steps were priests and elders talking and occasionally looking back. When at length they were all near the bridge in the gorge, Ben-Hur took the rope from the servant who had it and stepped past him.

"Master, master!" he said hurriedly, speaking close to the Nazarene's ear. "Do you hear, master? A word – one word. Tell me –"

The fellow from who he had taken the rope now claimed it.

"Tell me," Ben-Hur continued, "Do you go with these of your own accord?"

The people had come up now, and were asking angrily, "Who are you, man?"

"O master," Ben-Hur made haste to say, his voice sharp with anxiety, "I am your friend. Tell me, if I bring rescue will you accept it?"

The Nazarene never so much as looked up or allowed the slightest sign of recognition; yet the something which when we are suffering lets the onlooker know of it, failed not now. "Let him alone," it seemed to say. "He has been abandoned by his friends; the world has denied him; in bitterness of spirit, he has taken farewell of men; he is going he knows not where, and he cares not. Let him alone."

And to that Ben-Hur was now driven. A dozen hands were upon him, and from all sides there was shouting, "He is one of them. Bring him along; club him – kill him!"

With a gust of passion which gave him many times his ordinary force, Ben-Hur raised himself, turned once about with his arms outstretched, shook the hands off, and rushed through the circle which was fast hemming him in. The hands snatching at him as he passed tore his garments from his back, so he ran off the road naked; and the gorge, in keeping of the friendly darkness, received him safe.

Reclaiming his handkerchief and outer garments from the orchard wall, he followed back to the city gate; thence he went to the khan, and on the good horse rode to the tents of his people out by the Tombs of the Kings.

As he rode, he promised himself to see the Nazarene the next day – promised it, not knowing that the unfriended man was taken straight away to the house of Hannas to be tried that night.

The heart the young man carried to his couch beat so heavily he could not sleep; for now clearly his renewed Judean kingdom resolved itself into what it was – only a dream. It is bad enough to see our castles overthrown one after another with an interval between in which to recover from the shock, or at least let the echoes of the fall die away; but when they go altogether – go as ships sink, as houses tumble in earthquakes – the spirits which endure it calmly are made of stuffs sterner than common, and Ben-Hur's was not of them. In plainest speech, he was entering upon a crisis with which the morrow and the Nazarene would have everything to do.

NEXT MORNING, about the second hour, two men rode full speed to the doors of Ben-Hur's tents and, dismounting, asked to see him. He was not yet risen, but gave directions for their admission.

"Peace to you, brethren," he said, for they were of his Galileans, and trusted officers. "Will you be seated?"

"Nay," the senior replied bluntly, "to sit and be at ease is to let the Nazarene die. Rise, son of Judah, and go with us. The judgment has been given. The tree of the cross is already at Golgotha."

Ben-Hur stared at them.

"The cross!" was for the moment all he could say.

"They took him last night and tried him," the man continued. "At dawn they led him before Pilate. Twice the Roman denied his guilt; twice he refused to give him over. At last he washed his hands and said, 'Be it upon you then;' and they answered, 'His blood be upon us and our children.'"

"Holy Father Abraham!" cried Ben-Hur. "A Roman kinder to an Israelite than his own kin! And if he should indeed be the Son of God, what shall ever wash his blood from their children? It must not be – it is time to fight!"

His face brightened with resolution, and he clapped his hands.

"The horses – and quickly!" he said to the Arab who answered the signal. "And bid my servant send me fresh

garments, and bring my sword! It is time to die for Israel,
my friends. Wait outside till I come."

He ate a crust, drank a cup of wine, and was soon upon
the road.

"Where would you go first?" asked the Galilean.

"To collect the legions."

"Alas!" the man replied, throwing up his hands.

"Why alas?"

"Master" – the man spoke with shame – "master, I and
my friend here are all that are faithful. The rest follow the
priests."

"Seeking what?" and Ben-Hur drew rein.

"To kill him."

"Not the Nazarene?"

"You have said it."

Ben-Hur looked slowly from one man to the other. He
was hearing again the question of the night before: "The
cup my Father has given me, shall I not drink it?" In the
ear of the Nazarene he was putting his own question: "If I
bring rescue, will you accept it?" He was saying to himself,
"This death may not be averted. The man has been traveling towards it with full knowledge from the day he began
his mission: it is imposed by a will higher than his; whose
but the Lord's! If he is consenting, if he goes to it voluntarily, what shall another do?" Nor less did Ben-Hur see
the failure of the scheme he had built upon the fidelity of
the Galileans; their desertion, in fact, left nothing more of
it. But how singular it should happen that morning of all
others! A dread seized him. It was possible his scheming,
and labor, and expenditure of treasure, might have been
but blasphemous contention with God. When he picked
up the reins and said, "Let us go, brethren," all before him

was uncertainty. The faculty of resolving quickly, without which one cannot be a hero in the midst of stirring scenes, was numb within him.

"Let us go, brethren; let us to Golgotha."

They passed through excited crowds of people going south like themselves. All the country north of the city seemed aroused and in motion.

Hearing that the procession with the condemned might be met with somewhere near the great white towers left by Herod, the three friends rode there, passing around southeast of Akra. In the valley below the Pool of Hezekiah, passageway against the multitude became impossible, and they were compelled to dismount and take shelter behind the corner of a house and wait.

The waiting was as if they were on a riverbank watching a flood go by, for such the people seemed. Half an hour – an hour – the flood surged by Ben-Hur and his companions, within arm's reach, incessant, undiminished. They went by in haste – eager, anxious, crowding – all to behold one poor Nazarene die, a felon between felons. Studying the mass, it seemed the whole world was to be represented, and in that sense present, at the crucifixion.

The going was singularly quiet. A hoof-stroke upon a rock, the glide and rattle of revolving wheels, voices in conversation, and now and then a calling voice, were all the sounds heard above the rustle of the mighty movement. Yet was there upon every countenance the look with which men make haste to see some dreadful sight, some sudden wreck, or ruin, or calamity of war. And by such signs Ben-Hur judged that these were the strangers in the city come up to the Passover, who had had no part in the trial of the Nazarene and might be his friends.

At length, from the direction of the great towers, Ben-Hur heard, at first faint in the distance, a shouting of many men.

"Hark! They are coming now," said one of his friends.

The people in the street halted to hear; but as the cry rang on over their heads, they looked at each other, and in shuddering silence moved along.

The shouting drew nearer each moment; and the air was already full of it and trembling, when Ben-Hur saw the servants of the merchant Simonides coming with their master in his chair, and his daughter Esther walking by his side; a covered litter bearing the Wise Man Balthasar was behind them.

"Peace to you, O Simonides – and to you, Esther," said Ben-Hur, meeting them. "If you are for Golgotha, stay until the procession passes; I will then go with you. There is room to turn in by the house here."

The merchant's large head rested heavily upon his breast; rousing himself, he answered, "Speak to Balthasar; his pleasure will be mine. He is in the litter."

Ben-Hur hastened to draw aside the curtain. The Egyptian was lying within, his wan face so pinched as to appear like a dead man's. The proposal was submitted to him.

"Can we see him?" he inquired faintly.

"The Nazarene? Yes; he must pass within a few feet of us."

"Dear Lord!" the old man cried fervently. "Once more, once more! Oh, it is a dreadful day for the world!"

Shortly the whole party was in waiting under shelter of the house. They said but little, afraid, probably, to trust their thoughts to each other; everything was uncertain, and nothing so much so as opinions. Balthasar drew himself feebly from the litter and stood supported by a servant. Esther and Ben-Hur kept Simonides company.

Meantime the flood poured along, if anything more densely than before; and the shouting came nearer, shrill in the air, hoarse along the earth, and cruel.

"See!" said Ben-Hur bitterly. "That which cometh now is Jerusalem."

The advance was in possession of an army of boys, hooting and screaming, "The King of the Jews! Room, room for the King of the Jews!"

Simonides watched them as they whirled and danced along like a cloud of summer insects, and said gravely, "When these come to their inheritance, son of Hur, alas for the city of Solomon!"

A band of legionaries fully armed followed next, marching in sturdy indifference, the glory of burnished brass about them the while.

Then came the Nazarene!

He was nearly dead. Every few steps he staggered as if he would fall. A stained gown badly torn hung from his shoulders over a seamless undertunic. His bare feet left red splotches upon the stones. An inscription on a board was tied to his neck. A crown of thorns had been crushed hard down upon his head, making cruel wounds from which streams of blood, now dry and blackened, had run over his face and neck. The long hair, tangled in the thorns, was clotted thick. The skin, where it could be seen, was ghastly white. His hands were tied before him. Back somewhere in the city he had fallen exhausted under the transverse beam of his cross, which, as a condemned person, custom required him to bear to the place of execution; now a countryman carried the burden in his stead. Four soldiers went with him as a guard against the mob, who sometimes, nevertheless, broke through and struck him with sticks, and spit upon him. Yet no sound escaped him, neither remonstrance nor groan; nor did he look up until he was nearly in front of the house sheltering Ben-Hur and his friends, all of whom were moved with quick compassion. Esther clung to her father; and he, strong of will as he was, trembled; Balthasar fell down speechless. Even Ben-Hur cried out, "O my God! My God!" Then, as if he divined their feelings or heard the exclamation, the Nazarene turned his wan face towards the party and looked at them each one, so they carried the look in memory through life. They could see he was thinking of them, not himself, and the dying eyes gave them the blessing he was not permitted to speak.

"Where are your legions, son of Hur?" asked Simonides, aroused.

"Hannas can tell you better than I."

"What, faithless?"

"All but these two."

"Then all is lost, and this good man must die!"

The face of the merchant knit convulsively as he spoke, and his head sank upon his breast. He had borne his part in Ben-Hur's labors well, and he had been inspired by the same hopes, now blown out never to be rekindled.

Two other men succeeded the Nazarene bearing cross beams.

"Who are these?" Ben-Hur asked of the Galileans.

"Thieves appointed to die with the Nazarene," they replied.

Next in the procession stalked a mitered figure clad all in the golden vestments of the high priest. Policemen from the temple curtained him round about; and after him, in order, strode the Sanhedrin and a long array of priests, the latter in their plain white garments overwrapped by abnets of many folds and gorgeous colors.

"The son-in-law of Hannas," said Ben-Hur in a low voice.

"Caiphas! I have seen him," Simonides replied, adding, after a pause during which he thoughtfully watched the haughty pontiff, "and now I am convinced. With such assurance as proceeds from clear enlightenment of the spirit – with absolute assurance – now I know that he who first goes yonder with the inscription about his neck is what the inscription proclaims him – KING OF THE JEWS. A common man, an imposter, a felon, was never thus waited upon. For look! Here are the nations – Jerusalem, Israel. Here is the ephod, here the blue robe with its fringe, and purple pomegranates, and golden bells, not seen in the street since the day Jaddua went out to meet the Macedonian – proofs all that this Nazarene is king. Would I could rise and go after him!"

Ben-Hur listened, surprised; and directly, as if himself awakening to his unusual display of feeling, Simonides said impatiently, "Speak to Balthasar, and let us be gone. The vomit of Jerusalem is coming."

Then Esther spoke.

"I see some women there, and they are weeping. Who are they?"

Following the point of her hand, the party beheld four women in tears; one of them leaned upon the arm of a man of aspect not unlike the Nazarene's. Presently Ben-Hur answered, "The man is the disciple whom the Nazarene loves the best of all; she who leans upon his arm is Mary, the Master's mother; the others are friendly women of Galilee."

Esther pursued the mourners with glistening eyes until the multitude received them out of sight.

The demonstration was the forerunner of those in which, scarce thirty years later, under rule of the factions, the Holy City was torn to pieces; it was quite as great in numbers, as fanatical and bloodthirsty; boiled and raved, and had in it exactly the same elements – servants, camel-drivers, market-men, gate-keepers, gardeners, dealers in fruits and wines, proselytes, and foreigners not proselytes, watchmen and menials from the temple, thieves, robbers, and the myriad not assignable to any class, but who, on such occasions as this, appeared no one could say whence, hungry and smelling of caves and old tombs – bareheaded wretches with naked arms and legs, hair and beard in uncombed mats, and each with one garment the color of clay; beasts with abysmal mouths, in outcry effective as lions calling each other across desert spaces. Some of them had swords; a greater number flourished spears and javelins; though the weapons of the many were staves and knotted clubs, and slings, for which latter selected stones were stored in scrips, and sometimes in sacks improvised from foreskirts of their dirty tunics. Among the mass here and there appeared persons of high degree – scribes, elders, rabbis, Pharisees with broad fringing, Sadducees in fine cloaks – serving for the time as prompters and directors. If a throat tired of one cry, they invented another for it; if brassy lungs showed signs of collapse, they set them going again; and yet the clamor, loud and continuous as it was, could have been reduced to a few syllables – King of the Jews! – Room for the King of the Jews! – Defiler of the temple! – Blasphemer of God! – Crucify him, crucify him! And of these cries the last one seemed in greatest favor, because doubtless it was more directly expressive of the wish of the mob and helped to better articulate its hatred of the Nazarene.

"Come," said Simonides when Balthasar was ready to proceed. "Come, let us forward."

Ben-Hur did not hear the call. The appearance of the part of the procession then passing, its brutality and hunger for life, were reminding him of the Nazarene – his gentleness, and the many charities he had seen him do for suffering men; the miracle of Palm Sunday; and with these recollections, the thought of his present powerlessness stung him keenly, and he accused himself. He had not done all he might; he could have watched with the Galileans, and kept them true and ready; and this – ah! This was the moment to strike! A blow well given now would not merely disperse the mob and set the Nazarene free; it would be a trumpet-call to Israel, and precipitate the long-dreamt-of war for freedom. The opportunity was going; the minutes were bearing it away; and if lost! God of Abraham! Was there nothing to be done – nothing?

That instant a party of Galileans caught his eye. He rushed through the press and overtook them.

"Follow me," he said. "I would speak with you."

The men obeyed him, and when they were under shelter of the house, he spoke again:

"You are of those who took my swords and agreed with me to strike for freedom and the king who was coming. You have the swords now, and now is the time to strike with them. Go, look everywhere and find our brethren, and tell them to meet me at the tree of the cross making ready for the Nazarene. Haste all of you! Nay, stand not so! The Nazarene is the king, and freedom dies with him."

They looked at him respectfully, but did not move.

"Hear you?" he asked.

Then one of them replied, "Son of Judah" – by that time they knew him – "son of Judah, it is you who are deceived, not we or our brethren who have your swords. The Nazarene is not the king; neither has he the spirit of a king. We were with him when he came into Jerusalem; we saw him in the temple; he failed himself, and us, and Israel; at the Gate Beautiful he turned his back upon God and refused the throne of David. He is not king, and Galilee is not with him. He shall die the death. But hear you, son of Judah. We have your swords, and we are ready now to draw them and strike for freedom! and we will meet you at the tree of the cross."

The sovereign moment of his life was upon Ben-Hur. Could he have taken the offer and said the word, history might have been other than it is; but then it would have been history ordered by men, not God – something that never was, and never will be. A confusion fell upon him; he knew not how, though afterwards he attributed it to the Nazarene; for when the Nazarene was risen, he understood that his death was necessary to faith in the resurrection, without which Christianity would be an empty husk. The confusion, as has been said, left him without the faculty of decision; he stood helpless – wordless even. Covering his face with his hand, he shook with the conflict between his wish, which was what he would have ordered, and the power that was upon him.

"Come; we are waiting for you," said Simonides, the fourth time.

Thereupon he walked mechanically after the chair and the litter. Esther walked with him. Like Balthasar and his friends the Wise Men, the day they went to the meeting in the desert, he was being led along the way.

Robin Redbreast

Selma Lagerlöf

Translated by Velma Swanston Howard

IT HAPPENED AT THE TIME when our Lord created the world, when he made not only heaven and earth, but all the animals and the plants as well, and at the same time gave them their names.

Many stories have come to us from that time, and if we knew them all we should have light upon everything in this world which we cannot comprehend.

It happened one day, when our Lord sat in his paradise painting little birds, that the colors in his paint pot gave out. The goldfinch would have been without color if our Lord had not wiped all his paint brushes on its feathers.

It was then that the donkey got his long ears because he could not remember the name that had been given him. No sooner had he taken a few steps over the meadows of paradise than he forgot, and three times he came back to ask his name. At last our Lord grew somewhat impatient, took him by his two ears and said, "Your name is ass, ass,

ass!" And while he spoke, our Lord pulled both of his ears, so that the ass might hear better and remember what was said to him.

It was on the same day, also, that the bee was punished. When the bee was created, she began immediately to gather honey, and the animals and human beings who caught the delicious odor of the honey came and wanted to taste it. But the bee wanted to keep it all for herself, and with her poisonous sting pursued every living creature that approached her hive. Our Lord saw this and at once called the bee to him and punished her. "I gave you the gift of gathering honey, which is the sweetest thing in all creation," said our Lord, "but I did not give you the right to be cruel to your neighbor. Remember well that every time you sting any creature who desires to taste your honey, you shall surely die!"

Oh, yes! It was at that time, too, that the cricket became blind and the ant lost her wings. So many strange things happened on that day!

Our Lord sat and planned and created all day long, and toward evening he conceived the idea of making a little gray bird. "Remember, your name is Robin Redbreast," said our Lord to the bird as soon as it was finished. Then he held it in the palm of his open hand and let it fly.

After the bird had been testing his wings a while and had seen something of the beautiful world in which he was to live, he became curious to see what he himself was like. He noticed that he was entirely gray, and that his breast was just as gray as all the rest of him. Robin Redbreast twisted and turned in all directions as he looked at his reflection in the water, but he couldn't find a single red feather. Then he flew back to our Lord.

Our Lord sat there on his throne. Out of his hands came butterflies that fluttered about his head, doves that cooed on his shoulders; out of the earth beneath him grew the rose, the lily, and the daisy.

The little bird's heart beat heavily with fright, but with easy curves he flew nearer and nearer our Lord, till at last he rested on our Lord's hand. Then our Lord asked what the little bird wanted. "I only wish to ask you about one thing," said the little bird.

"What is it you wish to know?" asked our Lord.

"Why should I be called Redbreast, when I am all gray from the bill to the very end of my tail? Why am I called Redbreast, when I do not possess one single red feather?" The bird looked beseechingly at our Lord with his tiny black eyes – then turned his head. About him he saw pheasants, all red under a sprinkle of gold dust; parrots with marvelous red neck bands; cocks with red combs; to say nothing about the butterflies, the goldfish, and the roses! And, naturally, he thought how little he needed – just one tiny drop of color on his breast and he, too, would be a beautiful bird, and his name would fit him. "Why should I be called Redbreast when I am so entirely gray?" asked the bird once again, and waited for our Lord to say, "Ah, my friend, I see that I have forgotten to paint your breast feathers red, but wait a moment and it shall be done."

But our Lord only smiled a little and said, "I have called you Robin Redbreast, and Robin Redbreast shall your name be, but you must look to it that you yourself earn your red breast feathers." Then our Lord opened his hand and let the bird fly out once again into the world.

The bird flew out of paradise, deeply thoughtful.

What could a little bird like him do to earn red feathers for himself? The only thing he could think of was to make his nest in a brier bush. He built it in among the thorns in the close thicket. It would appear that he waited for a rose leaf to cling to his throat and give it color.

Countless years had come and gone since that day which was the happiest in all the world! Since then animals and people had left paradise and spread themselves over the earth. Human beings had already advanced so far that they had learned to cultivate the earth and sail the seas. They had procured clothes and ornaments for themselves, and long since had learned to build big temples and great cities – such as Thebes, Rome, and Jerusalem.

Then there dawned a new day, one that will always be remembered in the world's history. On the morning of this day, Robin Redbreast sat upon a little naked hillock outside Jerusalem's walls and sang to his young ones, who rested in a tiny nest in a brier bush.

Robin Redbreast told the little ones all about that wonderful day of creation, how the Lord had given names to everything, just as each Redbreast had told his children ever since the first Redbreast had heard God's word and gone out of God's hand. "And mark you," he ended sorrowfully, "so many innumerable years have gone, so many roses have bloomed, so many little birds have come out of their eggs since Creation Day, but Robin Redbreast is still a little gray bird. He has not yet succeeded in gaining his red feathers."

The little young ones opened wide their tiny bills, and asked if their forebears had never tried to do any great thing to earn the priceless red color.

"We have all done what we could," said the little bird, "but none of us has succeeded. One day the first Robin Redbreast met another bird exactly like himself, and immediately began to love it with such a mighty love that he could feel his breast glow. 'Ah!' he thought, 'now I understand! It was our Lord's meaning that I should love with so much ardor that my breast would grow red in color from the very warmth of the love that lives in my heart.' But it did not happen; nor did it happen to any who followed, nor will it happen to you."

The little ones twittered sadly and began to mourn because the red color would not come to beautify their downy little grey breasts.

"We had also hoped that singing would help us," said the old one in long-drawn-out notes. "The first Robin Redbreast sang until his heart swelled within him, he was so carried away, and he dared to hope anew. 'Ah!' he thought, 'it is the glow of the song which lives in my soul that will color my breast feathers red.' But he was mistaken, as were all his descendants – even as you will be too." Again was heard a sad "peep" from the young ones' half-naked throats.

"We had also counted on our courage and valor," said the bird. "The first Robin Redbreast fought bravely with other birds, until his breast flamed with the pride of conquest. 'Ah!' he thought, 'my breast feathers will become red from the love of battle which burns in my heart.' But that too failed for him and all who came after him, even as it will happen to you." The little ones chirped courageously, for they still wished to try and win the much-sought-for prize, but the bird answered them sorrowfully that it would be impossible.

What hope could they have when so many splendid ancestors had not managed it? What more could they do than love, sing, and fight? What could . . . the little bird stopped short, for out of one of the gates of Jerusalem came a crowd of people marching, and the whole procession rushed toward the hillock where the bird had its nest. There were riders on proud horses, soldiers with long spears, executioners with nails and hammers. There were dignified judges and priests in the procession, weeping women, and above all a mob of mad, loose people running about – a filthy, howling mob of vagabonds.

The small grey bird sat trembling on the edge of his nest. He feared each instant that the little briar bush would be trampled down and his young ones killed!

"Be careful!" he cried to the defenseless young ones. "Creep close together and be quiet. Here comes a horse that will ride right over us! Here comes a warrior with iron-shod sandals! Here comes the whole wild, storming mob!" All at once the bird ceased his cry of warning and was silent. He almost forgot the danger hovering over him. Suddenly he hopped down into the nest and spread his wings over his young ones.

"Oh! this is too terrible," he said. "I don't want you to witness this awful sight! There are three criminals who are going to be crucified!" And he spread his wings so that the little ones could see nothing. They caught only the sound of hammers, the cries of anguish, and the wild shrieks of the mob.

Robin Redbreast followed the whole spectacle with his eyes, which grew big with terror. He could not take his glance from the three unfortunates.

"How cruel human beings are!" said the bird after a while. "It isn't enough that they nail these poor creatures to a cross, but they must place a crown of piercing thorns upon the head of one of them. I see that the thorns have wounded his forehead so that the blood flows," he continued. "And this man is so beautiful and looks about him with such mild glances that everyone ought to love him. I feel as if an arrow were piercing my heart when I see him suffer!"

The little bird began to feel a stronger and stronger pity for the thorn-crowned sufferer. "Oh! if I were only my brother the eagle," thought he, "I would draw the nails from his hands and with my strong claws I would drive away all those who torture him!" He saw how the blood trickled down from the brow of the crucified one, and he could no longer remain quiet in his nest. "Even if I am little and weak, I can still do something for this poor tormented one," thought the bird. Then he left his nest and flew out into the air, describing wide circles around the crucified one.

He flew around him several times without daring to approach, for he was a shy little bird who had never dared to go near a human being. But little by little he gained courage, flew close to him, and drew with his little bill a thorn that had been imbedded in the forehead of the crucified one. And as he did this there fell on his breast a drop of blood from the crucified one; it spread quickly and colored all the little fine breast feathers.

As soon as the bird had returned to his nest his young ones cried to him, "Your breast is red! Your breast feathers are redder than the roses!"

"It is only a drop of blood from the poor man's forehead," said the bird. "It will vanish as soon as I bathe in a pool or a clear spring."

But no matter how much the little bird bathed, the red color did not vanish – and when his young ones grew up, the blood-red color shone also on their breast feathers, just as it shines on every Robin Redbreast's throat and breast until this very day.

The Atonement

Ludwig von Gerdtell

Translated by Hela Ehrlich and Nicoline Maas

THERE WAS ONCE A KING, a true father of his country, just and gentle toward all his subjects, who had to contend with a powerful revolutionary party that wanted to raise its leader to the throne.

One day this king noticed that important state and family papers had been stolen from his desk. Beside himself because of the possibility of a political scandal which could arise through the misuse of these stolen papers, he immediately had his heralds proclaim the following decree: "I swear by God and my honor as king that I shall without fail execute the one who misuses the stolen papers against my throne and the welfare of the state, and that anyone who dares again to steal my secret papers shall be punished publicly by the executioner with a hundred strokes of the lash, no matter who it is."

To the king's great pain, a few days after this decree was published a palace guard seized the king's dearly loved mother and his two sisters, just as they were about to open the king's secret cabinet with a master key. Investigations immediately set in operation proved beyond doubt that all three were participants in the conspiracy.

The news that the thieves, in the person of the queen mother and the two princesses, were caught in the act and that their guilt was proven, was immediately published in every newspaper in the kingdom. Some spite-filled articles emphasized that His Majesty now had an unusual opportunity to show his much-vaunted justice and to prove to the opposition that he placed the laws of the kingdom above his selfish family interests.

The queen mother and the king's two sisters fell on their knees before the king and promised to give up all connection with the rebels and to be all the more faithful to him in the future. The king did not doubt the sincerity of their remorse. In his double position as son and as ruler he was thrown into terrible agitation of heart and conscience. He locked himself into his study for a whole day and did not eat or drink. The king in him became a tyrant toward the mother's son he was and demanded equal rights for all. The son and brother in him, on the other hand, became a rebel against the king and demanded pardon.

What was he to do? If he carried out his decree, he must allow his dearly loved mother, as well as his own sisters, to be publicly disgraced by the executioner. He knew that they would not survive the shame and suffering of this dreadful punishment. If, on the other hand, he did not carry out his proclamation, the king would stand perjured, unjust, and dishonored before his whole people and his enemies. And yet he knew that only the personal trust of his people in his justice, honesty, and generosity could still save his throne and the state. Thus the conspiracy had penetrated into the heart of the king himself. What was he to do? The one was just as impossible for him as the other.

On the following morning, after a terrible night, the king ordered the executioner and the people to assemble before the palace. Many thousands crowded around the throne which had been hastily erected in the palace square.

Finally the king came, leading his trembling old mother reverently by the arm, while his sisters, burning with shame, followed them. Then the king, pale and deeply earnest, but manly and composed, stepped beneath the canopy of his throne and said to the crowd, which immediately became deathly still: "So that my people and my enemies may see that in my kingdom there is equal justice for all, I now hand over to you, executioner, my old mother, for the immediate execution before all your eyes of the punishment merited according to my decree."

A dreadful moment followed. Broken, the king sank down to the seat of his throne, burying his pale face in his hands to hide his tears. The princesses, their backs to the people, had broken down sobbing before the throne. For one second the humming of the whip was heard.

Then, just as the executioner was about to strike the old lady unmercifully, the king sprang up, grabbed the executioner by the arm, and called out with a lion's voice which awakened an echo from the palace walls, "Give me the hundred strokes! But let these three go!" And without a sound the king broke down under the hundred whiplashes, and half an hour later was carried, half-dead and streaming with blood, into his palace. Even his enemies wept.

The king recovered but slowly from this terrible chastisement, but he had won even his opponents and was from then on beloved by all his people. In this way, through his justice, love, and a wisdom greater than Solomon's, the king saved his kingdom and his family from ruin.

The Flaming Heart of Danko

Maxim Gorky

Translated by A. S. Rappoport

I T WAS BESIDE the sea, near Akkerman in Bessarabia, that I heard the following tale from the old woman Izergil. She was drowsing off, nodding her head and whispering something, softly, very softly . . . perhaps a prayer.

Dark, heavy, gloomy-looking clouds were rising over the sea, looking like a chain of mountains. They were traveling slowly towards the steppe. Fragments broke away from the summit and, flying forward, hid the stars in succession. The sea was murmuring. Close to us among the green vines there was kissing, and whispering, and sighing. A dog howled in the distance, far away across the steppe. The air became stifling, and some curious odor assailed one's nostrils and irritated the nerves. Flights of shadows thrown by the clouds passed slowly over the earth, disappearing only to make room for others. The moon was almost hidden; nothing but a patch of dull opal filled its place, over which from time to time swept a ragged blue-black cloud. Far off on the horizon, where the steppe had grown dark and terrible, as if hiding some fearful mystery, little blue flames kept shooting up. They shone for a moment, first here, then there, and then disappeared, as if there were men wandering far apart from one another about the steppe looking for something with matches, which they had no sooner lighted than the wind blew them out. They were curious, these blue flames, with their fantastic little gleaming lights.

"Do you see those sparks?" asked Izergil.

"The blue sparks over there?" I said, pointing towards the steppe.

"Yes, those blue sparks, those are the ones. So they are still flying about . . . but I can no longer see them. There are many things now which I cannot see."

"Where do they come from, those little flames?" I asked her.

I had been told something once about the origin of these sparks, but I wanted to hear what Izergil had to say upon the subject.

She looked at me, then replied:

Those sparks come from Danko's burning heart. There was once a heart that caught fire and those sparks flew from it. I will tell you all about it . . . It is another old tale. Everything is old – everything. You see how many things happened in the past . . . Now there is nothing, neither deeds, nor men, nor tales such as we had in the old days. And why? Tell me that . . . But you are not able. What do you know? What do any of you young ones know? Well, well! . . . Keep your eye fixed on the times that are past; it is there only that you will find the answer to the riddle, the meaning of everything.

But you do not care to learn about old times, and that is why you do not understand life . . . But I, do not I know it? Yes, I understand it, and I see everything, although my eyes are old and weak. I can see that men now do not really live, that they do nothing more than just accommodate themselves to existence, exhausting all their strength merely on this, and then, having robbed themselves and spent their time in this useless fashion, they begin to rail at destiny. Everyone is master of his own fate! I see plenty of men nowadays, but I see no strong men. Where are they gone to? Handsome men are becoming rarer and rarer.

The old woman went on asking herself why there were now so few strong and handsome men, and as she meditated on the matter, she looked out over the dark steppe as if seeking a reply.

I was waiting for her tale, and I said nothing, fearing to make any remark that might turn her from the subject we were now upon. I was aware that when she embarked on the stormy sea of her own memories she grew philosophical, and it often happened that some legend or other became lost in the labyrinth of this philosophy. It was a very simple and liberal philosophy; but when old Izergil was expounding it, one could only think of a strange ball of many-colored threads which had become cunningly entangled by the hand of time.

She began again:

In the good old days there were men living in the world, I cannot say exactly where, I only know that their dwelling place was surrounded by huge, impenetrable forests, and that one side opened onto the steppe. They were free, light-hearted, powerful men, who wanted nothing – probably gypsies. But at last a great trouble fell upon them. Other races of people arrived and drove the first settlers away into the depths of the forest. There all was darkness and swamp, for the trees were so old that their thick branches had grown interlaced, hiding the sky above them, so that the sun's rays could hardly penetrate through the solid screen of foliage. When by chance they touched the stagnant water of the marsh, the exhalation was so poisonous that the people died one after another. The women and children began to lament, and became sad and thoughtful. It was evident that they must leave the forest.

There were two ways of exit to choose from: one led back to where their strong and cruel enemies were stationed; the other, which led forward, was overgrown by the enormous forest trees barring the road with their solid network of boughs and their knotted roots, which struck deep into the sticky mud of the swamp. A kind of twilight reigned throughout the forest during the day; the trees reared their mighty forms, silent and motionless, like giants of stone. At night, when the men lit their fires, the encircling trees seemed to draw even more closely around them, threatening, it appeared, to fall and crush these free creatures, accustomed to the splendid immensity of the steppe.

It was more terrible still when the tops of these colossal figures were shaken by the storm, and the forest resounded with menacing voices that rang like the funeral dirge of the men who had taken refuge there – and yet they were strong men who might well have fought to the death with those who had vanquished them; they had, however, been forbidden to die in battle, for they were the guardians of certain sacred precepts which would be lost forever when they died – and so it was that they lingered on there, in a dreamy state of existence, through the long nights, amid the smothered murmurs of the forest and the empoisoned air of the swamp. There they remained, the shadows thrown by their fires leaping around them in silent fantastic dance; and at times it seemed to the men that they were not merely shadows, but rather the evil spirits of the forest and swamp celebrating their triumph. And so the men spoke little, and sat on, thinking.

There is nothing, not even work, or women, which so exhausts body and soul as unquiet thoughts that suck the heart's blood like a vampire. This perpetual state of meditation robbed them of their vitality. They became prey to a terror which made their strong hands helpless; and the terror took possession of the women as they wept over the bodies of the men who had been killed by the infectious air, and over the living ones enslaved by fear.

Words of dread and apprehension began to be whispered about the forest, at first timid and hardly audible, but then louder. The men were proposing to go straight to the enemy and offer themselves and their own wills in homage, for the thought of slavery no longer appalled them.

Then Danko appeared, and single-handedly saved the whole tribe.

The old woman spoke much of Danko's flaming heart; her sentences followed one another with a rhythm that suggested long, self-colored ribbons, unwinding themselves like a drawn-out melody, while in her dull, harsh voice I seemed to hear the shuddering of the forest, in the midst of which the unhappy exiles had succumbed to the poisonous atmosphere. She went on:

Danko – one of the men – was young and handsome. Handsome men are always courageous, and addressing his companions he said:

"Thinking alone will not even move a stone out of the path. Nothing ever comes to him who does nothing. Why do we waste our energy in weeping? Rise – let us be going!

"Rise – let us go straight away into the forest and force our way through! It is not without limits! Everything in this world has an end! See now! Let us be going!"

The men looked at him. They recognized his authority, for his eyes were alight with a fire of strength and determination.

"Lead us," they said.

And he led them on.

The old woman paused, gazing in the direction of the steppe where the shadows were deepening. The sparks from Danko's flaming heart could be seen in the distance, like blue aerial flowers blooming for the space of a moment. Then she resumed her story:

Danko put himself at their head. They followed him in a body; they had perfect confidence in him. But the way was indeed difficult! There, amid the darkness, the swamp opened its hungry, fetid jaws to swallow them, and every step of the way was won with sweat and blood. So they went on for a long, long time.

The forest grew thicker as the men's strength became less! They began to murmur against Danko, saying that he was young, inexperienced, and that he had done wrong to drag them along like this. And he, quiet and courageous, still marched ahead and led them on.

One day a fearful storm broke over the forest; a low and terrible sound crept up among the trees. The forest grew dark, as if all the nights that had been since the world began were reassembled within it. The men marched on under the gigantic trees like pygmies amid the hideous roar of the tempest, while the trees tore the air with their evil voices and the cold blue glare of the lightning lit up the forest at intervals, filling the hearts of the cowering men with dread. The trees seemed to start into life as the cold fire fell on them; they stretched forth their long, gaunt hands as if to keep back these men who were trying to escape from the bondage of darkness. The men, worn out with their efforts, began to lose courage. They were ashamed, however, to confess their weakness.

And now, all at once, they fell upon Danko – on the man who was guiding them! They began to reproach him with his incapacity.

"You! You are a good-for-nothing and harmful man! You have dragged us here, and we are dead with fatigue; you shall die for it!"

And the thunder and lightning added emphasis to their words.

Danko looked at the people for whom he had sacrificed himself and saw that they were as the brute beasts. He looked at the men who were crowding round him; there was no nobility on their faces, no hope, as he saw, that he would meet with mercy at their hands. His indignation rose, but out of pity for his brothers he held it in check. He would meet with no mercy at their hands. Yet he loved these men, and without his help he feared that they would perish.

Then his heart grew aflame with the desire to save them, and the vivid light of that flame leaped into his eyes. And they, seeing this, thought that he was furious with anger. They rose like wolves, believing that he was going to fight them, and drew round him in a circle, that they might get better hold of him to kill him. But he had already read their souls, and his heart burnt with a fiercer fire, for their suspicious thoughts filled him with sorrow.

And still the forest chanted its mournful dirge, and still the thunder roared and the rain rattled.

"What shall I do for these men?" Danko cried in a voice that rang louder than the thunder. And he rent open his chest with his two hands, tore out his heart, and held it up high over his head.

And the flaming heart blazed with a light more dazzling than that of the sun.

Then the forest depths, illumined by this torch of supreme love for man, grew silent. The shadows fled trembling from before this aurora, driven into the far corners of the forest, into the jaws of the poisonous swamp. The men stood dumb with astonishment, as if turned to stone.

"Forward!" cried Danko, rushing onward as he held aloft his flaming heart to light the road.

They threw themselves after him, full of ecstasy and wonder. The trees shook their leafy summits with astonishment, and again the forest became full of sound, but now it was covered by that of the tramping of the men's feet. They marched along, inspired with courage, led on by the marvelous spectacle of the flaming heart.

And suddenly the forest in front opened. Mute and impenetrable, it now lay at last behind them. Danko and his companions found themselves plunging into a vast sea of light and pure air, washed by the rain. The storm still hung over the forest, but here around them was the warm light of the sun, the grass sprinkled with bright diamonds of rain, while the river sparkled gold as it glided along. It was evening, and as the rays of the setting sun fell on the water, it ran crimson like the blood that flowed from Danko's torn chest.

The dying Danko, proud and fearless, cast a look of joy before him over the immensity of the steppe – over that land of liberty that rolled away on either side; then with one last smile, he fell and breathed his last.

The wondering trees looking on from behind whispered softly among themselves, and the grass, wet with Danko's blood, made answer to them.

And the people, full of joy and hope, did not even notice that their leader was dead; they did not see that his heart was still burning brightly beside his body. One man alone, perceiving this, and seized with some feeling of fear, put his foot on the proud heart. The flame broke into a shower of sparks and went out.

And these are the blue sparks which you see over the steppe before a storm breaks!

As the old woman finished her beautiful tale, a terrifying silence fell upon the steppe, as if it too had been struck dumb by this deed of the courageous Danko, who had allowed his heart to burn away for the love of his fellow men and had died asking for no return. The old woman, slumbering and shivering at intervals, was leaning back against the baskets which were piled with grapes. I looked at her and thought of all the tales and of all the recollections with which her memory must be filled. I thought of Danko's flaming heart, and of the curious, imaginative power in man that had created so many fine and charming legends of the old times with their heroes and wonderful deeds, of the sad times in which we were living, so poor in men of power and in great events, so rich in the cynical contempt that mocks at everything – unhappy times, with their swarms of miserable men, whose hearts were only half alive . . .

The wind blew, lifting the rags that covered the shrunken bosom of the old woman, whose sleep grew more and more profound. I drew the garments over her aged form, and lay down myself beside her on the ground. The steppe was wrapped in gloom and silence. The clouds slowly and mournfully dragged themselves across the sky, while the sea murmured low and plaintively. And still old Izergil slept on . . .

It was possible she might never wake again.

John

Elizabeth Goudge

IT STRUCK HIM suddenly that it was odd to be bothering to sweep the floor when the world had come to an end and love was dead. What was the use? And by the light of a candle too. One could not see to sweep properly by the light of a candle. But there had to be a candle, because it was night. The light of the world had been put out, and it was night.

He stopped and looked down for a moment in the dim light at the broom handle and his thin brown hands tautly holding it, clutching at it in a stupid, desperate sort of way, as though it was a spar of wood that kept him from drowning. Well, so it was. The everyday tasks, chopping the wood, carrying the water from the well, washing the dishes, sweeping the floor, did keep one from drowning in grief, going mad from the shock of what one had seen, what one remembered, what one had done.

What one had *done.* That was the worst of it. He had run away. They had all run away. If they hadn't it might not have happened. Not that he was concerned with what the others had done; it was his own running away that was the weak trembling of his limbs, the tight band of pain jammed down over his temples, the stabbing through his hands and feet, the appalling knowledge in his mind that his pain was only the feeblest echo of the pain he had seen. And yet his friend who had borne it had never run away. Courage forsaken by cowardice, truth betrayed by lies, love tortured by hatred, life put out by death. And then darkness and the ending of the world. He had run away. He'd come back, of course, but it had been too late. Nothing to be done then but stand there through the endless hours and watch it happen, the sight searing through his brain and the agony of his helplessness choking him. Too late then. It had taken him exactly two minutes to run away, but the agony of his friend had gone on for hours. If he could only have back that two minutes and do it again, do it differently. But he couldn't. It was too late. And love was dead. In spite of a confused feeling of unbelief, he knew that must be true, because for a moment or two, while Joseph smoothed out the winding sheet, he had held love dead in his arms. Dead because he had run away. Lord God, help me, he prayed. I'll go mad if I go on like this, like those poor devils who used to fall screaming at the Master's feet, and he'd put out his hands and hold them steady. But there was no one now to hold him steady, to hold any poor wretch steady. He'd seen to that by running away.

Stop it, you fool! Stop thinking! He began to sweep the floor again, and the dust went around and around in whirls. He couldn't seem to get the dust where he wanted it. He was a complete fool. When he'd carried in water from the well last night, he'd only stumbled over the doorsill and upset the bucket. And Mary, his mother too now, had mopped up the water and comforted him. In greater grief than any of them, yet it was she who was their strength. But then she had not run away. She only, of them all, was guiltless in the darkness of this night. She had the strength of her sinlessness, and of some memory to which she clung; something her son had said about "the third day." There was a vague memory of that in John's mind too; it was the source of that feeling he had that death could not be true, but his confused mind could not seem to get hold of it.

What was happening? The candle flame dipped and swayed, the floor seemed slipping away beneath him, and there was a rumble like thunder. Only another earthquake shock. He steadied himself. Usually earthquakes terrified him, only nothing mattered now. But he hoped the women would be safe, going through the dark streets to the garden. But there was no further shock. That was all; except that the atmosphere seemed curiously freshened, as though a clean wind blew down the world. Yet there was no wind. There was something, though. He blinked his sleepless, red-rimmed eyes and looked about him. What was it? Light! The endless night was over and the first light of dawn was slowly filling the little room, flowing into it like water through the small square window. The light lapped about his body, which ached with such an intolerable weariness. It seemed to rise about him, taking away the pain. It was a brightness about the broom handle and it touched his hands.

He felt that it held his hands. He had always been a highly strung, restless sort of creature, and when he was nervous and excited his hands would shake. Sometimes the Master had put his own hand over them, holding them still. Not often, because the Master had never been very free with his caresses, his love not being of that type; the grasp of the hand, the word of endearment were given when they were necessary, but not when they were not. Yet now, as the light rose and strengthened, he distinctly felt the grasp of a living hand. He knew the feel of that hand so well: wide across the palm because accustomed to the handling of an oar, hardened by the tools of his trade, the fingers very strong and supple. Yet the hardness and the strength had given a reassurance more comforting than any softness, and the warmth of the hand had always sent a glow of courage right through one's body. He felt that glow now. It rose with the light and reached his heart, which had been thumping so oddly. It reached his sore eyes and aching temples. Just his fancy, of course, about the touch, for the Master was dead; but straightening himself, he found that day had come. And his splitting headache had gone. The broom was not so heavy now, and there was strength in his body. He got the dust where he wanted it, opened the door, and swept it out of doors.

He knocked the broom handle against the side of the door and then paused, for it was such an extraordinarily lovely dawn. It struck him as odd that he should be able to notice the loveliness, but he did. It was still very early, yet the pearly light held already some faint rumor of the coming glory of the sunrise. It held colors soft and delicate as the colors of a reflected rainbow, incredibly gentle yet pervasive, as though the world in sleep had soaked up mercy like the air we breathe. Why did the word "mercy" come to his mind? There had been no mercy in the world two days ago. Mercy, with love, had died. Yet today, in this dawn, it was alive again.

John

There was still that freshness in the air. He took great gulps of it as though it were cool water from a well. He leaned against the door and the blessed coolness of it seemed gently to close his eyes. It was incredible relief to keep his eyes shut for a little while. He had scarcely been able to close them the last two nights because of what he saw when the lids came down. He had not known before that memory could paint such pictures upon closed lids. Perhaps that was one of the things that drove men mad – looking at the pictures they saw when they closed their eyes, things they'd seen, things they'd done. Perhaps that was what was torturing Peter, for he'd lain all night with closed lids, yet not sleeping. But no, it wouldn't be what he saw that he could hardly bear, for he hadn't been there. It would be what he heard. His own voice speaking. Three times over he'd said it. At the first cockcrow this morning a rigor like the rigor of death had seemed to take his body. John, lying beside him on his mat, had got up and come downstairs to sweep the floor, for he had known that the only thing he could do for the man at that moment was to leave him alone.

He wished Peter could hear what he was hearing now – the singing of birds. They were waking in the gardens of Jerusalem, and their liquid notes were cool as the air and beautiful as the newborn light. Were they singing like this in the garden where love was laid in the tomb, the garden where the women were? The women had left the house very early, while it was yet dark, with the spices for the embalming. There had not been time for that on that fearful Friday night. They had not been able to do more than wrap their dead Master in his grave clothes . . . dead . . . But the word that in spite of his queer unbelief had been stabbing him like a spear in his side for so many hours no longer stabbed him. It was as though the wound had healed, as though the word itself was dead. He opened his eyes and saw the whole of the sky covered with small, crisp, rosy clouds like feathers, with behind them an incredible depth of blue. And the scent of flowers came on the wind.

It was then that he heard the running feet, coming so quickly and lightly yet with such a desperate urgency. He stood braced now, one hand pressed against the door, his heart beating in sickening thuds. For he knew even before he saw her who it was who was running down the street. Only Mary of Magdala had such fleetness of foot, only she could put such a note of eager desperation into all she did and was.

She was with him in a moment, clinging to him like a child, the veil fallen back from her bright head, and like a child she was crying and gasping and talking all at once, so that he could make out nothing of what she was trying to tell him. Her clamor hurt him. It hurt the stillness and peace of the heavenly dawn. He pulled her inside the house and shut the door.

"Mary, be quiet! Don't cry like that. What's the good? And I can't understand."

But he held her gently, for he was gentle by nature, and grief had so completely locked them all together through these dreadful days that all of them who loved their Master seemed now one body. And then the passionate simplicity of Mary's childlike nature always called forth protectiveness. She poured her whole being into the joy or despair of the moment, so that like a child she must be held in safety till the storm was past.

"They have taken him away! They have taken him away! He's not there!" she gasped.

"Who have taken him away? What are you talking about?"

"The robbers. He's gone. John! John! Robbers have stolen the Master."

"No, that's not possible. They sealed the stone and set a guard."

It was not John who had spoken now but Peter. He had heard her crying and had come to them, and though he was in greater misery than John, he was at the moment more clearheaded. For him the impossible thing had happened and the unbearable thing was being borne. He knew his Master had died. He knew it better than John did, who had seen him die. There is a sense in which it is easier to know a thing if you have not seen it. John's mind these last two nights had beaten this way and that in confusion among the unbelievable things he had seen, so that he had become exhausted by unbelief, but his had lain still with the impossible in cold agony until at last he knew it true. And the truth about himself he knew too. The loyal, courageous hero of his daydreams, the man whose love would never deny or forsake however hard the test, did not exist at all. He was a man without courage, without loyalty, without truth, and without love. For two nights he had lain with the unbearable knowledge, but at the sound of Mary's crying he had got up, bearing it, and had gone to see what he could do. Such acceptance had made him very clearheaded, but it had also aged him. The sight of his face, when she raised her head and looked at him over John's shoulder, stilled Mary's lamentations as John's gentle endearments had not been able to do. She had not known before that a man could become old so quickly as this.

"Sit down, Mary," said Peter quietly. He took her from John's arms and sat her down on the stool. He stood by her and awkwardly stroked the braids of her hair. For the moment she was quieted and said sensibly, "The stone has been rolled away and the guard has gone. They fled in a panic. You can see they did because there's a lantern over-turned and a couple of spears left behind. And the grass and the flowers are trampled where they ran. It was grave robbers. You can see it was." And then the horror of it came over her again and she jumped up, twisted herself free from John's detaining hand and ran for the door. She collided there with Salome, John's mother, and Mary Cleopas, but she pushed them away and ran out into the street and away again like the wind. It seemed to her bruised mind that if she went back to the garden again perhaps she would find him.

"Mary!" cried Salome. "Come back!"

"Let her alone," said Peter heavily. "Is it true, Salome?"

Both the older women, breathless and panting, for they too had run through the streets, began to talk at once. Until now they had been calmer than Mary, for they had lived longer in this world and had known the death of many hopes and stood by many graves, but now they were nearly as incoherent as she had been. But with joy, not despair. For the tomb was not empty, they said. There were two men there. Sunlit, they seemed. Yes, sunlit in that dark place. They sat one at the head and one at the foot where the body of Jesus had lain, and they said the Lord was risen. Not stolen, but risen. Mary, poor girl, had not seemed to see anything. She had not waited to hear and see.

She had never had much patience, poor Mary, and without patience there is neither hope nor faith nor vision. But they had heard and seen. Not seen, exactly, for they had not been able to look on those shining faces. Nor heard, really; not like you hear men speaking in the ordinary way. Yet they *had* heard, like you hear news that shakes you in the song of a bird, a shepherd's pipe calling in the hills, a child singing at the well; you hear and you set down your pitcher and the tears are on your face. But they knew what they had to say. They had to come quickly and say, "He is alive. He is risen. Lo, I have told you."

The bird told you, the shepherd's pipe, the child singing at the well, the sunlit man who had looked down at the slab of holy stone and then passed his hand across his shining eyes. They said the same thing.

Afterward John could hardly disentangle the women's confused words from the thoughts that had lit into flame in his own mind. Nor did he remember how he had got himself out into the street, away from the women's talk and from Peter's sad eyes that looked pitifully upon them and thought they talked the nonsense of silly women who have borne too much. There seemed wings on his feet for a while, and then he heard Peter calling after him and slackened speed that the older man might catch up. They ran for a little side by side, but they could not speak, Peter because he was panting with the exhaustion of John's speed, John because of the tumultuous hope that was in him. Now and then he looked at Peter, but the man's rugged, furrowed face was still set in the lines of his stony grief. He ran so doggedly and so desperately because he thought they might yet catch the robbers. But he could not stay the course. The sweat started out on his forehead and he gasped and stumbled as the pain caught his side. John ran on and came first to the tomb.

But he could not go in. His nature, fine-drawn and sensitive, was not disciplined enough as yet to have attained to that perfect poise he had so worshiped in his Master. His own will was still beloved by him. His Master, though far more highly strung, more intensely sensitive than he, had been held in perfect balance by the iron strength of his devotion to the will of God. But John swung this way and that, intensely happy when things went as he wanted them to go, miserable when they did not, now courageous, now afraid. When he was with his Master he had felt like a small boat, swinging with the tides, yet safely moored to a great strength; he would not be swept to disaster, either one way or the other, while the rope held. But two days ago it had seemed to break, and there had seemed no bottom to the misery into which he had fallen. But there had been a bottom, because there had come that unbelief in the fact of death, the peace of the fair dawn, his winged feet, his hope that, as the misery had only seemed to be bottomless, so the rope had only seemed to break. But now – he could not go in. His frail boat had swung the other way. If he were to go in now and see no shining ones, *see* only the empty slab of cold and cruel stone or, worse still, a heap of tumbled graveclothes flung there by thieves, then it would kill him. It would be the last thing he could not bear. He leaned against the rock, panting from his run, his heart thudding, his head buried in the crook of his arm, and the pictures began again in his mind, this time not pictures of what he had seen but of what he might have seen if he had watched the thieves in the tomb. Peter came up to him, paused a moment, and then with something of his old impetuosity went on into the tomb. But John could not follow him. If he went in he would see the tumbled graveclothes.

But he had courage and it returned to him as the thudding of his heart quieted. He must go in. He must know one way or the other. And he could not leave Peter alone in there. Moving gallantly now, with the grace of his youth, he bent his comely head and went in. He saw no heavenly spirits and the light was dim. He saw Peter on his knees staring stupidly at the slab of rock where the Master had lain. And then he saw what he had dreaded to see, the graveclothes left behind, and it was in truth as though he died. He could not groan or cry out. He was too cold. He just stood there, gripped by the cold. This was death, this cold. To have had the glorious hope and lost it. To be forsaken of hope. To be forsaken in this cold. Was this what the Master had felt when in the dark garden they had forsaken him and fled? His mind, which had been so hot and confused, was suddenly coldly clear, as Peter's had been. He and Peter had changed places now, for looking at Peter's face he saw only bewilderment there, not a full comprehension of the fearful thing that had happened. He looked back again at the graveclothes, and the whole terrible clarity of his mind became focused upon them.

They were not in a tumbled heap. They lay in dignity, every fold in place. No human hands had touched them since the hands of the Marys had so disposed those folds. And the small bunches of herbs that the women had placed here and there among the folds were still where they had put them. Only as there was no body within the graveclothes, they had sunk gently to the stone by their own weight, just as a lily flower might fall softly to the ground below, still keeping its perfect shape. The shape of the graveclothes was very perfect. Naturally, thought John, for the shape of the body that had been withdrawn had been perfect. And the shape of his head too. The napkin, lying apart by itself, kept the shape of the head. No one had disturbed it. God had taken to himself his human body once again with supreme gentleness as well as supreme power. But the gentleness and the power had for John a most dear familiarity.

Without knowing what he did, he too fell on his knees. He wondered why he had thought the tomb so dark, for the light of the sun filled it. He saw no heavenly spirits; for him they were not necessary. He heard no voice speaking, but he heard the birds singing outside in the garden. Was the Master outside in the garden? Mary, perhaps, had seen him. Yet John stayed where he was, for he who had forsaken his Lord did not deserve to see his Lord. But he knew that he would see him again, if not in this life then in another, because the gentleness and the power were but different aspects of eternal mercy. John could wait. Length of time no longer mattered. Nothing mattered but the fact of life.

The Legend of Christophorus

Adapted from Hans Thoma

ONCE UPON A TIME a boy was born, and his parents named him Opherus. He was a very strong boy and did not know what to do with all his strength. Even as a young child he broke tools and agricultural equipment. His father often was at a loss for how to occupy him, because in spite of his good will he did more harm than his work was worth. All his father's tools were too weak for his strong arms. You should have seen his muscles!

By the time he became a young man, Opherus looked like a giant. One day his father sent him to the fields to plow. Since the horses were too slow for Opherus, he set them loose and pushed the plow through the field himself at great speed. After a few hours the plow fell to pieces. His father was sad because Opherus always meant well; he was simply too strong. He said to his son, "Opherus, you must serve a greater and stronger master, so that you can use your strength in a right and proper way."

So Opherus left home. He traveled from land to land, from town to town, and everywhere he asked where the mightiest lord was to be found. At last he came to a king's court, where a young lad told him that this king was the mightiest far and wide. Opherus had himself led to the throne, and there he offered his services.

Now on that very day the king had summoned all the knights of his country to form an army, because a neighboring king had invaded and burnt down a town. The king intended to send a great force against the invader. When he saw the powerful Opherus he said, "You have come at the moment of my greatest need. You shall be above all my soldiers, and with you I shall win every battle."

With all speed the royal armorer forged a gigantic sword for Opherus, for no other sword was nearly big enough for him. The very next day the king went off to battle, with Opherus leading the troops.

On the third day of the battle, a messenger raced back to the palace and announced, "Our army has gained the victory! It was wonderful to behold how Opherus fought – there was hardly anything left for the other soldiers to do. The enemy fled from the sweep of his gigantic sword and was scattered in the neighboring mountains. The invader is vanquished!"

Victory wreaths were hung from the gates and towers of the palace. Bells were rung throughout the town. The king commanded that the table in the great hall be set for a feast of celebration.

In the evening the hall was lit with many lights and the feasting commenced. A harper sang to the music of the strings, and the best talent of the court performed sword dances. Opherus sat beside the king. But he noticed that, as the harper played and sang a song in which the devil was mentioned, the king unobtrusively made the sign of the cross over his brow.

"That is odd," Opherus thought to himself.

The singing ended, and the festive throng lifted their goblets and drank with great cheer. When the king asked Opherus how he had liked the song, he replied, "There is one thing I am wondering about, Your Majesty. Why did you make the sign on your brow during the song?"

"Oh," replied the king, "I do that whenever I hear the name of the devil!"

"Well," Opherus persisted, "is the devil's power superior to yours?"

"I rule over just one country, but the devil has dominion over the whole world!" replied the king.

Never having heard of the devil before, Opherus thought to himself, "If there is another who is mightier than this king, I shall go and find him. I want to serve the *very greatest* king."

The next day Opherus said farewell, even though the king was unwilling to see him go. He wandered through the countries of the world. Everywhere, he asked where the devil's kingdom was, but no one would tell him. Indeed, many people took fright at the question, at which his respect for the unknown king grew even greater.

One day when Opherus was making his way through a deep forest, a stranger came up to him from behind. Opherus at once asked him, "Wayfarer, can you tell me where I may find the devil, who people say is the most powerful king on earth?"

"He is walking beside you: I am he," replied the stranger.

"Is it true that you have power over the whole world?"

"That is correct," answered the devil.

"Then allow me to be your servant, Your Majesty!"

And that is how Opherus became a faithful servant of the devil. In the service of evil he did terrible things, but he was glad because he had found a strong master.

One day the devil took Opherus to a building site for a new chapel. After weeks of labor, the rafters and roof-timbers were finally in place, and bright ribbons decorated a little fir-tree set on the gable-end. It was evening, and the workers had already left, intending to tile the roof the following morning.

"Strike it down!" cried the devil, pointing to the building. Immediately Opherus uprooted a tree and struck the roof with it, smashing the walls so that not one stone remained upon another.

"You have done your work well," said the devil, grinning.

When the workmen came to the chapel next morning, they stared sadly at the ruins of the building.

"That has been done by the Evil One," exclaimed one of them. "Let us set up a cross here on the path before we resume building. That will keep him away."

They did as the man directed, and set up a wooden cross in the middle of the road leading up to the chapel ruins. Then, before setting to work to restore the building, they sang a hymn.

After some time, when the walls and roof had been restored over the holy place, the devil returned with Opherus. But when he came near the cross the builders had erected, he trembled, sprang aside, and made a wide circuit around it. Opherus stopped, surprised.

"Tell me, Your Majesty: why did you jump aside from the cross in the path?"

"Do not ask, but strike the roof. Look, the tiles are already on it."

"I will not strike even one blow unless you explain the meaning of the cross."

"The cross is the sign of a great lord, whose name I dare not speak," the devil replied.

"Is his name so dangerous that even you cannot mention it?" asked Opherus. "Is this other lord mightier than the devil?"

Then the devil sidled up close and whispered, "He is the one whose power is supreme in earth and in heaven. But ask no more. Come, strike the roof!"

"If there is a lord who has power over not only earth but also heaven, then surely he is the greatest king, and him only will I serve," said Opherus; and the devil left him, cursing.

Early next morning the workmen arrived. They found Opherus asleep within the chapel walls. Awakened by their noise, he jumped up, and pointing to the wooden cross asked, "To what king does this sign belong?"

They answered, "The king's name is Christ."

Opherus forsook the devil that very moment and began seeking Christ. He inquired everywhere if anyone had heard of him or knew where he could be found. As he was searching, lonely and burdened with many evil deeds, Opherus met a hermit, who told him that if he wanted to find Christ, he must first find remorse and repentance. But Opherus told the hermit he wanted to do more than just sit and repent.

The hermit replied: "Listen then to my advice. If you wish to find Christ, you must serve mankind with all your strength. Do you see the broad river down there? It has no bridge, yet every day many wayfarers wish to cross. Go down there, build a hut by the stream, and ferry people over on your strong shoulders. If you do this out of love, you may find what you seek."

For many years, Opherus did as the hermit said. He did not spare himself; day or night he was ready to help the travelers who passed. He built himself a little hut at the edge of the river, and if someone called, he carried them across the dangerous waters. But in all this time, his longing to find Christ grew stronger.

It happened once on a very stormy night that he heard a voice crying, "Opherus, Opherus, carry me over." He left his house and searched up and down the riverbank, but found no one. So he returned to his hut and fell asleep again. But the voice called again, coming to him weakly through the tempest: "Opherus, Opherus, carry me over." Again he went out, but no one was there. Thinking it must be the wind, he lay down again. But before long he heard the voice a third time. It sounded at first like a cry, and then he heard his name through the wind: "Opherus, Opherus, come carry me over the water."

This time he found a small child huddled on the riverbank. He lifted the little boy onto his shoulder, where he seemed quite light; but when he entered the water, the child became increasingly heavier. Soon the burden grew so great that Opherus almost broke down under its weight. He cried out, "Oh, little child, you seem to be so very heavy – it is as if I were carrying the whole earth on my shoulders."

Then the child answered, "You not only carry the earth and the heavens, but you carry him who bears the whole need of the world upon himself. I am Jesus Christ, your King whom you seek."

And the child spoke further to Opherus, "From now on you will fear neither death nor the devil. You will walk through the suffering of this world and your name will be Christ-Opherus, which means 'bearer of Christ.' Your soul will be illumined with the love of God, and you will show mercy to men."

Then the child disappeared; but Christophorus obeyed his command and went out to the people of the earth. Wherever he went, he witnessed to the love and power of the child, his King.

Many of his old friends did not like the change in Opherus. They began to persecute him and drive him away, for they did not want to hear his message. Finally, their hatred became so strong that they banded together and killed him. But his voice and his challenge to become carriers of Christ could not be killed.

Let us open our ears, then, so that we too may hear the voice calling us to carry the King over.

Robert of Sicily

Sara Cone Bryant

Adapted from Henry Wadsworth Longfellow

AN OLD LEGEND says that there was once a king
named Robert of Sicily, who was brother to the great
pope of Rome and to the emperor of Allemaine. He was
a very selfish king, and very proud; he cared more for his
pleasures than for the needs of his people, and his heart
was so filled with his own greatness that he had no thought
for God.

One day this proud king was sitting in his place at
church, at vesper service; his courtiers were about him in
their bright garments, and he himself was dressed in his
royal robes. The choir was chanting the Latin service, and
as the beautiful voices swelled louder, the king noticed one
particular verse which seemed to be repeated again and
again. He turned to a learned clerk at his side and asked
what those words meant, for he knew no Latin.

"They mean, 'He hath put down the mighty from their
seats and hath exalted them of low degree,'" answered the
clerk.

"It is well the words are in Latin, then," said the king angrily, "for they are a lie. There is no power on earth or in heaven which can put me down from my seat!" And he sneered at the beautiful singing as he leaned back in his place.

Presently the king fell asleep, while the service went on. He slept deeply and long. When he awoke, the church was dark and still and he was all alone. He, the king, had been left alone in the church, to awake in the dark! He was furious with rage and surprise, and stumbling through the dim aisles he reached the great doors and beat at them madly, shouting for his servants.

The old sexton heard someone shouting and pounding in the church and thought it was some drunken vagabond who had stolen in during the service. He came to the door with his keys and called out, "Who is there?"

"Open! Open! It is I, the king!" came a hoarse, angry voice from within.

"It is a crazy man," thought the sexton; and he was frightened. He opened the doors carefully and stood back, peering into the darkness. Out past him rushed the figure of a man in tattered, scanty clothes, with unkempt hair and white, wild face. The sexton did not know that he had ever seen him before, but he looked long after him, wondering at his wildness and his haste.

In his fluttering rags, without hat or cloak, not knowing what strange thing had happened to him, King Robert rushed to his palace gates, pushed aside the startled servants, and hurried, blind with rage, up the wide stair and through the great corridors, toward the room where he could hear the sound of his courtiers' voices. Men and women servants tried to stop the ragged man who had somehow got into the palace, but Robert did not even see them as he fled along. Straight to the open doors of the big banquet hall he made his way, and into the midst of the grand feast there.

The great hall was filled with lights and flowers; the tables were set with everything that is delicate and rich to eat; the courtiers, in their bright clothes, were laughing and talking; and at the head of the feast, on the king's own throne, sat a king. His face, his figure, his voice were exactly like Robert of Sicily; no human being could have told the difference; no one dreamed that he was not the king. He was dressed in the king's royal robes, he wore the royal crown, and on his hand was the king's own ring. Robert of Sicily, half-naked, ragged, without a sign of his kingship on him, stood before the throne and stared with fury at this figure of himself.

The king on the throne looked at him. "Who art thou, and what dost thou here?" he asked. And though his voice was just like Robert's own, it had something in it sweet and deep, like the sound of bells.

"I am the king!" cried Robert of Sicily. "I am the king, and you are an impostor!"

The courtiers started from their seats and drew their swords. They would have killed the crazy man who insulted their king; but he raised his hand and stopped them, and with his eyes looking into Robert's eyes he said, "Not the king; you shall be the king's jester! You shall wear the cap and bells and make laughter for my court. You shall be the servant of the servants, and your companion shall be the jester's ape."

With shouts of laughter, the courtiers drove Robert of Sicily from the banquet hall; the waiting-men, with laughter too, pushed him into the soldiers' hall; and there the pages brought the jester's wretched ape, and put a fool's cap and bells on Robert's head. It was like a terrible dream; he could not believe it true; he could not understand what had happened to him. And when he woke next morning, he believed it was a dream, and that he was king again. But as he turned his head, he felt the coarse straw under his cheek instead of the soft pillow, and he saw that he was in the stable with the shivering ape by his side. Robert of Sicily was a jester, and no one knew him for the king.

Three long years passed. Sicily was happy and all things went well under the king who was not Robert. Robert was still the jester, and his heart was harder and bitterer with every year. Many times during the three years, the king, who had his face and voice, had called him to himself, when none else could hear, and had asked him the one question, "Who art thou?" And each time that he asked it his eyes looked into Robert's eyes to find his heart. But each time Robert threw back his head and answered proudly, "I am the king!" And the king's eyes grew sad and stern.

At the end of three years, the pope bade the emperor of Allemaine and the king of Sicily, his brothers, to a great meeting in his city of Rome. The king of Sicily went, with all his soldiers and courtiers and servants – a great procession of horsemen and footmen. Never had been a merrier sight than the grand train, men in bright armor, riders in wonderful cloaks of velvet and silk, servants, carrying marvelous presents to the pope. And at the very end rode Robert the jester. His horse was a poor old thing, many-colored, and the ape rode with him. Everyone in the villages through which they passed ran after the jester and pointed and laughed.

The pope received his brothers and their trains in the square before Saint Peter's. With music and flags and flowers he made the king of Sicily welcome and greeted him as his brother. In the midst of it, the jester broke through the crowd and threw himself before the pope. "Look at me!" he cried. "I am your brother, Robert of Sicily! This man is an impostor who has stolen my throne. I am Robert, the king!"

The pope looked at the poor jester with pity, but the emperor of Allemaine turned to the king of Sicily, and said, "Is it not rather dangerous, brother, to keep a madman as jester?" And again Robert was pushed back among the serving-men.

It was Holy Week, and the king and the emperor, with all their trains, went every day to the great services in the cathedral. Something wonderful and holy seemed to make all these services more beautiful than ever before. All the people of Rome felt it: it was as if the presence of an angel were there. Men thought of God and felt his blessing on them. But no one knew who it was that brought the beautiful feeling. And when Easter Day came, never had there been so lovely, so holy a day: in the great churches, filled with flowers and sweet with incense, the kneeling people listened to the choirs singing, and it was like the voices of angels; their prayers were more earnest than ever before, their praise more glad – there was something heavenly in Rome.

Robert of Sicily went to the services with the rest and sat in the humblest place with the servants. Over and over again he heard the sweet voices of the choirs chant the Latin words he had heard long ago: "He hath put down the mighty from their seat, and hath exalted them of low degree." And at last as he listened, his heart was softened. He too felt the strange blessed presence of a heavenly power. He thought of God, and of his own wickedness; he remembered how happy he had been, and how little good he had done; he realized that his power had not been from himself at all. On Easter night, as he crept to his bed of straw, he wept, not because he was so wretched, but because he had not been a better king when power was his.

At last all the festivities were over, and the king of Sicily went home to his own land again with his people. Robert the jester came home too.

On the day of their homecoming, there was a special service in the royal church, and even after the service was over for the people, the monks held prayers of thanksgiving and praise. The sound of their singing came softly in at the palace windows. In the great banquet room the king sat, wearing his royal robes and his crown, while many subjects came to greet him. At last he sent them all away, saying he wanted to be alone; but he commanded the jester to stay. And when they were alone together the king looked into Robert's eyes, as he had done before, and said softly, "Who art thou?"

Robert of Sicily bowed his head. "Thou knowest best," he said. "I only know that I have sinned."

As he spoke, he heard the voices of the monks singing, "He hath put down the mighty from their seat," – and his head sank lower. But suddenly the music seemed to change; a wonderful light shone all about. As Robert raised his eyes, he saw the face of the king smiling at him with a radiance like nothing on earth, and as he sank to his knees before the glory of that smile, a voice sounded with the music, like a melody throbbing on a single string:

"I am an angel, and thou art the king!"

Then Robert of Sicily was alone. His royal robes were upon him once more; he wore his crown and his royal ring. He was king. And when the courtiers came back they found their king kneeling by his throne, absorbed in silent prayer.

Two Old Men

Leo Tolstoy

Translated by Louise and Aylmer Maude

I

THERE WERE ONCE two old men who decided to go on a pilgrimage to worship God at Jerusalem. One of them was a well-to-do peasant named Efím Tarásitch Shevélef. The other, Elisha Bódrof, was not so well off.

Efím was a staid man, serious and firm. He neither drank nor smoked nor took snuff, and had never used bad language in his life. He had twice served as village elder, and when he left office his accounts were in good order. He had a large family: two sons and a married grandson, all living with him. He was hale, long-bearded, and erect, and it was only when he was past sixty that a little grey began to show itself in his beard.

Elisha was neither rich nor poor. He had formerly gone out carpentering, but now that he was growing old he stayed at home and kept bees. One of his sons had gone away to find work, the other was living at home. Elisha was a kindly and cheerful old man. It is true he drank sometimes, and he took snuff, and was fond of singing, but he was a peaceable man and lived on good terms with his family and with his neighbors. He was short and dark, with a curly beard, and, like his patron saint Elisha, he was quite bald-headed.

The two old men had taken a vow long since and had arranged to go on a pilgrimage to Jerusalem together: but Efím could never spare the time; he always had so much business on hand; as soon as one thing was finished he started another. First he had to arrange his grandson's marriage; then to wait for his youngest son's return from the army; and after that he began building a new hut.

One holiday the two old men met outside the hut and, sitting down on some timber, began to talk.

"Well," asked Elisha, "when are we to fulfil our vow?"

Efím made a wry face.

"We must wait," he said. "This year has turned out a hard one for me. I started building this hut thinking it would cost me something over a hundred rubles, but now it's getting on for three hundred and it's still not finished. We shall have to wait till the summer. In summer, God willing, we will go without fail."

"It seems to me we ought not to put it off, but should go at once," said Elisha. "Spring is the best time."

"The time's right enough, but what about my building? How can I leave that?"

"As if you had no one to leave in charge! Your son can look after it."

"But how? My eldest son is not trustworthy – he sometimes takes a glass too much."

"Ah, neighbor, when we die they'll get on without us. Let your son begin now to get some experience."

"That's true enough, but somehow when one begins a thing one likes to see it done."

"Eh, friend, we can never get through all we have to do. The other day the womenfolk at home were washing and housecleaning for Easter. Here something needed doing, there something else, and they could not get everything done. So my eldest daughter-in-law, who's a sensible woman, says: 'We may be thankful the holiday comes without waiting for us, for however hard we worked we should never be ready for it.'"

Efím became thoughtful.

"I've spent a lot of money on this building," he said, "and one can't start on the journey with empty pockets. We shall want a hundred rubles apiece – and it's no small sum."

Elisha laughed.

"Now, come, come, old friend!" he said. "You have ten times as much as I, and yet you talk about money. Only say when we are to start, and though I have nothing now I shall have enough by then."

Efím also smiled.

"Dear me, I did not know you were so rich!" said he. "Why, where will you get it from?"

"I can scrape some together at home, and if that's not enough, I'll sell half a score of hives to my neighbor. He's long been wanting to buy them."

"If they swarm well this year, you'll regret it."

"Regret it! Not I, neighbor! I never regretted anything in my life, except my sins. There's nothing more precious than the soul."

"That's so; still it's not right to neglect things at home."

"But what if our souls are neglected? That's worse. We took the vow, so let us go! Now, seriously, let us go!"

II

ELISHA SUCCEEDED in persuading his comrade. In the morning, after thinking it well over, Efím came to Elisha.

"You are right," said he, "let us go. Life and death are in God's hands. We must go now, while we are still alive and have the strength."

A week later the old men were ready to start. Efím had money enough at hand. He took a hundred rubles himself, and left two hundred with his wife.

Elisha, too, got ready. He sold ten hives to his neighbor, with any new swarms that might come from them before the summer. He took seventy rubles for the lot. The rest of the hundred rubles he scraped together from the other members of his household, fairly clearing them all out. His wife gave him all she had been saving up for her funeral; and his daughter-in-law also gave him what she had.

Efím gave his eldest son definite orders about everything: when and how much grass to mow, where to cart the manure, and how to finish off and roof the cottage. He thought out everything and gave his orders accordingly. Elisha, on the other hand, only explained to his wife that she was to keep separate the swarms from the hives he had sold, and to be sure to let the neighbor have them all, without any tricks. As to household affairs, he did not even mention them.

"You will see what to do and how to do it as the needs arise," he said. "You are the masters and will know how to do what's best for yourselves."

So the old men got ready. Their people baked them cakes, and made bags for them, and cut them linen for leg-bands. They put on new leather shoes and took with them spare shoes of platted bark. Their families went with them to the end of the village and there took leave of them, and the old men started on their pilgrimage.

Elisha left home in a cheerful mood, and as soon as he was out of the village forgot all his home affairs. His only care was how to please his comrade, how to avoid saying a rude word to anyone, how to get to his destination and home again in peace and love. Walking along the road, Elisha would either whisper some prayer to himself or go over in his mind such of the lives of the saints as he was able to remember. When he came across anyone on the road, or turned in anywhere for the night, he tried to behave as gently as possible and to say a godly word. So he journeyed on, rejoicing. One thing only he could not do, he could not give up taking snuff. Though he had left his snuff-box behind, he hankered after it. Then a man he met on the road gave him some snuff; and every now and then he would lag behind (not to lead his comrade into temptation) and would take a pinch of snuff.

Efím too walked well and firmly, doing no wrong and speaking no vain words, but his heart was not so light. Household cares weighed on his mind. He kept worrying about what was going on at home. Had he not forgotten to give his son this or that order? Would his son do things properly? If he happened to see potatoes being planted or manure carted as he went along, he wondered if his son was doing as he had been told. And he almost wanted to turn back and show him how to do things, or even do them himself.

III

THE OLD MEN had been walking for five weeks; they had worn out their homemade bark shoes, and had to begin buying new ones when they reached Little Russia. From the time they left home they had had to pay for their food and for their night's lodging, but when they reached Little Russia the people vied with one another in asking them into their huts. They took them in and fed them, and would accept no payment; and more than that, they put bread or even cakes into their bags for them to eat on the road.

The old men traveled some five hundred miles in this manner free of expense, but after they had crossed the next province, they came to a district where the harvest had failed. The peasants still gave them free lodging at night, but no longer fed them for nothing. Sometimes, even, they could get no bread: they offered to pay for it, but there was none to be had. The people said the harvest had completely failed the year before. Those who had been rich were ruined and had had to sell all they possessed; those of moderate means were left destitute, and those of the poor who had not left those parts, wandered about begging, or starved at home in utter want. In the winter they had had to eat husks and goosefoot.

One night the old men stopped in a small village; they bought fifteen pounds of bread, slept there, and started before sunrise, to get well on their way before the heat of the day. When they had gone some eight miles, on coming to a stream they sat down, and, filling a bowl with water, they steeped some bread in it and ate it. Then they changed their leg-bands and rested for a while. Elisha took out his snuff-box. Efím shook his head at him.

"How is it you don't give up that nasty habit?" said he.

Elisha waved his hand. "The evil habit is stronger than I," he said.

Presently they got up and went on. After walking for nearly another eight miles, they came to a large village and passed right through it. It had now grown hot. Elisha was tired out and wanted to rest and have a drink, but Efím did not stop. Efím was the better walker of the two, and Elisha found it hard to keep up with him.

"If I could only have a drink," said he.

"Well, have a drink," said Efím. "I don't want any."

Elisha stopped.

"You go on," he said, "but I'll just run into the little hut there. I will catch you up in a moment."

"All right," said Efím, and he went on along the high road alone, while Elisha turned back to the hut.

It was a small hut plastered with clay, the bottom a dark color, the top whitewashed; but the clay had crumbled away. Evidently it was long since it had been re-plastered, and the thatch was off the roof on one side. The entrance to the hut was through the yard. Elisha entered the yard and saw, lying close to a bank of earth that ran round the hut, a gaunt, beardless man with his shirt tucked into his trousers, as is the custom in Little Russia. The man must have lain down in the shade, but the sun had come round and now shone full on him. Though not asleep, he still lay there. Elisha called to him and asked for a drink, but the man gave no answer.

"He is either ill or unfriendly," thought Elisha; and going to the door he heard a child crying in the hut. He took hold of the ring that served as a door-handle, and knocked with it.

"Hey, masters!" he called. No answer. He knocked again with his staff.

"Hey, Christians!" Nothing stirred.

"Hey, servants of God!" Still no reply.

Elisha was about to turn away, when he thought he heard a groan the other side of the door.

"Dear me, some misfortune must have happened to the people! I had better have a look."

And Elisha entered the hut.

IV

ELISHA TURNED THE RING; the door was not fastened. He opened it and went along up the narrow passage. The door into the dwelling-room was open. To the left was a brick oven; in front against the wall was an icon-stand and a table before it; by the table was a bench on which sat an old woman, bareheaded and wearing only a single garment. There she sat with her head resting on the table, and near her was a thin, wax-colored boy with a protruding stomach. He was asking for something, pulling at her sleeve and crying bitterly. Elisha entered. The air in the hut was very foul. He looked round and saw a woman lying on the floor behind the oven: she lay flat on the ground with her eyes closed and her throat rattling, now stretching out a leg, now dragging it in, tossing from side to side; and the foul smell came from her. Evidently she could do nothing for herself, and no one had been attending to her needs. The old woman lifted her head and saw the stranger.

"What do you want?" said she. "What do you want, man? We have nothing."

Elisha understood her, though she spoke in the Little-Russian dialect.

"I came in for a drink of water, servant of God," he said.

"There's no one – no one – we have nothing to fetch it in. Go your way."

Then Elisha asked:

"Is there no one among you, then, well enough to attend to that woman?"

"No, we have no one. My son is dying outside, and we are dying in here."

The little boy had ceased crying when he saw the stranger, but when the old woman began to speak, he began again, and clutching hold of her sleeve cried:

"Bread, Granny, bread."

Elisha was about to question the old woman, when the man staggered into the hut. He came along the passage, clinging to the wall, but as he was entering the dwelling-room he fell in the corner near the threshold, and without trying to get up again to reach the bench, he began to speak in broken words. He brought out a word at a time, stopping to draw breath and gasping.

"Illness has seized us . . . ," said he, "and famine. He is dying . . . of hunger."

And he motioned towards the boy and began to sob.

Elisha jerked up the sack behind his shoulder and, pulling the straps off his arms, put it on the floor. Then he lifted it onto the bench and untied the strings. Having opened the sack, he took out a loaf of bread, and cutting off a piece with his knife, handed it to the man. The man would not take it, but pointed to the little boy and to a little girl crouching behind the oven, as if to say:

"Give it to them."

Elisha held it out to the boy. When the boy smelled bread, he stretched out his arms, and seizing the slice with both his little hands, bit into it so that his nose disappeared in the chunk. The little girl came out from behind the oven and fixed her eyes on the bread. Elisha gave her also a slice. Then he cut off another piece and gave it to the old woman, and she too began munching it.

"If only some water could be brought," she said, "their mouths are parched. I tried to fetch some water yesterday – or was it today – I can't remember; but I fell down and could go no further, and the pail has remained there unless someone has taken it."

Elisha asked where the well was. The old woman told him. Elisha went out, found the pail, brought some water, and gave the people a drink. The children and the old woman ate some more bread with the water, but the man would not eat.

"I cannot eat," he said.

All this time the younger woman did not show any consciousness, but continued to toss from side to side. Presently Elisha went to the village shop and bought some millet, salt, flour, and oil. He found an axe, chopped some wood, and made a fire. The little girl came and helped him. Then he boiled some soup and gave the starving people a meal.

V

THE MAN ATE A LITTLE, the old woman had some too, and the little girl and boy licked the bowl clean, and then curled up and fell fast asleep in one another's arms.

The man and the old woman then began telling Elisha how they had sunk to their present state.

"We were poor enough before," said they, "but when the crops failed, what we gathered hardly lasted us through the autumn. We had nothing left by the time winter came, and had to beg from the neighbors and from anyone we could. At first they gave, then they began to refuse. Some would have been glad enough to help us but had nothing to give. And we were ashamed of asking: we were in debt all round, and owed money, and flour, and bread."

"I went to look for work," the man said, "but could find none. Everywhere people were offering to work merely for their own keep. One day you'd get a short job, and then you might spend two days looking for work. Then the old woman and the girl went begging further away. But they got very little; bread was so scarce. Still we scraped food together somehow, and hoped to struggle through till next harvest, but towards spring people ceased to give anything. And then this illness seized us. Things became worse and worse. One day we might have something to eat, and then nothing for two days. We began eating grass. Whether it was the grass, or what made my wife ill, I don't know. She could not keep on her legs, and I had no strength left, and there was nothing to help us to recovery."

"I struggled on alone for a while," said the old woman, "but at last I broke down too for want of food, and grew quite weak. The girl also grew weak and timid. I told her to go to the neighbors – she would not leave the hut, but crept into a corner and sat there. The day before yesterday a neighbor looked in, but seeing that we were ill and hungry she turned away and left us. Her husband has had to go away, and she has nothing for her own little ones to eat. And so we lay, waiting for death."

Having heard their story, Elisha gave up the thought of overtaking his comrade that day and remained with them all night. In the morning he got up and began doing the housework, just as if it were his own home. He kneaded the bread with the old woman's help and lit the fire. Then he went with the little girl to the neighbors to get the most necessary things, for there was nothing in the hut: everything had been sold for bread – cooking utensils, clothing, and all. So Elisha began replacing what was necessary, making some things himself and buying some. He remained there one day, then another, and then a third. The little boy picked up strength and, whenever Elisha sat down, crept along the bench and nestled up to him. The little girl brightened up and helped in all the work, running after Elisha and calling, "daddy, daddy."

The old woman grew stronger and managed to go out to see a neighbor. The man too improved, and was able to get about holding onto the wall. Only the wife could not get up, but even she regained consciousness on the third day and asked for food.

"Well," thought Elisha, "I never expected to waste so much time on the way. Now I must be getting on."

VI

THE FOURTH DAY was the feast day after the summer fast, and Elisha thought:

"I will stay and break the fast with these people. I'll go and buy them something, and keep the feast with them, and tomorrow evening I will start."

So Elisha went into the village, bought milk, wheat flour, and dripping, and helped the old woman to boil and bake for the morrow. On the feast day Elisha went to church, and then broke the fast with his friends at the hut. That day the wife got up, and managed to move about a bit. The husband had shaved and put on a clean shirt which the old woman had washed for him; and he went to beg for mercy of a rich peasant in the village to whom his plow-land and meadow were mortgaged. He went to beg the rich peasant to grant him the use of the meadow and field till after the harvest; but in the evening he came back very sad and began to weep. The rich peasant had shown no mercy but had said, "Bring me the money."

Elisha again grew thoughtful. "How are they to live now?" thought he to himself. "Other people will go haymaking, but there will be nothing for these to mow; their grassland is mortgaged. The rye will ripen. Others will reap (and what a fine crop mother earth is giving this year), but they have nothing to look forward to. Their three acres are pledged to the rich peasant. When I am gone, they'll drift back into the state I found them in."

Elisha was in two minds, but finally decided not to leave that evening but to wait until the morrow. He went out into the yard to sleep. He said his prayers and lay down;

but he could not sleep. On the one hand he felt he ought to be going, for he had spent too much time and money as it was; on the other hand he felt sorry for the people.

"There seems to be no end to it," he said. "First I only meant to bring them a little water and give them each a slice of bread: and just see where it has landed me. It's a case of redeeming the meadow and the cornfield. And when I have done that, I shall have to buy a cow for them, and a horse for the man to cart his sheaves. A nice coil you've got yourself into, brother Elisha! You've slipped your cables and lost your reckoning!"

Elisha got up, lifted his coat, which he had been using for a pillow, unfolded it, got out his snuff-box, and took a pinch, thinking that it might perhaps clear his thoughts.

But no! He thought and thought and came to no conclusion. He ought to be going; and yet pity held him back. He did not know what to do. He refolded his coat and put it under his head again. He lay thus for a long time, till the cocks had already crowed once: then he was quite drowsy. And suddenly it seemed as if someone had roused him. He saw that he was dressed for the journey, with the sack on his back and the staff in his hand, and the gate stood ajar so that he could just squeeze through. He was about to pass out, when his sack caught against the fence on one side: he tried to free it, but then his leg-band caught on the other side and came undone. He pulled at the sack and saw that it had not caught on the fence, but that the little girl was holding it and crying, "bread, daddy, bread!"

He looked at his foot, and there was the tiny boy holding him by the leg-band, while the master of the hut and the old woman were looking at him through the window.

Elisha awoke, and said to himself in an audible voice:

"Tomorrow I will redeem their cornfield, and will buy them a horse, and flour to last till the harvest, and a cow for the little ones; or else while I go to seek the Lord beyond the sea, I may lose him in myself."

Then Elisha fell asleep and slept till morning. He awoke early, and going to the rich peasant, redeemed both the cornfield and the meadowland. He bought a scythe (for that also had been sold) and brought it back with him. Then he sent the man to mow, and himself went into the village. He heard that there was a horse and cart for sale at the public-house, and he struck a bargain with the owner and bought them. Then he bought a sack of flour, put it in the cart, and went to see about a cow. As he was going along he overtook two women talking as they went. Though they spoke the Little-Russian dialect, he understood what they were saying.

"At first, it seems, they did not know him; they thought he was just an ordinary man. He came in to ask for a drink of water, and then he remained. Just think of the things he has bought for them! Why, they say he bought a horse and cart for them at the publican's only this morning! There are not many such men in the world. It's worthwhile going to have a look at him."

Elisha heard and understood that he was being praised, and he did not go to buy the cow, but returned to the inn, paid for the horse, harnessed it, drove up to the hut, and got out. The people in the hut were astonished when they saw the horse. They thought it might be for them, but dared not ask. The man came out to open the gate.

"Where did you get a horse from, grandfather?" he asked.

"Why, I bought it," said Elisha. "It was going cheap. Go and cut some grass and put it in the manger for it to eat during the night. And take in the sack."

The man unharnessed the horse and carried the sack into the barn. Then he mowed some grass and put it in the manger. Everybody lay down to sleep. Elisha went outside and lay by the roadside. That evening he took his bag out with him. When everyone was asleep, he got up, packed and fastened his bag, wrapped the linen bands round his legs, put on his shoes and coat, and set off to follow Efím.

VII

WHEN ELISHA HAD WALKED rather more than three miles, it began to grow light. He sat down under a tree, opened his bag, counted his money, and found he had only seventeen rubles and twenty kopeks left.

"Well," thought he, "it is no use trying to cross the sea with this. If I beg my way it may be worse than not going at all. Friend Efím will get to Jerusalem without me, and will place a candle at the shrines in my name. As for me, I'm afraid I shall never fulfil my vow in this life. I must be thankful it was made to a merciful Master, and to one who pardons sinners."

Elisha rose, jerked his bag well up on his shoulders, and turned back. Not wishing to be recognized by anyone, he made a circuit to avoid the village and walked briskly homeward. Coming from home the way had seemed difficult to him, and he had found it hard to keep up with Efím, but now on his return journey, God helped him to get over the ground so that he hardly felt fatigue. Walking seemed like child's play. He went along swinging his staff, and did his forty to fifty miles a day.

When Elisha reached home the harvest was over. His family were delighted to see him again, and all wanted to know what had happened: Why and how he had been left behind? And why he had returned without reaching Jerusalem? But Elisha did not tell them.

"It was not God's will that I should get there," said he. "I lost my money on the way, and lagged behind my companion. Forgive me, for the Lord's sake!"

Elisha gave his old wife what money he had left. Then he questioned them about home affairs. Everything was going on well; all the work had been done, nothing neglected, and all were living in peace and concord.

Efím's family heard of his return the same day, and came for news of their old man; and to them Elisha gave the same answers.

"Efím is a fast walker. We parted three days before St. Peter's day, and I meant to catch him up again, but all sorts of things happened. I lost my money, and had no means to get any further, so I turned back."

The folks were astonished that so sensible a man should have acted so foolishly: should have started and not got to his destination, and should have squandered all his money. They wondered at it for a while, and then forgot all about it, and Elisha forgot it too. He set to work again on his homestead. With his son's help he cut wood for fuel for the winter. He and the women threshed the corn. Then he mended the thatch on the outhouses, put the bees under cover, and handed over to his neighbor the ten hives he had sold him in spring, and all the swarms that had come from them. His wife tried not to tell how many swarms there had been from these hives, but Elisha knew well enough from which there had been swarms and from which not. And instead of ten, he handed over seventeen swarms to his neighbor. Having got everything ready for the winter, Elisha sent his son away to find work, while he himself took to platting shoes of bark and hollowing out logs for hives.

VIII

ALL THAT DAY while Elisha stopped behind in the hut with the sick people, Efím waited for him. He only went on a little way before he sat down. He waited and waited, had a nap, woke up again, and again sat waiting; but his comrade did not come. He gazed till his eyes ached. The sun was already sinking behind a tree, and still no Elisha was to be seen.

"Perhaps he has passed me," thought Efím, "or perhaps someone gave him a lift and he drove by while I slept and did not see me. But how could he help seeing me? One can see so far here in the steppe. Shall I go back? Suppose he is on in front, we shall then miss each other completely and it will be still worse. I had better go on, and we shall be sure to meet where we put up for the night."

He came to a village, and told the watchman, if an old man of a certain description came along, to bring him to the hut where Efím stopped. But Elisha did not turn up that night. Efím went on, asking all he met whether they had not seen a little, bald-headed old man? No one had seen such a traveler. Efím wondered, but went on alone, saying, "We shall be sure to meet in Odessa, or on board the ship," and he did not trouble more about it.

On the way, he came across a pilgrim wearing a priest's coat, with long hair and a skull-cap such as priests wear. This pilgrim had been to Mount Athos and was now going to Jerusalem for the second time. They both stopped at the same place one night and, having met, they traveled on together.

They got safely to Odessa, and there had to wait three days for a ship. Many pilgrims from many different parts were in the same case. Again Efím asked about Elisha, but no one had seen him.

Efím got himself a foreign passport, which cost him five rubles. He paid forty rubles for a return ticket to Jerusalem, and bought a supply of bread and herrings for the voyage.

The pilgrim began explaining to Efím how he might get onto the ship without paying his fare; but Efím would not listen. "No, I came prepared to pay, and I shall pay," said he.

The ship was freighted and the pilgrims went on board, Efím and his new comrade among them. The anchors were weighed and the ship put out to sea.

All day they sailed smoothly, but towards night a wind arose, rain came on, and the vessel tossed about and shipped water. The people were frightened: the women wailed and screamed, and some of the weaker men ran about the ship looking for shelter. Efím too was frightened, but he would not show it, and remained at the place on deck where he had settled down when first he came on board, beside some old men from Tambof. There they sat silent, all night and all next day, holding onto their sacks. On the third day it grew calm, and on the fifth day they anchored at Constantinople. Some of the pilgrims went on shore to visit the Church of St. Sophia, now held by the

Turks. Efím remained on the ship, and only bought some white bread. They lay there for twenty-four hours, and then put to sea again. At Smyrna they stopped again; and at Alexandria; but at last they arrived safely at Jaffa, where all the pilgrims had to disembark. From there it was still more than forty miles by road to Jerusalem. When disembarking the people were again much frightened. The ship was high and the people were dropped into boats which rocked so much that it was easy to miss them and fall into the water. A couple of men did get a wetting, but at last all were safely landed.

They went on on foot, and at noon on the third day reached Jerusalem. They stopped outside the town at the Russian inn, where their passports were endorsed. Then, after dinner, Efím visited the Holy Places with his companion, the pilgrim. It was not the time when they could be admitted to the Holy Sepulcher, but they went to the Patriarchate. All the pilgrims assembled there. The women were separated from the men, who were all told to sit in a circle, barefoot. Then a monk came in with a towel to wash their feet. He washed, wiped, and then kissed their feet, and did this to everyone in the circle. Efím's feet were washed and kissed with the rest. He stood through vespers and matins, prayed, placed candles at the shrines, handed in booklets inscribed with his parents' names, that they might be mentioned in the church prayers. Here at the Patriarchate food and wine were given them. Next morning they went to the cell of Mary of Egypt, where she had lived doing penance. Here too they placed candles and had prayers read. From there they went to Abraham's Monastery, and saw the place where Abraham intended to slay his son as an offering to God. Then they visited the spot where Christ appeared to Mary Magdalene, and the Church of James, the Lord's brother. The pilgrim showed Efím all these places and told him how much money to give at each place. At midday they returned to the inn and had dinner. As they were preparing to lie down and rest, the pilgrim cried out and began to search his clothes, feeling them all over.

"My purse has been stolen, there were twenty-three rubles in it," said he – "two ten-ruble notes and the rest in change."

He sighed and lamented a great deal, but as there was no help for it, they lay down to sleep.

IX

AS EFÍM LAY THERE, he was assailed by temptation.

"No one has stolen any money from this pilgrim," thought he. "I do not believe he had any. He gave none away anywhere, though he made me give and even borrowed a ruble of me."

This thought had no sooner crossed his mind than Efím rebuked himself, saying, "What right have I to judge a man? It is a sin. I will think no more about it." But as soon as his thoughts began to wander, they turned again to the pilgrim: how interested he seemed to be in money, and how unlikely it sounded when he declared that his purse had been stolen.

"He never had any money," thought Efím. "It's all an invention."

Towards evening they got up and went to midnight Mass at the great Church of the Resurrection, where the Lord's

Sepulcher is. The pilgrim kept close to Efím and went with him everywhere. They came to the Church; a great many pilgrims were there, some Russians and some of other nationalities: Greeks, Armenians, Turks, and Syrians. Efím entered the Holy Gates with the crowd. A monk led them past the Turkish sentinels to the place where the Savior was taken down from the cross and anointed, and where candles were burning in nine great candlesticks. The monk showed and explained everything. Efím offered a candle there. Then the monk led Efím to the right, up the steps to Golgotha, to the place where the cross had stood. Efím prayed there. Then they showed him the cleft where the ground had been rent asunder to its nethermost depths; then the place where Christ's hands and feet were nailed to the cross; then Adam's tomb, where the blood of Christ had dripped onto Adam's bones. Then they showed him the stone on which Christ sat when the crown of thorns was placed on his head; then the post to which Christ was bound when he was scourged. Then Efím saw the stone with two holes for Christ's feet. They were going to show him something else, but there was a stir in the crowd, and the people all hurried to the Church of the Lord's Sepulcher itself. The Latin Mass had just finished there, and the Russian Mass was beginning. And Efím went with the crowd to the tomb cut in the rock.

He tried to get rid of the pilgrim, against whom he was still sinning in his mind; but the pilgrim would not leave him, but went with him to the Mass at the Holy Sepulcher. They tried to get to the front but were too late. There was such a crowd that it was impossible to move either backwards or forwards. Efím stood looking in front of him, praying and every now and then feeling for his purse. He was in two minds: sometimes he thought that the pilgrim was deceiving him, and then again he thought that if the pilgrim spoke the truth and his purse had really been stolen, the same thing might happen to himself.

X

EFÍM STOOD THERE gazing into the little chapel in which was the Holy Sepulcher itself, with thirty-six lamps burning above it. As he stood looking over the people's heads, he saw something that surprised him. Just beneath the lamps in which the sacred fire burns and in front of everyone, Efím saw an old man in a grey coat, whose bald, shining head was just like Elisha Bódrof.

"It is like him," thought Efím, "but it cannot be Elisha. He could not have got ahead of me. The ship before ours started a week sooner. He could not have caught that; and he was not on ours, for I saw every pilgrim on board."

Hardly had Efím thought this, when the little old man began to pray, and bowed three times: once forwards to God, then once on each side, to the brethren. And as he turned his head to the right, Efím recognized him. It was Elisha Bódrof himself, with his dark, curly beard turning grey at the cheeks, with his brows, his eyes and nose, and his expression of face. Yes, it was he!

Efím was very pleased to have found his comrade again, and wondered how Elisha had got ahead of him.

"Well done, Elisha!" thought he. "See how he has pushed ahead. He must have come across someone who showed him the way. When we get out, I will find him, get rid of this fellow in the skullcap, and keep to Elisha. Perhaps he will show me how to get to the front also."

Efím kept looking out so as not to lose sight of Elisha. But when the Mass was over, the crowd began to sway, pushing forward to kiss the tomb, and pushed Efím aside. He was again seized with fear lest his purse should be stolen. Pressing it with his hand, he began elbowing through the crowd, anxious only to get out. When he reached the open, he went about for a long time searching for Elisha both outside and in the Church itself. In the cells of the Church he saw many people of all kinds, eating, and drinking wine, and reading and sleeping there. But Elisha was nowhere to be seen. So Efím returned to the inn without having found his comrade. That evening the pilgrim in the skull-cap did not turn up. He had gone off without repaying the ruble, and Efím was left alone.

The next day Efím went to the Holy Sepulcher again, with an old man from Tambof whom he had met on the ship. He tried to get to the front but was again pressed back; so he stood by a pillar and prayed. He looked before him, and there in the foremost place under the lamps, close to the very Sepulcher of the Lord, stood Elisha, with his arms spread out like a priest at the altar, and with his bald head all shining.

"Well, now," thought Efím, "I won't lose him!"

He pushed forward to the front, but when he got there, there was no Elisha: he had evidently gone away.

Again on the third day Efím looked, and saw at the Sepulcher, in the holiest place, Elisha standing in the sight of all men, his arms outspread, and his eyes gazing upwards as if he saw something above. And his bald head was all shining.

"Well, this time," thought Efím, "he shall not escape me! I will go and stand at the door, then we can't miss one another!"

Efím went out and stood by the door till past noon. Everyone had passed out, but still Elisha did not appear.

Efím remained six weeks in Jerusalem, and went everywhere: to Bethlehem, and to Bethany, and to the Jordan. He had a new shirt sealed at the Holy Sepulcher for his burial, and he took a bottle of water from the Jordan, and some holy earth, and bought candles that had been lit at the sacred flame. In eight places he inscribed names to be prayed for, and he spent all his money except just enough to get home with. Then he started homeward. He walked to Jaffa, sailed thence to Odessa, and walked home from there on foot.

XI

EFÍM TRAVELED the same road he had come by; and as he drew nearer home, his former anxiety returned as to how affairs were getting on in his absence. "Much water flows away in a year," the proverb says. It takes a lifetime to build up a homestead, but not long to ruin it, thought he. And he wondered how his son had managed without him, what sort of spring they were having, how the cattle had wintered, and whether the cottage was well finished. When Efím came to the district where he had parted from Elisha the summer before, he could hardly believe that the people living there were the same. The year before they had been starving, but now they were living in comfort. The harvest had been good, and the people had recovered and had forgotten their former misery.

One evening Efím reached the very place where Elisha had remained behind; and as he entered the village, a little girl in a white smock ran out of a hut.

"Daddy, daddy, come to our house!"

Efím meant to pass on, but the little girl would not let him. She took hold of his coat, laughing, and pulled him towards the hut, where a woman with a small boy came out into the porch and beckoned to him.

"Come in, grandfather," she said. "Have supper and spend the night with us."

So Efím went in.

"I may as well ask about Elisha," he thought. "I fancy this is the very hut he went to for a drink of water."

The woman helped him off with the bag he carried, and gave him water to wash his face. Then she made him sit down to table, and set milk, curd-cakes, and porridge before him. Efím thanked her and praised her for her kindness to a pilgrim. The woman shook her head.

"We have good reason to welcome pilgrims," she said. "It was a pilgrim who showed us what life is. We were living forgetful of God, and God punished us almost to death. We reached such a pass last summer that we all lay ill and helpless with nothing to eat. And we should have died, but that God sent an old man to help us – just such a one as you. He came in one day to ask for a drink of water, saw the state we were in, took pity on us, and remained with us. He gave us food and drink, and set us on our feet again; and he redeemed our land, and bought a cart and horse and gave them to us."

Here the old woman, entering the hut, interrupted the younger one and said:

"We don't know whether it was a man or an angel from God. He loved us all, pitied us all, and went away without telling us his name, so that we don't even know whom to pray for. I can see it all before me now! There I lay waiting for death, when in comes a bald-headed old man. He was not anything much to look at, and he asked for a drink of water. I, sinner that I am, thought to myself, "What does he come prowling about here for?" And just think what he did! As soon as he saw us, he let down his bag, on this very spot, and untied it."

Here the little girl joined in.

"No, Granny," said she, "first he put it down here in the middle of the hut, and then he lifted it onto the bench."

And they began discussing and recalling all he had said and done, where he sat and slept, and what he had said to each of them.

At night the peasant himself came home on his horse, and he too began to tell about Elisha and how he had lived with them.

"Had he not come we should all have died in our sins. We were dying in despair, murmuring against God and man. But he set us on our feet again; and through him we learned to know God, and to believe that there is good in man. May the Lord bless him! We used to live like animals; he made human beings of us."

After giving Efím food and drink, they showed him where he was to sleep, and lay down to sleep themselves.

But though Efím lay down, he could not sleep. He could not get Elisha out of his mind, but remembered how he had seen him three times at Jerusalem, standing in the foremost place.

"So that is how he got ahead of me," thought Efím. "God may or may not have accepted my pilgrimage, but he has certainly accepted his!"

Next morning Efím bade farewell to the people, who put some patties in his sack before they went to their work, and he continued his journey.

XII

EFÍM HAD BEEN AWAY just a year, and it was spring again when he reached home one evening. His son was not at home but had gone to the public-house, and when he came back, he had had a drop too much. Efím began questioning him. Everything showed that the young fellow had been unsteady during his father's absence. The money had all been wrongly spent and the work had been neglected. The father began to upbraid the son; and the son answered rudely.

"Why didn't you stay and look after it yourself?" he said. "You go off, taking the money with you, and now you demand it of me!"

The old man grew angry and struck his son.

In the morning Efím went to the village elder to complain of his son's conduct. As he was passing Elisha's house, his friend's wife greeted him from the porch.

"How do you do, neighbor," she said. "How do you do, dear friend? Did you get to Jerusalem safely?"

Efím stopped.

"Yes, thank God," he said. "I have been there. I lost sight of your old man, but I hear he got home safely."

The old woman was fond of talking:

"Yes, neighbor, he has come back," said she. "He's been back a long time. Soon after Assumption, I think it was, he returned. And we were glad the Lord had sent him back to us! We were dull without him. We can't expect much work from him anymore, his years for work are past; but still he is the head of the household, and it's more cheerful when he's at home. And how glad our lad was! He said, 'It's like being without sunlight, when father's away!' It was dull without him, dear friend. We're fond of him, and take good care of him."

"Is he at home now?"

"He is, dear friend. He is with his bees. He is hiving the swarms. He says they are swarming well this year. The Lord has given such strength to the bees that my husband doesn't remember the like. 'The Lord is not rewarding us according to our sins,' he says. Come in, dear neighbor, he will be so glad to see you again."

Efím passed through the passage into the yard and to the apiary to see Elisha. There was Elisha in his grey coat, without any face-net or gloves, standing under the birch trees looking upwards, his arms stretched out and his bald head shining, as Efím had seen him at the Holy Sepulcher in Jerusalem: and above him the sunlight shone through the birches as the flames of fire had done in the holy place, and the golden bees flew round his head like a halo, and did not sting him.

Efím stopped. The old woman called to her husband.

"Here's your friend come," she cried.

Elisha looked round with a pleased face, and came towards Efím, gently picking bees out of his own beard.

"Good day, neighbor, good day, dear friend. Did you get there safely?"

"My feet walked there, and I have brought you some water from the river Jordan. You must come to my house for it. But whether the Lord accepted my efforts . . ."

"Well the Lord be thanked! May Christ bless you!" said Elisha.

Efím was silent for a while, and then added, "My feet have been there, but whether my soul, or another's, has been there more truly . . ."

"That's God's business, neighbor, God's business," interrupted Elisha.

"On my return journey I stopped at the hut where you remained behind . . ."

Elisha was alarmed, and said hurriedly: "God's business, neighbor, God's business! Come into the cottage, I'll give you some of our honey." And Elisha changed the conversation, and talked of home affairs.

Efím sighed, and did not speak to Elisha of the people in the hut, nor of how he had seen him in Jerusalem. But he now understood that the best way to keep one's vows to God and to do his will, is for each man while he lives to show love and do good to others.

The Golden Egg

Ivy Bolton

THE SUN WAS SETTING over the city of London in a golden glory, a little dimmed by the haze from the river. There was a freshness of spring in the air and the slender little maid, standing by the Thames, lifted her pale face joyously as the soft breezes fanned a tinge of color into her cheeks. She was neatly dressed, though her shoes were worn and her homespun dress patched, as well as her faded hood and cloak.

"Daydreaming, Winnie?" asked a boy's voice, and she turned to see a lad about her own age standing at her side.

"Not so much as enjoying the springtime, Stephen," she answered as she seated herself on a low parapet which overhung the river. "I got through with my weaving and spinning early today, and Mother sent me out for a breath of air. It has been so close today in the Fleet. But here one can see the trees bursting into leaf and the flowers on the bank and know that Easter is almost here."

"The day after tomorrow, and on Easter Monday, the great egg rolling takes place. Are you going to be able to go out on Richmond Hill with us all, Winnie?"

"Mother says that I may."

"The egg rolling is going to be in Master Oglethorpe's grounds, and he is giving a big prize, Winnie. There is going to be hidden a golden egg, and they say it will be worth fifty guineas. Think of the luck of getting that!"

"Oh, if I only could!" She clasped her hands. "I think I would be willing almost to give my life for those fifty guineas."

"What do you want them for so badly?" He looked at her curiously.

She choked back a little sob. "For my father, Stephen. You know he is in the Debtors' Prison, and he has been there for seven of my thirteen years. Of course, he has to bide in the prison itself, and we live in that little house in the Debtors' Ward. I do not remember much else, only once a big green field when I was a baby, and lovely yellow cowslips which Mother made into balls and threw to me."

"You poor little wench." He patted her hand awkwardly. "Do not cry, Winnie. Perhaps your father will get free some day."

"If I could get the golden egg, perhaps he would. It was only fifty guineas that sent him to prison, and it was no fault of his that he got into debt. He borrowed it first when Mother was ill, and he had the money all ready to pay when it was stolen. That is what hurts so. The creditor was so angry, and he called Father a cheat and said he had hidden the money himself, and then he put him in prison. Father cannot earn anything in prison, and Mother and I can only make enough to feed ourselves and Martin."

"I hope you win it, Winnie. I will help you if I can. It would be wonderful if your father could get out and you could go away from the Fleet back to the country again."

"It would mean so much." She smiled radiantly. "Martin does not remember the green fields at all. You see, he was only one year old. Then there is Mother. She had such rosy cheeks and she was always laughing, and now she is thin and pale and so tired all the time. Thank you, Stephen." She rose, and he watched her out of sight.

Stephen Mellett had run across Winifred Cheatham in strange fashion. His pet dog had disappeared, and he had sought it far and wide. Then one day he saw it following a maid along the Cheap, and the two had turned into the Fleet. The boy had followed, and the dog, catching sight of his master, had fawned upon him. The girl had spoken joyously.

"Why, he must be yours," she said. "I found him with a broken leg close by the Thames, and I brought him home. Mother set it, and he is almost well now. I am so glad you have found him."

Their friendship dated from that afternoon. Winifred had refused a reward, and Stephen had often longed to find some way of serving her.

"You had better do the hiding, Randolph," a grave voice said, and the boy saw two men approaching. They did not notice him below the bank. He recognized the speaker as James Oglethorpe, whose great estate was to be the scene of the festivity on Easter Monday. His companion was unknown to the lad.

"Where shall I hide it?" Randolph asked. "It must be well concealed, for we shall have half of London out with such a prize as this."

"You remember the great oak tree at the left of the tower?" James Oglethorpe said. "In that is an old owl's nest which was my boyhood's hidey-hole. Put it there and it will take a clever lad or lass to find it. The egg rolling will be in front, and I have planned a good meal to be served in the great hall afterward."

"You love your poor, Oglethorpe."

"Aye, I want to do something for them. I am hoping to be able to help some. I have my Charter, Randolph, to a large tract of land south of the Carolinas in the New World. I hope to transport some of my poor thither."

They passed on, and Stephen sat thinking. Here was a clue for Winnie. Surely between them they could find the great oak and the owl's nest. He looked at the sun. He would have time to go down to the Fleet and find her.

Winifred made her way home slowly. Her heart was light now. Surely she would be able to find the golden egg. If she only could – there was no one in London to whom it would mean more. She stole into the Church of St. Mary-le-Bow opposite to Newgate prison and went into a shady corner. The rays of the sunset came through a stained-glass window, and she raised her face to the Divine One pictured there, a face which seemed to smile at her.

"Please thee, Lord," she prayed, "let me find the golden egg. Thou knowest how long Father has been in prison. Thou knowest how lovely are the fields and home, and Martin has never seen them. Lord, please let me find the egg and set them free. Amen."

She rose and went on her way again. Surely the Lord of the children would hear and help.

"Winnie!" She turned at Stephen's call, and he ran to her, excited and flushed. "I have the greatest news," he burst out. "Master Oglethorpe himself came by just after you went, and I heard where the egg will be hidden. It is to be in the owl's nest in the big oak tree near the tower. We will go right there, and just as soon as the signal is given we will get it."

He ran off without waiting for her reply, and she stood looking after him with a light in her eyes. "Why, our Lord has answered almost before I had finished my prayer," she thought. With happy heart she lifted the latch of her home and went in.

"You are late, little daughter." Her mother looked up from her work. "I have to finish this sewing for Dame Gurden tonight, so you must get the supper. It is a good one tonight, for Mistress Pettigill has sent in one of her great loaves, and there is a big bowl of milk for each of us as well. Master Hendricks had some left over, and he gave me just double. How kind folks are!"

"That is true, Mother." Winnie was spreading the worn, checked cloth on the table and setting out pewter spoons and bowls. "Mother, would it not be wonderful if we could go to the country again and live there in a wee cottage with Father?"

Mistress Cheatham sighed. "Wonderful indeed, my maid. But it is a long way off for us I fear. Fifty guineas is a huge sum for those who can make but a few pence a day. But we will go on hoping, and your father never loses courage."

Winifred smiled. "And I will go on hoping too," she said half aloud.

Martin looked up from his primer in the corner. "What does h-o-n-o-r-a-b-l-e spell, Winnie?" he asked. He was a fair-haired little lad with a small pinched face and great wistful grey eyes that seemed all too big for it. Winnie went over to him.

"Honorable, little brother," she said. "What a big word it is!"

"And what does it mean?"

"Being honest and truthful and – oh, just not able to do a mean thing."

"I see." He nodded his head. "It is more than being just truthful; it is not taking advantage, like the old knights you tell me about." He looked puzzled. "Is it right to listen secretly and take advantage, Winnie? A boy told me it is all right, but I do not think it is honorable, is it?"

"It is not; why of course not, be . . ."

"What is the matter, Winnie? Why are you so white?"

"It – it is nothing . . ." Winifred stammered. "Supper is ready, Martin. Come Mother."

She choked down her supper somehow. This was nothing she wanted her mother to see. It was something she must fight out first. She went about her usual duties and saw Martin started for bed. At last she lay down on her own little pallet in the corner of the living room, but not to sleep. Things were too tragic for that.

Would it be wrong to use her knowledge and find the golden egg? Oh surely it would not be. The golden egg just meant added pleasures for the others; to her it meant everything – home, love, perhaps even the lives of those she loved. Her mother's strength was failing; Martin was frail indeed, and this court by the Fleet was airless and cheerless and no place for a child.

"Dear Lord, please let me use it," she prayed again and again. But her conscience would not rest, and at last she dropped into an uneasy sleep.

"You look tired, child," her mother said at the breakfast table. "Have you not slept?"

Winnie went over and put her arms about her lovingly. "Not very well," she owned. "May I go over and speak to Father today?"

"He will be in the yard now. Go before you begin work; the air will do you good, little daughter."

Winnie donned her cloak. The guard knew her well and smiled at her as he let her into the prison precincts.

There, near the iron grating where the debtor's purses hung to beg a few pence from the passers-by, she saw her father. He never hung his purse up. "We have not begged yet," he told his wife, and it was his own idea to sit and watch the purses of the others. He was whittling now with clever fingers. He raised his haggard face, and his lips broke into a smile as he saw Winnie. He showed her his work. "It's a boat for Martin," he said. "You can take him to the heath and he can sail it in the pond there."

"He will love that." She sat down beside him, and he looked at her wistful eyes.

"Are you worrying, my maid? Is anything wrong?" he asked.

"Nothing is wrong; it is just something I cannot decide," she said. "Father, I came to ask your advice. Is it never right to do something – well, just a little dishonorable, if there is a lot involved?"

"No, my maid. You ought to be able to answer that for yourself."

"I ought, but I cannot." Her eyes filled. "If there was a lot involved – if it meant freedom for you, Father, and happiness for us all – would it be so very wrong to take an advantage?"

He put an arm about her and she leaned an aching head on his shoulder.

"Little daughter, I would rather die in a Debtors' Prison than have you even a shade dishonorable," he said. "But you have answered the question for yourself. You knew it was wrong or you would not have asked the question, and I know you well enough to know you will choose aright. I am proud of my maid."

She blinked back the tears. "You shall not be ashamed of me," she whispered. "I must go back and help Mother now."

It was almost dusk before she was able to go out again, and she went slowly to the church of St. Mary-le-Bow. Into its coolness she went and knelt in her corner again.

"Dear Lord, I am giving it up," she said aloud. "I cannot ask you for the golden egg now, but oh Lord, please help me somehow."

She rose and slipped out. Stephen came up to her.

"What is the matter, Winnie?"

She smiled. "It is just that we cannot take the golden egg, Stephen. You see, they did not know you heard. You see, it would not be honorable."

"I – I had not thought of that," he faltered. "Oh, Winnie, does it mean you have to give it up?"

She nodded. "It is all right; we just have to give it up," she said bravely. "I am going, Stephen, for Martin wants the fun."

Easter Morning dawned bright and clear, and Stephen joined Winnie and Martin as they came out at Richmond. Master Oglethorpe's mansion was a quaint Elizabethan one, and the great park stretched far around it. There the dappled deer strayed, a little alarmed now as the laughing bands of children ran through, up to the great house. There they were marshalled into lines, and a breathless hush came as James Oglethorpe explained his plan.

The egg rolling began and the hunt as well, and the whole scene was a merry one. Stephen took care of Martin, and Winnie slipped away to the shade of a great oak on the left. She could see the other oak by the tower and the owl's nest well within reach. Her eyes filled and with a little sob, she buried her face in the soft moss.

"What is the matter? Have you found no eggs, little maid? Why do you not hunt with the rest?"

She raised her tear-stained face and scrambled to her feet as she saw that it was James Oglethorpe himself who was addressing her.

"I – I may not hunt the golden egg, sir," she faltered. "You see, I know where it is – over yonder – and, oh, I wanted it so."

The sobs came faster now. James Oglethorpe put an arm about her and seated her beside himself on a big stone bench.

"How did you know?" he asked.

"Stephen overheard you telling Master Randolph where to hide it," Winnie answered. "We knew then we must not hunt it and . . ."

"Why do you want it so much?"

"For my father. He has been in Debtors' Prison for seven years now, and we cannot earn fifty guineas, Mother and I."

He looked at her little work-worn hand. "I think you and Mother may toil overhard," he said. "You are an honorable little maid."

A tall boy came up waving the golden egg. "Well, lad, so you found it! May it bring you good luck!"

"It will, sir," the boy answered joyously. "I can go to the Bluecoat School now."

"It is time that we had our supper," James Oglethorpe said. "Come, Giles, and you, Winifred Cheatham, is that the name? We must call them all to the feast."

"I am glad you got it," Winifred said shyly to the tall boy. "I hope you are happy in the Bluecoat School."

"I am coming to see your mother sometime," James Oglethorpe said as he bade her farewell. He watched her as she trudged off with Martin.

She was not at home when he came, and it was near the river that she met him.

"I have been to see your father, Winifred," he said. "He will be free tomorrow. We have struck a bargain. How would you like to fare forth to the New World, Winnie? To a place where you can make your home and sow great crops and beat a pathway for others to follow? That is what your father has agreed to do. I had not thought of the Debtors before, but they are the folk I could help with this new grant of mine.

"He will go with me next month and you all with him. Your friend Stephen is going, too. I had made arrangements with his family some months ago. Are you happy, little maid? No, do not kiss my hand, but hold out your own."

"This is your golden egg," he said. "It will make a faring for you."

"I – I don't know how to thank you," Winnie faltered.

"Your happy eyes do that," he said as he turned away.

Clutching her golden egg, Winnie slipped into the quiet church. "You did find a way," she whispered rapturously. "Oh, I do not know how to thank you, dear Lord. I love you."

The Case of Rachoff

Karl Josef Friedrich

Translated by Eileen Robertshaw

This is an imaginative story inspired by the life of Vasily Osipovich Rakhov (born ca. 1861), who wandered through Russia serving the poor and was imprisoned for eight years in the Suzdal Monastery. Accounts of the historical Rakhov's death vary.

READER, BEHOLD YOUR HAND. Sometimes I watch my own as I write; or as I hold it up, fingers spread, so that it gleams like a pale star against the dark background of books piled on my table. The human hand – this bundle of bones, flesh, and nerves – think of all it can do. It can bless or curse. It can draw blood or bind a wound. It is gentle, agitated, vicious; supplicating, ardent, tender. It can weld an iron bridge or caress a child's head. It possesses the power to both harm and heal.

RACHOFF WAS FOURTEEN when the devout old Timofei, a dealer in wheat and a guest in his father's house, laid a blessing on him. Taking the young man's hands in his,

Timofei reverently made the sign of the cross on them and said, "Vassili Ossipovich Rachoff, I hereby set a seal on your two hands, that you may never use them for anything evil, impure, or shameful, but only to comfort, give, and heal. Your hands shall rest tenderly on brows furrowed with pain and care; they shall gently rub weary backs. They shall carry food, drink, and warm clothes to the poor. They shall be a blessing to everyone."

Deeply stirred, Rachoff knelt before the old man for a long time, his large, earnest eyes searching the wooden floor, his ears reddening with a sense of inadequacy. Timofei's words had struck him and sunk quickly to the depths, and yet he could still hear their echoes, their strange and wonderful sound. What did they mean?

Timofei turned and went, and not long afterward he died. But his words did not die. "Your hands shall be a blessing to everyone." That was at once a consecration and a call. God himself had put the words into Timofei's mouth, and they had power. Power to change and to purify. Power to grant a vision that grew ever clearer.

Rachoff was born in 1861, the son of a respected citizen in Archangelsk, a city far in the North between the vast Russian tundra and the White Sea. Like Timofei, his father was a grain merchant, though well-to-do. Rachoff grew up in his father's large, stone townhouse near the harbor and was expected to follow in his father's footsteps. After he turned seventeen he was apprenticed to a family friend, a merchant who owned a large German export firm, and every day he went to this man's house to learn all he could about commerce.

Though successful, Rachoff's master was not a worldly man but a sincere believer who was more concerned with inner, rather than outer, things. On Rachoff's eight-eenth birthday, he presented the young man with a Bible. Looking at him intently he said, "You are as a son to me, dear Rachoff, and I have long wished to seal your eyes as a father would. See clearly when you read this book. Everything depends on it. If your eyes are not truly open, you may as well be blind." Then he blessed Rachoff, saying: "I seal your eyes as a father would, so that God's Word is not an obstacle to you but a source of comfort, wisdom, and peace. Your eyes shall see nothing in this holy book but Jesus' power and great love." Rachoff stood there, startled and perplexed as the strange word "seal" rang again in his ears. What could it mean?

Soon Rachoff was reading the Bible almost every evening. He had to read it secretly, for his father, an Orthodox believer who felt that the study of God's Word was better left to priests, would not have approved. But that did not matter, for the merchant's words were true: Jesus spoke to him from every page – and not only spoke, but turned his life upside down, robbing him of complacency and setting him on edge. And that is how it should be, because it is written, "He who draws near to me draws near to the fire."

The next winter a distant cousin moved into the city with his family. He was a poor man and did not wait long to inform Rachoff's father where he lived and how he was related, so one Sunday after dinner, Rachoff's father, who was tired of his pestering, set out with his son to visit the man and see for themselves whether something could be done.

As they entered the house – really a squalid, cavern-like cellar – they saw that the entire family of seven lived in one room. The children huddled in it were famished and half-naked, and the floor so dirty it made Rachoff's skin creep. The man motioned them to take seats in two peeling painted chairs, and as he did, his wife darted forward to wipe a brown smear from one of them. Rachoff grimaced, then sat down anyway. What else was there to do? He looked around. There was one window, a small, high opening in one wall, but the light it let in was wan, and the draft that seeped from it sour and chilly.

Rachoff's father sent for food from a nearby inn, and meat was brought. As soon as it came, the man, hunger-crazed, thrust his fingers into it, snatched up a piece, and devoured it. The rest of the family followed suit. It was a dreadful sight, one Rachoff would never forget. What filth – what degradation! His heart tightened at the sight of such broken, animal-like beings. And to think that they were his own relatives!

That evening his thoughts kept turning to Jesus. For was it not Jesus who had forced his eyes open, searing them as if with sparks flung from a burning fire? He broke down, weeping. What would Jesus have done? Waves of shame rolled over him, for he knew the answer. His hands would have soothed and healed and given blessing.

After that night new insights burst upon Rachoff at every turn, driving him forward and dismantling every cherished and long-held assumption. Even the church brought him no peace. Previously the bells had rung out sweetly, dispelling all his troubles and inspiring him to prayer. Now their chimes unsettled him, reminding him only of the bishop's endless wealth and the grinding poverty of the peasants who flocked to hear him. Previously the statues of the saints had awed him, as did the candles (some weighing a hundred pounds and costing a thousand rubles apiece), the gilded images, and the wall hangings. Now, however, he saw that such beauty was really a pious distraction from reality – from the wretchedness of the poor who sought comfort in its intoxicating veil.

At length, driven by his disquiet, Rachoff attempted his first act of charity. It was a gray, rainy day in February, and from his window he saw a ragged old man tottering along the street. Without a word to anyone, he went out and called the beggar into his room, bathed him, dressed him in clean clothes, fed him, and offered him his own bed. Stupefied, the man stared first at Rachoff, then at his fine furniture, then at the tapestries on his walls. He shook his head. Rachoff, equally tongue-tied, let him go – and with him, his gold watch, as he was embarrassed to discover the next morning.

After this incident, a period of disillusionment set in, and Rachoff began to doubt the value of generosity. For a while he even adopted his father's way of thinking, whereby the poor were all classed as one kind: cheats and liars responsible for their own plight; undeserving riffraff who had no sense of what it meant to earn money.

Yet Jesus continued to work in him, and soon Rachoff was again restless and unable to find peace. In his turmoil he went to a Marxist, a preacher who believed that the state would one day be replaced by a just economic system and a citizenry of equals. Such was his dream. At first Rachoff was attracted by his oratory, but when he realized that the man was intent on seizing political power, by armed struggle if necessary, he turned away. The Jesus he knew was a humble man.

IN 1881, WHEN RACHOFF WAS TWENTY, his old master, the merchant, sent him to manage a sugar-beet factory in a village not far from the city. Rachoff was happy to go, but after a year and a half the desolate, unending landscape began to depress him, as did his employees, many of them uncouth peasants given to heavy drinking and wild behavior. Rachoff tried hard to reform them, but nothing he did seemed to work.

Then he met Irina Nesterova. The wife of a peasant farmer and dealer, Irina was a kindly, bespectacled little woman of about fifty, and a devoted disciple of Jesus. When she spoke her eyes shone, and her warmth of heart and kindly voice won over everyone who met her, including Rachoff. Four families lived in Irina's house, and though they had once been rough and disorderly, their manners had gradually yielded to her steady calm. Irina belonged to a small group of believers, and once a week (on Fridays, the day Jesus died) she gathered its members at her house, where they frankly confessed their sins, encouraged one another, and prayed and sang.

Unlike the upper half of the village, where Rachoff's factory stood, Irina's half – the so-called lower village – was transformed by her. When someone was sick, she visited him. On cold days she brought tea to the laborers in the fields; on hot days she carried them water. When a woman was beaten by her drunken husband, Irina would be the first one at the house, mellowing him with friendly gestures and then admonishing him with firm words. In Irina, the spirit of Jesus was at work.

"Little mother," Rachoff asked her one day, "what are your teachings? What are your beliefs about God, about the rich and poor?"

"In my eyes they all live in bondage," Irina replied, "the rich just as much as the poor."

"The rich!" exclaimed Rachoff. "How can they be, when they live in such warmth and comfort?"

"No one is free just because he has possessions," said Irina. "And money does not necessarily mean wealth. Yes, even the richest man is poor. And so is every other being. The whole creation moans under the weight of a terrible sadness. The earth itself cries out as if in pain. There is sighing among the animals and the trees, in the springs and the rocks, in the fire and the stars. But Jesus will come. He hears every groan, and he will come to rescue us from our grief. His spirit heals and reconciles and blesses; it comes to us and dwells in our midst, and it can – through grace and hard work – pry us free from our bondage and make us like children."

"Children?" Rachoff puzzled.

"Yes, children," Irina repeated. "True children are joyous, whether they are fed with a hundred rubles or three kopeks a day, for the spirit of Jesus lives within them."

"You are right, Mother Irina," said Rachoff. "I remember my friends, the Lupkins of Archangelsk, whose son is ill all the time. He suffers from a chest infection and has undergone surgery many times, but nothing will help him, so wrapped up he is in his own misery. His sister is healthy, but just as unhappy. Spoiled and bored, she stands hour after hour at the window, dreary and sullen, though surrounded by comforts and possessions of every kind. Their parents are both given to bad moods and violent quarrels, and even on the best days they live in a state of continual nervous tension."

Irina nodded. "There is coldness wherever people are not yet healed by the Spirit. But how different it can be with Jesus! You know my Natasha. She's been bedridden for three years with tuberculosis, but never cries or complains. She's rarely unhappy, for she is filled with hope and love."

Rachoff listened to her words, and longing for the same spirit, asked her, "Give me your blessing, Mother Irina."

"Gladly," she answered, "I will set a seal on your heart." And with that she made the sign of the cross over his heart, saying, "Jesus alone shall rule in this heart. Away with all sadness and complaining! Come, spirit of God, dwell here within this man, and grow until he is filled with your purifying love."

Rachoff trembled and his eyes welled with tears, for it was now three times that he had been thus blessed. A threefold seal! And now it was clear to him what it meant. His hands must become like Jesus' hands: tender and eager to serve. His eyes must become like Jesus' eyes: clear, loving, and sincere. Finally, his heart must become one with Jesus' heart, finding peace in the Father with the same trust and certainty that Jesus had.

Youth is never clear sailing, however, and many storms still lay ahead for Rachoff. He confronted greed and cruelty, self-righteousness, lust, and deceit, yet still he did not fully accept the task that had been laid on him. And though he knew he must serve Jesus, it seemed as though the Master did not welcome his attention, but stood constantly at his shoulder, wielding the whip of another exacting demand, calling him to sacrifice and give still more. What torment it brought him! For Rachoff did not yet see how everything that opposes God must be destroyed within a man before he can find peace, and before there is release from the anguish of unanswered searching.

Back in Archangelsk, Rachoff was consumed both with a feeling of restlessness and a premonition of approaching fulfillment. He was twenty-two now, and his mother meant to find him a wife. In fact, she claimed to have found one – a kind and well-off woman. But things turned out quite differently.

One autumn night, after hours of inner striving, Rachoff had a dream. In it he saw a fallow field stretching far into the distance, sloping gently upward until it met the sky. Suddenly a shining light appeared above the horizon and began to move slowly toward him. He saw that the radiance surrounded a simply dressed yet noble figure, a man in a brown robe, guiding a plow and coming down the newly turned furrow. The man was not alone, but accompanied by an adoring throng.

All at once the air was pierced by a sound – the thin, steady tone of a bow being drawn across the string of a violin. Or was it the muted cry of a baby? The man at the plow looked up and listened. The crowd held its breath. The sound was coming from a nearby hut. The man walked over and entered it.

Rachoff followed, and saw that the sound was coming from a baby. Silent, he watched as the man gathered it up and kissed it, at which the crying stopped. A natural gesture, one might think. But it was so tender, so infinitely compassionate, that Rachoff was moved to tears. Stumbling blindly back out of the hut, he returned to the crowd. It had changed to a mob, and the cheers to contemptuous scoffing.

Rachoff was unable to stop weeping. He could not have explained it, but he had just seen what he had longed for through all the years of his unrest. He had seen Jesus – Jesus, stooping to pick up a little child.

Suddenly Rachoff was wide awake. Jumping from his bed, he knelt down on the floor and gave fervent thanks for his dream; then, with nothing but the clothes on his back, he slipped silently out of his parents' house.

The moon was bright; a soft breeze tousled his hair. He strode down the road with a light, glad step. Once he stood still for a moment, contemplating the meaning of his vision, but then his heart rose high within him, and he stepped out again, even more briskly. This was no time to interpret a dream. He had seen Jesus – that was all that mattered – and Jesus was no longer a goad, a piercing arrow, a source of unrest. He was a well of peace, a fire of love, a sun of joy. He was cause for unbroken praise.

Gratitude and exultation swept over Rachoff. He broke into a run, and ran on and on toward the dawn, shouting into the darkness and the springing wind, "Brother Jesus, here I am. I am coming! I am coming!"

FOR FIVE DAYS Rachoff traveled eastward, until he reached the district capital of Pinega, and on the sixth day he walked further, to Radinovka, a village of poor workers. Twilight was falling when he came, and a light autumn rain stirred the dust of the unpaved streets.

In front of the first house Rachoff passed he met a rough-looking woman with untidy red hair, driving a herd of pigs.

"Is there a holy man in the village?" he asked.

"Yes, there's a dear old father here," she replied. "He usually prays and sings, but he's lying sick just now. Come with me."

The woman brought Rachoff into a nearby house, and there he found an old man with swollen feet, lying near a brick stove with his legs wrapped in a fleece.

"Tell me, dear brother, are you a man of God?" Rachoff asked him. "I greet you with joy in the name of Jesus Christ. What is your name? Mine is Rachoff."

"My greetings to you, too, wandering brother," replied the man. "But how sad that you have a name. I have no name; I am nameless."

"What do you mean by that, my brother?" asked Rachoff.

"The one who is above is nameless," the man returned, pointing upwards. Then, pointing to himself, he went on, "And the one who is above is the one who lives here. The two are one and the same. I am a part of him, a part of the nameless one. That is what Gregor Petrov told me when I was in Tambov with the army. Gregor was a God-fearing peasant, and he read this in a holy book, written in the holy language and given to him by a venerable man."

"Come here to me, and I will make you better, dear Father Nameless," Rachoff said.

The old man obeyed, and Rachoff took a bucket of warm water from the stove and washed and massaged his legs. He was like a child, Rachoff thought.

"What else was written in the holy book, dear Father Nameless?" he inquired.

"It said, my dear friend, that true faith is a daily fight, and fasting a good aid in overcoming the flesh. It said, too, that men should live singly and pure, like the angels in heaven. Even if they are married, they ought to abstain, praying until every desire is conquered, and doing so with the help of a copper cross around their neck. Look, here is mine!"

At this the old man tugged at his crucifix, then went on: "One day judgment will come, and God's people will be counted, and only those will be saved who wear a cross, like I do."

The old man rambled on, talking now wisely and now foolishly, while Rachoff finished tending to his sores. Night had come, and the room was filling with curious women and children. The men were at the tavern. Later Rachoff knelt and prayed with his listeners, and read to them from the Gospels.

Afterward the women returned to their shacks, and then the men returned, stumbling in the dark, beating their wives and children and causing one petulant outburst after another. Rachoff sat in the darkness and listened to their angry shouts, waiting for the uproar to subside. He knew now that this was the place for him to stay.

Rachoff stayed two years in Radinovka, going from house to house and sharing in the work of the villagers. Above all he chose jobs that no one else wanted to do. He helped care for the sick, scrubbed dirty wooden floors, scraped molding walls and whitewashed them, cleansed neglected animals, and shoveled out overflowing stalls.

He taught the children to speak Russian, for they knew only the local dialect, and how to read and write. He also read the Gospel to them and told them stories about Jesus, saying, "It is not enough to have his image in a little shrine in a corner of the house. We must keep him in our eyes and hands, and in our hearts."

In the evenings he gathered the villagers and strengthened them in faith, teaching them that not asceticism – not fasting or abstaining – but Jesus alone is the power that overcomes the world. They took his words to heart, and as they did, the men were weaned from their drunken ways, and the women from their gossip and backbiting. Eyes became gentler, hands more peaceable, and words kinder and more understanding. Husbands stopped mistreating their wives, who in turn showed new respect to them, and children began to honor and obey their parents.

Before long Rachoff was accepted as a friend throughout the village. Even the smallest children were entrusted to his care, and though he was only twenty-four, they fondly called him Father Vassili.

But there was one exception. When Rachoff had arrived in Radinovka, the Orthodox priest had kept to his home, suffering from an infectious disease. No one was willing to look after him, not even his wife, so frightened was she of contagion. Only Rachoff was courageous enough to visit him, and he brought hot compresses and eased his inflammation. Eventually Rachoff's attentive care cured him.

Others might have thanked him, but the priest did not. Jealous of Rachoff's popularity and suspicious that his kindness was really a ruse to get him out of bed and back to work, he looked on the young man with growing mistrust. As for the young man's condemnation of strong drink, it made him fairly bristle, for there was little he loved like the bottle. "Have you any idea, little brother," he would complain, "what a sacrifice it is for me to sit here year after year in this godforsaken place, toiling and half starving, stranded with a wife and children, surrounded by nothing but the frozen wastes? Over in Pinega, my hometown, I was a man among men. Here I am a man among swine, and drinking is my only salvation. With it I can at least escape this miserable hole for a while and fly back to my good friends – back to the days of my youth. Wine is the gift of a good God. Why, it is even praised in the Psalms!"

To which Rachoff replied, "That may be so, but if you would stop drinking and turn Radinovka from the hell-hole you describe into a place of warmth and love – into a garden for Jesus – you would no longer hate your life, or want to flee it in a drunken fog."

"A garden for Jesus?" retorted the priest, rolling his eyes. "That's just what infuriates me about you. You talk of nothing but Jesus. Always Jesus! It's enough to make one think you're from a sect. Can't you see that the peasants are too thickheaded for him? Find me one who's not a shameless rascal. The two don't go together. Praying is religion enough. Anyone can do it."

"No," insisted Rachoff, "it is not enough. A Jesus who is only there for people to pray to is an idol in the clouds, and what good is that? We must help each villager to receive him into his heart, his eyes, his hands. We must let his love live right here among us. He is already at work. Look at Taras, or at Anissa. Look at almost every other. Jesus has made his home with them; they have become sons and daughters of God."

But the priest continued to mistrust him. It didn't help much that the peasants now recoiled from him in disgust as he staggered along the street, cursing or guffawing and reeking of cheap wine. In earlier days they had hurried to him, confiding in him as one of their own. They had drunk and joked with him; they had kissed his hand. And now – now they turned to Rachoff, that intruder from

Archangelsk. Oh, what wouldn't he give to be rid of him!

One day about half a year later a government order arrived from Pinega, forbidding Rachoff to remain in the village. The women wept, and the men, too, broke down when they heard the news. Only Rachoff remained calm. "It is only I, a twenty-five-year-old man of no consequence, who has been banned. Jesus still remains in Radinovka; he can still work among you. Only I am journeying on."

Rachoff set out for Archangelsk again, and when he arrived back home, it was May. Everywhere the wintry tundra was carpeted in green. Alder catkins nodded along the water, and flowers bloomed; the fresh-turned furrows breathed with new life. In later years Rachoff's mother would look back on it as a heavenly spring: her son was home, and she could once more care for him. And what was more, Rachoff, who had previously resisted every gesture, now allowed her to show love to him.

Then, as suddenly as he had come, Rachoff disappeared. He did so without a word, leaving only a terse note: "Jesus is calling, and I must answer." And then: "Jesus is still with you." That was all he wrote.

When his mother found the sheet of paper Rachoff was already long gone. His gait was confident and upright; his bearded face weathered, creased by sunshine, wind, and rain. He crossed new vistas daily, for he aimed to wander all of Russia. Everywhere, people were drawn by his love and loved him in return. And whether they admitted it or not, everyone who returned his earnest gaze felt his blessing.

Rachoff demonstrated his love in practical ways. In each village he came to, he pulled out his cache of tools – hammer and nails, hand-saw, knife, and string – and offered his services to any who would take them. When a goat broke into a widow's garden, he mended the fence for her; when a cripple ran short of winter fuel, he split firewood for a day. Once he cared for a sickly young woman until she was strong enough to hold her newborn child. Another time he sat with a dying old man until his last breath. Rachoff told him so vividly about the joys of the world beyond that the man thought an angel had come to him.

"You are sure it is not a place of darkness and decay?" he asked about death.

"Oh, no!" Rachoff reassured him. "You are about to enter the fullness of life – a glorious, bright morning as brilliant as the sun at Easter." And as Rachoff went on to describe the beauty of the heavenly realm, the man grew more and more peaceful, so that at the end he was happy, even eager, to pass into the land of eternal spring.

Sometimes people joined Rachoff for a stretch along the road. Once two devoted young women, friends who had heard his call to serve, even followed him for several weeks. They begged food and cooked for him, washed his tunic and mended his cloak. They might never have left his side, had he not shaken himself loose from them. Crowds often came after him as he left a village where he had stayed, but though kindly and gentle, he always evaded them. Before long a rumor was circulating that Jesus himself was journeying through Russia. And truly, his behavior and speech were so selfless, so pure, that Jesus' spirit did shine from him, penetrating many a heart and bearing good fruit.

Once in the far southern reaches of Russia, Rachoff came upon a sect led by a certain Jacob Istomin, who asked him, "Are you one of us?"

"That depends who you are, dear brother," replied Rachoff warm-heartedly.

"We are wanderers, travelers, pilgrims," said the man. "We go from place to place. An ascetic named Ivan taught us that a true worshipper of God is continually on the run from the Antichrist. And so we move on ceaselessly, for the whole world is ruled by the Antichrist, our enemy from the beginning, and all priests and ministers and soldiers are his servants. We are unable to resist them in battle, so we flee on and on, across the endless plains of our native land and through the vast and kindly forests.

"We have broken all ties with church and state and disdain all excuses for contact with the world. We refuse to pay taxes, to serve in the army, to obey government authorities, to respect bishops or priests. We have no use for documents such as passports, but tear them up or burn them. Money is meaningless to us, and we never keep any on hand. We depend on the devout. They give us food and clothing enough.

"The only thing we honor is the small cross that each of us carries. See, here is mine. Look what is written on it – it was endorsed in Jerusalem itself. That is the only real passport, for what are true Christians but pilgrims and strangers in this life? And is it not so, that only those who escape the world will not be condemned to destruction with it?"

Rachoff listened quietly until the man was finished. Then, humbly but passionately, he began to speak, reminding Jacob Istomin of the simple love of Jesus, and showing up his own complex ideas as delusion: "Jesus is the true king over the earth, and it is he, not the Antichrist, who shall have the final say. Jesus reigns wherever people welcome him, and wherever this happens, the Antichrist will sense his active, living presence, and turn and flee.

"It is not the disciples of Jesus, but the followers of the Antichrist, who are always on the run. No, Jesus' disciples hold their ground with valiant and determined hearts. Jesus builds up, gathers, and affirms. You tear down; you scatter; you run and hide. Jesus blesses; you curse. Jesus unites; you divide. Jesus heals and comforts; he brings peace, joy, and love; and wherever he rules, the Antichrist gives way to him. Kneel down, proud man! Kneel to Jesus! He alone has power!"

In the end, Jacob Istomin saw the truth of Rachoff's words and followed after him, though eventually Rachoff threw him off his trail.

Down by the Sea of Asov, at the mouth of a great river, Rachoff met a withered old hermit named Abrossim. An anchorite who made his home in a cave, Abrossim was well versed in the lives of the saints, and, after the manner of one of them, believed that peace was found only by withdrawing from the daily affairs of men.

Abrossim went down to the river each day to catch the fish he lived on; otherwise, he spent his hours in contemplation and prayer. At midday he danced in the gray-green grasses of the steppe, circling slowly on the top of the hill, long beard streaming, cloak fluttering in the wind. That symbolized the dancing of the saints and friends of God on the holy meadows of paradise. At evening he knelt down in front of his cave, gazing in rapture at the eternal movement of the stars. That symbolized the adoration to come, the holy time when all men will behold God. At midnight he lay down in a grave that he had dug for himself. That symbolized dying, and the importance of readiness for death. Then, on the following morning, he began the day by bowing, then running toward the sunrise, his hands uplifted in prayer. That symbolized resurrection. So every day Abrossim lived in expectation, acting out a parable of man's passage from this life to the next.

When Rachoff found the anchorite, however, he lay sick, so Rachoff stayed in the cave for several weeks, caring for him and learning a great deal. When they parted, the old man wept and said: "You have been like a mother to me, dear brother. Ancient as I am, I thought of my own mother when you tended me with your gentle hands. I thank you for your love. Oh, how I wish my life were still before me, so I might go out as you do, and in the strength of Jesus fill the whole world with his spirit! But I cannot. So receive my blessing, and give me yours."

Rachoff traveled on, learning, teaching, and healing as he went. Finally he left Russia and made his way to Jerusalem. Once there, he wandered the city and took in its storied sights, but though deeply moved, he was at the same time heartbroken. Everywhere the poor pilgrims were shamefully exploited, and it wasn't the hucksters but the priests who cheated them the worst. With deep pain, he recognized that, holy as it was, Jerusalem had no room for Jesus. Just as the city had rejected him in the past, so it did now. Judas, the betrayer, would have felt right at home.

One day, while watching a great procession, Rachoff could hold back his indignation no more. A Greek patriarch, seated on a white, silken throne borne aloft by four strong priests, was making his way down the street. Trumpets sounded, and the procession moved like a white cloud toward a magnificent church.

Following the throng inside, Rachoff watched as the patriarch was reverently lowered in front of the gold-encrusted altar. Then, rising to his full height, he cried out,

"You on the white throne, Jesus is calling you! If you are a shepherd, then take care of your flock! Look how your sheepdogs are treating the sheep: they are scattering the ewes and devouring the lambs. Woe to such dogs! And woe to the shepherd who cannot control them!"

Everyone stood petrified by this outburst. Blood reddened cheeks; faces burned with shame. But the bold young stranger's words hit home to many. How many of them had traveled from great distances, simple, perhaps, and poor, but devout in their longing? And how many more pinched and scraped for years, hoping to nourish their souls by walking where Christ had walked on earth? And here, at the end of it all, what awaited them other than greedy priests who demanded coins for every foolish rite: gold to touch the hole where the cross had stood, silver to kiss the place where the sacred body had lain, copper to have a candle lit, or to place a hand in the crack of some holy temple wall! It was a just denunciation, they knew, and they began to tremble.

Meanwhile the rash heckler was seized by guards, who pulled him from the gaping crowd and dragged him outside and away. Throwing Rachoff in a fortress room, they left him imprisoned for a day and a night, with nothing but a jug of water to sustain him.

Yet he was not forgotten. At morning, as a cool breeze ran through the alleys, a young woman stood under his barred window – a pilgrim who had found him after many hours of searching. Craning her neck to see into the dark opening, she pled, "Oh, where are you, my Jesus? If only I might see you, here in this city where your feet once trod!" Rachoff did not answer, but fell on his knees in the gloom, shaken and humbled to his very depths.

BANNED FROM THE HOLY LAND, Rachoff traveled north again, until he reached the great city of Odessa on the Black Sea. Everywhere, lavish displays of wealth met his eyes: imposing mansions on broad, tree-lined boulevards; expensive cafés filled with laughing women and haughty men; luxurious hotels for travelers from faraway places such as Paris and Berlin.

There were magnificent parks, too, bright with roses and oleanders and freshened by fountains and pools. In one square Rachoff passed a towering glass sunroom. Behind its windows, elegantly attired visitors strolled among potted date palms and orange trees, plucking ripe fruit as they went. In another he passed a well-tended garden in which a maid sat grooming a miniature dog. Beside her, exotic, fantailed fish swam in a tiny pond whose sides and bottom appeared to be painted with gold leaf.

But that was not all he saw. On the outskirts of the city, only half an hour's walk away, he found coal yards and slaughterhouses, and beyond them, shacks, tents, and mud. Here lived Odessa's homeless poor, on bare fields allotted to them by the authorities.

Drunken men stumbled through puddles, and bitter-eyed women hauled pails of brackish water. Gaunt children and wizened crones poked about in steaming garbage heaps (the city's daily refuse, carted out by horse) and stuffed their pickings into sacks. The food was scanty and only remotely edible – vegetable peels, meat bones and other half-rotten scraps – but they hoarded it as if it were gold. Rachoff was horrified.

Still, despite the acrid odors and the raucous, tattered crowds; despite the grubby boys and girls who flung themselves at Rachoff, vying for his attention and clamoring for coins; despite the clouds of mosquitoes, and the mangy, yapping dogs – or was it because of all these? – he knew he must stay.

At first the squatters stared when they saw he meant to take up quarters with them. Then they mocked him, especially when he spoke of Jesus, whom they scoffed at with foul gestures and jeers. But Rachoff was not easily discouraged. Knowing that God's love is best shown in deeds, he did not try to convince them with words. Eventually he stopped talking altogether. For the next half year, he said almost nothing to anyone. Diligently, silently, and simply, he brought Jesus to the people through his hands, eyes, and heart.

Rachoff helped here, there, and everywhere. In spring he begged planks and nails, rakes, hoes, and seeds from a kindly woman of means, and with her gifts built sheds and straightened paths, dug gardens and sowed vegetables. Soon even the most suspicious no longer looked at him askance, but offered their time and help.

Then, in one night, it all came to an end. Vandals burned his lumber, broke his tools, and scattered his supplies. They even uprooted his seedlings and plants. Heartbroken, Rachoff went back to the donor and threw himself at her feet. This time she refused to help him. Meanwhile the squatters lost confidence in him as well, and on his return they treated him with contempt.

That night Rachoff sequestered himself and prayed for hours. He remained alone the next day too. Then, in the evening, he went into Odessa, to the heart of its grandeur: the opera house.

Rachoff could not have looked more out of place in the brightly lit square. It was opening night, and everywhere he turned there was wealth to be seen. Ornate, horse-drawn carriages came and went, disgorging smiling ladies in evening gowns. Trim escorts breezed by in tails and top hats; ivory canes tapped paving stones; jewels glinted; glasses clinked. But he did not hesitate. Mounting the imposing marble steps, he climbed them, bought (with his last savings) a ticket for a front seat, and walked boldly into the great baroque hall.

Inside, the splendor almost overwhelmed him. Upholstered red seats were filling with well-to-do patrons, and from the velvet-covered balcony boxes above them, cologne wafted down. The air vibrated with titters of anticipation.

Near Rachoff's chair, it is true, the mood was decidedly different. As he seated himself, there was silence, and then looks of revulsion and disbelief. Who was this filthy scoundrel, this unwashed tramp? Who had let him in? Why didn't someone throw him out? Tongues clicked indignantly and someone called for an usher, but it was too late. Already the lights were going out, the curtain lifting. The performance had begun.

Rachoff sat quietly, praying, through the first act. Then, as the curtain fell, he rose suddenly to his feet. Stepping calmly onto his chair, he turned to the audience and spoke in a strong, clear voice.

"Hear me, for Jesus' sake! Rich brothers, rich sisters, for his sake listen quietly to a poor servant of Jesus. If you knew half of what I have seen outside this city, it would bring tears to every kind eye, wrench every compassionate heart. What misery there is; what destitution! Your fellow humans there – no, your brothers – they live like wild animals. Your lapdogs live better than their children! But it need not be so, and wouldn't be, if you shared even a smidgen of your food and clothing, your warmth, comfort, power, or education with them."

There was silence in the great hall, and then a commotion as several guards entered from the back and began to make their way toward Rachoff. He went on, louder: "In a moment I will be removed. But let me first beg you to take this simple message to heart: Jesus is crying out in grief. Jesus is waiting for you to act. May Jesus plant his seed of love within you, and stir every man and woman of good will!"

Then, turning to the guards, who had just surrounded him, Rachoff stretched out his arms. "Here are my hands," he cried. Until this moment, the audience had remained as still as death, but now an astonished murmur rose. Opera glasses were trained on him, and hundreds stood. Few saw his face as he was led away, but those who did said it shone with joy. And those nearest him heard him whisper, as if to himself, "Thank you, dear Jesus, for standing by me."

After his arrest, Rachoff was dragged off to prison, and for weeks nothing more was heard of him. But the uproar he had already caused animated dinner parties and made headlines for days. "A Blow Struck for Jesus." "Madman at the Opera." "Lunatic, or Early Christian?" "A Conspirator for Christ." It was mostly nervous excitement, and after a while the papers lost interest in the story. Some first exploited it shamelessly, of course: one reporter investigated the squatters' camp and wrote the most twisted piece, praising its primitivism and waffling about the "serenity of life untouched by modern complications."

Yet here and there the seeds Rachoff had planted took root and began to grow. Certain reform-minded citizens were so horrified by the poverty they found on the outskirts of town that they rallied the city fathers for measures of relief, pressed local merchants for building supplies and food, and continued to agitate until housing was improved, filth cleared, streets paved, and schools established.

Rachoff never saw the fruits of their work. Charged with inciting a riot, tried, convicted, and banned, he was long gone from Odessa, and out on the steppes, alone with the grass and the sheltering sky, and the songbirds in the clear, blue air.

Turning up some time later in Kiev, or rather in the slums on its outskirts, Rachoff, who was now about thirty, continued to work with the poor. He still spoke of Jesus, too, though his words mostly fell on deaf ears. "Here in Kiev we don't need your Jesus," people told him, shaking their heads or elbowing him good-naturedly. "We have the saints; they're good enough to save the likes of us."

It was true. Kiev did have saints, and plenty of them, as Rachoff soon learned. His guide was Mironoff, a steward in the Lavra Monastery, and one of the only men in the city interested in Rachoff's stories of Jesus.

"Deep in the cellars," Mironoff told him, "lie the saints in which the poor have such great faith. There are hundreds of them. But they are not really saints. They are the embalmed bodies of dead pilgrims and monks, or effigies with heads of wax, and clothing stuffed with wood shavings or straw. The bodies lie one apiece on biers covered with black altar cloths; they are dressed in fine silk, embroidered with silver and gold." Rachoff shuddered. But the next day, after gathering his courage, he joined a troop of worshipers as they entered the underground vaults.

At the entrance stood a corpulent monk with a whip in his hand, demanding the so-called offering without which no one could go in. After pocketing the pilgrims' coins, the monk instructed them not to touch the saints, not to do this, not to do that. The only thing they could do was kiss the saints on the soles of their feet.

Rachoff burned with anger. He looked around at the peasants kneeling everywhere. He breathed in the clamminess of the morgue-like air. He peered at the motionless figures, a cross in each pair of ashen hands, hair combed severely back, a hood drawn stiffly over each lifeless head. A colored lamp swung above him, casting dismal, quivering shadows; a burning censer moved in slow, steady arcs.

Suddenly Rachoff knelt down and called on Jesus in a loud voice, beseeching him to reveal the trickery and put an end to the vile show. Then he sprang up, snatched the whip from the gaping monk, and turned towards the pilgrims. With one kick he knocked a stuffed figure from its platform. "Look!" he cried, as it fell apart in a cloud of shavings. "Here's a good idol for you! Out with you, poor blinded creatures! Out of this cavern of lies!" And he cracked his whip so furiously that the pilgrims fled in terror, the fat monk screaming at their heels.

Rachoff fled the ensuing confusion, but during the night he was found and seized. Lying in prison, he awaited the day of his trial. He planned to defend himself with Holy Writ itself: "Jesus instituted the lash as a sacrament," he would say. "It is a tool with which to drive out hypocrites and liars. And Jesus' disciples, too, must wield it. That is all I have done."

Rachoff spent many days behind bars, but he remained courageous and full of cheer. He knew that the seeds he had planted would remain in the soil of every open heart, and in time they would grow into healing herbs. He planted seeds in the prison too. Formerly the guards had treated the inmates as wild beasts. Now a few, softened by Rachoff's kindness, and made vulnerable by his love, began to see them as brothers – fallen, but still their own kind.

Some even approached Rachoff in his cell, wanting to know how they could find happiness for themselves. But he only said: "We must be hated for Jesus' sake. Suffering is a badge of honor to me." And this was true, for whenever Rachoff met with new humiliations or indignities, he did not grumble, but laughed: "Another medal, then!" That was the secret of his indestructible joy.

Rachoff was never brought to trial, for in order to avoid the shame of public exposure, the monastery decided to suppress the incident. Eventually he was released and banished to his hometown, Archangelsk.

At first he stayed at his father's house. Then he moved into the city, where he walked the poorest districts from morning till night, listening and comforting, teaching and offering a helping hand. In this street he bought books and taught the people to write; in the next he gathered the children and read to them from the Gospels. In one alley he made peace between a quarrelling couple; in another he found decent work for a prostitute. Wherever he went he spread Jesus' love, though also his sharpness against lust and deceit. That never earned him praise, of course, but only angry kicks and blows.

With money given him by his parents, Rachoff rented two rooms in the worst place he could find, converted them, and opened a simple restaurant. Even his admirers were skeptical of this venture, for he had no steady source of income. But he did have faith, and that proved sufficient. "Do something for Jesus," was all he ever asked. And he rarely made such an appeal without receiving enough to buy food and fuel, and pay his monthly dues besides.

No meat or alcohol was served at Rachoff's table – no alcohol because it led to drunkenness; no meat because he opposed the slaughter of animals for food. Meals began only when everyone present was seated, and then with a prayer or a few verses from the Bible. Afterward, Rachoff said a blessing: "May this food keep you strong in body and soul. And may it not feed anger or a cruelly lifted arm, but only the hand stretched out in love, only the heart lit by Jesus. May your limbs be turned solely to compassionate and selfless deeds. May your spirit reflect solely the spirit of Jesus."

Word spread, and soon Rachoff was feeding more than a hundred people every day. Many came not only to satisfy their physical hunger but also because they sought comfort, and found it in his words.

Before long, however, shop owners made nervous by the downtrodden hordes alerted the authorities, and citing failure to comply with city regulations, they closed the little restaurant, and then shuttered it for good.

Rachoff was undeterred. "I may be defeated," he said, "Yet Jesus never is. He goes on from victory to victory, and no one can hinder him." And so he went on as confidently as ever.

It was winter now, but he was up with the sun every morning, loading a large sled with provisions and making his way through the drifts. "Perhaps I cannot gather the hungry for food," he explained, "But no one can stop me from carrying it to them." From one wretched house to another he went, pausing to unpack whatever the inhabitants needed most – bread, flour, wood, or coal; sugar or salt; tea or blankets – and then leaving again before they could ask his name.

In one place Rachoff found the men especially coarse and given to drink. Staying with them, he soon found out why: a tavern near the sawmill where most of them worked sold liquor on credit. Many families had been destroyed, and many more faced ruin. He decided to intervene. Arriving at the mill each day before the first shift began, he gathered the workers and led them in prayer. He also set up a fund for mutual aid, organized the purchase of allotments for gardens, and encouraged those who could to further their studies.

Later, with a sizable contribution from the owners of the sawmill, who were impressed by Rachoff's influence on their workers (and by their increased productivity, now that they no longer drank), he founded an orphanage. Or so people said. Rachoff himself insisted, as he did about everything, that Jesus was behind it all: "I only oversaw construction."

At first the orphanage took in only street urchins, of whom there were plenty in the city; later it also welcomed children from families who couldn't make ends meet. Eventually it held some forty boys and girls. Rachoff cared for his charges day and night: teaching and tending them, feeding them and lulling them to sleep. He sang with them, told them stories, sorted out arguments, and helped them with their chores. He played and laughed with them; he taught them finger games and rhymes. Visitors remarked at his tenderness and patience – at how a man could be both father and mother at once.

Rachoff encouraged the older children to do at least one good or chivalrous deed every day. "Go out into the streets," he would say, "and see if there is anyone in need of love. Look out for the old, the weak, the poor, the ill-treated. Do not go by yourselves, but in small groups, and be sure you are back at sunset."

By evening they were traipsing back in twos and threes, glowing with pride and eager to report everything they had done: "We helped a granny stack firewood for her stove." "We washed bad words off a harbor wall!" "We helped a drunk find his way back home." One had run errands for a housewife; another had sat and stroked a wounded dog; these two had swept glass from a shopkeeper's floor; those two had carried coal for a sickly old man. All had wished every person they met a good day, and told them that they brought greetings from Jesus.

"EVERYTHING FOR OTHERS, nothing for myself," and, "Fear no one, love everyone." These were Rachoff's mottoes, and he truly lived by them. He shared everything he had with the poor – with "those dearest to Jesus," as he called them. Once his father gave him a fur coat, but the next day Rachoff met a half-dressed beggar shivering in the street and gave it to him. And he never wore gloves, even though he was always receiving them from people who noticed his red hands. "Don't worry about me," he would say, accepting them, but telling the donor that he planned to pass them on. "The poor hardly know what gloves look like. I can always beg a pair if I really need to."

There were two other mottoes Rachoff followed as well: "Do not eat if you know of someone who needs the food more than you do," and, "Do not go to sleep before everyone you know has found a bed." That is why he could often be seen at night, roaming the streets and making sure that there was no one without shelter.

By this time there was hardly a citizen in the area who did not know of Rachoff. Most admired him, though some affirmed his goodness secretly, for he was (how should they put it?) so mystical, so eccentric, so naïve. To the poor, of course, he was nothing less than a saint. A few even took him to be the Savior himself, and now and then an old woman would try to kiss his hand. When that happened, it took all Rachoff had to keep from exploding. "How could I be Jesus?" he would passionately exclaim. "I am only a man, whereas Jesus is both man and God. He is eternal. Yes, he lives within me, but I am only a house of clay. I will perish, and when I crumble into dust, Jesus will travel on until he finds a new heart in which to make his home."

But if the masses in Archangelsk looked up to Rachoff, the authorities (especially the heads of the Orthodox Church) lost little love on him. Unnerved by his growing fame, they shook their heads and muttered of heresy. Then they approached the secret police. After that spies kept watch over his daily activities, though try as they might they could find no grounds for arrest.

Some people said he spoke against the saints. Yet there stood every icon, displayed in the prescribed way, in a prayer corner hung with red cloth. Others said he used only the Bible, and dismissed all other holy books. Yet when they searched his simple room, nothing heretical could be found; indeed, every book in it bore the seal of official approval.

Nevertheless the evil intrigue continued. Forget the particulars: it was clear to anyone that Rachoff was an apostate from the Church, that his teachings were unorthodox, that his charisma was dangerous, and that he confused all who listened to him with his endless talk of Jesus.

One bright autumn morning Rachoff was unexpectedly seized, charged with heresy, and thrown behind bars. News of his arrest spread like wildfire, and when word got out that he had declined the assistance of a lawyer – "God will represent me," he reportedly said – the entire city buzzed.

Fortunately for him, his judge (one Engelhardt, the chief officer of the district administration) was a broad-minded man. His sympathies lay with Rachoff, and he believed him to be innocent. Indeed, he considered dismissing the case and letting Rachoff go, if only to shake up the "lazy, drunken priests." Yet the law was the law, and proceedings were proceedings, so he brought Rachoff before the bench, duly questioned him about his faith, and demanded that he enlighten the court as to the teachings he espoused.

"My teachings?" Rachoff asked, as if surprised. "I advocate nothing but the teachings of Jesus. My sole aspiration is to follow him. That is my life task, and it is in fact every man's. That is all I have ever taught. But do with me as you like; I do not matter. Jesus has lived in my heart for many years, and from the moment he entered it, I ceased to exist. Rachoff is long dead, though he must yet die a thousand deaths. What of it? Jesus lives, and he is always victorious."

Engelhardt was so deeply moved by these simple words that he sat tongue-tied in his chair, and later he sent wheat cakes and milk to Rachoff's cell, and ordered him released. Yet even this was not enough to save Rachoff, for the same day he was recaptured by the spies of the powerful ecclesial court.

To satisfy the indignant people of Archangelsk, a statement was issued by the Orthodox Church: Rachoff was a revolutionary, and on top of that, insane. He was confusing the faithful and disrupting their lives. None of these charges would have stood the glare of truth had they been held to its light, but that did not prevent the church authorities from pressing them.

On the one hand it was sloth. As Rachoff himself had once put it, "The wind from the heights is too strong for those who prefer to drowse amid votive candles." On the other, it was guilt, that burden with which the mildest spring breeze takes on an unkind edge. Finally, it was fear: they knew they were hypocrites and sensed judgment was near. In short, every churchman in Archangelsk knew exactly what drove Rachoff, and it rattled and stung him. It was the spirit of Christ, which those who serve falsehood can neither fathom nor bear.

ON OCTOBER 20, 1894, at eight o'clock in the morning, Rachoff was secretly removed from the city. He was not allowed to bid farewell to anyone. Like his Master he was thirty-three years old. One month later and a thousand kilometers to the south, the forbidding dungeon of the Suzdal Monastery received him into its silence.

Tears were shed in Archangelsk when word of his banishment reached those who loved him. For his parents, the news was a mortal blow. Three months later his mother died of grief, and soon afterward his embittered father, who made repeated unsuccessful petitions on his son's behalf, gave up and died of a broken heart too.

As for Rachoff, he suffered a living death. Held in solitary confinement, he was denied all companionship except that of the vermin who shared his damp cell. All creaturely comforts were denied him, too, save for a musty leaf pile that served as his bed. A small barred window, set high in the wall and impossible to open, let in a small pool of filtered light by day, but otherwise there was none. It was achingly cold. There was food, but it came only at uncertain intervals, and consisted of unappetizing scraps.

Soon fever wracked Rachoff's wasted body. He lay and dreamed a great deal. Often he was delirious, and the visions that tortured him made sleep a descent into hell. "Turn back, you deluded fools!" he would cry in great distress, as if seeing the world's tormented about to fall over a cliff. "You are headed for the Pit. Stop, before it is too late. Stop! Stop!" And then, with muffled screams, "It is arrogance! murder! lust! deceit! Turn away, and follow Jesus! Let Jesus come to you!"

Eventually the warden, a troubled old man made uneasy by Rachoff's words, arranged for him to be transferred to a small stone shed in the monastery garden. The move came almost too late. Rachoff's limbs, once strapping, were now wasted and white, and though he had once brimmed with confidence, his spirit now seemed utterly crushed.

Sunlight, fresh air, and regular food worked wonders, however, and soon Rachoff turned a corner. His emaciated body grew slowly stronger, his dreams became less oppressive, and a new radiance – an ethereal, innocent expression of joy – transfigured his face and did not fade. His mind was now like that of a little child, incapable of anything but simple speech. He was mad, one might say, mentally deranged. Yet who is to say how such matters are viewed in the world beyond?

Rachoff spent the last days of his life sitting in a corner of a small enclosed garden, his eyes closed, a smile playing on his face, his hands folded, his stooped shoulders warmed by the sun. On occasion he circled or swayed with slow steps. "I am dancing," he explained, "for I shall soon see God." He said this almost incredulously, as if not quite able to apprehend such happiness.

Then one day at twilight, in the middle of such a dance, he was seen to stop suddenly and kneel down. Opening his eyes wide, he cried loudly, "Jesus!" Then he slumped forward, his head sinking gently into the thick, deep grass. He saw God.

But that is not all. For though every man's life must come to its end, God's spirit can never be quenched. And even as Rachoff was readied for burial, others were setting out across the land, leaving their plows and nets to follow Him who said, "I am the Way." Thus Jesus wanders on, over steppes and through forests, into hearts and homes. He looks into the eyes of beggars; he blesses children. No spies can prevent him, no magistrates can arrest him, no prison can hold him fast. He can cross every frontier, and walk among us, too. Pray that he may, for we have long had need of him.

Jesus wanders on. So ends the story of every Rachoff.

The Deserted Mine

Ruth Sawyer

Based on a story by Vladimir Nemirovich-Dantchenko

A T THE ENTRANCE of the new mine stood a group of miners. They wore leather jerkins and small lamps that flickered at their belts. The young overseer was talking to the oldest miner, whose gray beard fell untidily over his hollow chest. The old man's breath came in thin, whistling sounds; his black eyes burned like black holes shot through with strange, fantastic light; his feeble arms hung at his sides, his legs tottered under him. They called him Ivan the Silent.

"Listen, old man," said the overseer. "You can never manage the ladders. We'll put you in the bucket and lower you in."

The other miners laughed good-humoredly. "Think of old Father Ivan thinking he could go down the ladders with the best of us. Ho ho!"

Ivan looked at the bucket they were making ready. He hadn't been lowered in a bucket since he was a baby, eighty years ago. He had been born in the old mine – the deserted one. His father had been killed in it; his mother had gone on working in his place so there might be food enough for two when he was born. He had been born down there in the eternal darkness. The first noises he remembered were sounds of picks and blasting rocks. He lay all through his babyhood on an old blanket in a hole, sucking away at his milk rag. His eyes followed the flickerings of his mother's lamp. He learned to walk in the mine, his hand on the ledges of rock; and as he grew he came to know new sounds – rushing water, sudden crashing, swishing, hollow echoes. Sometimes a miner sang; sometimes he swore or groaned. Sometimes there was silence. The silences were terrible.

"Get in, old man," said the overseer.

He pushed him in and Ivan squatted down at the bottom.

"Now in the name of God you'll turn round a bit," said one.

"Look you, we'll get him down in the wink of an eye," said another.

Nevertheless, there was time for many memories as old Ivan swung and creaked down on the rusty chain. He watched the square of daylight over his head dim out until it was only a speck of gray. The lamp at his belt threw timid shadows on the damp trickling walls of the shaft. At last the daylight above him closed its gray eye and he was in the dark.

"Already the shaft is old. Old and rotten. Someday it will come crashing in with all the earth on top of it. Then those who are inside will stay in, and those that are out will stay out."

He said all this to himself. He never spoke aloud. No one had heard him speak in ten years. He stirred his memories about and pulled out one that he liked. He was still very little – talking some – walking as one does in such darkness – listening to everything. He had a friend, an old miner, old as he was himself now. Down there in what he called the comfortable darkness, he had told him about the Lord Jesus Christ.

"I tell you, Ivanovich," he would say, "He has his kingdom here, under the earth, the same as above. He is here, moving about us, often. Listen some day and you will see it is the truth. You will hear the rustle of his garments as he passes through the long galleries. If you are lucky you will see him; if not today, why, then tomorrow."

"And do you see him?"

At the question his friend had laughed in his throat. "Now why should I see him! I am old – everything has grown too thick about me. But when I was little like you, Ivanovich, I heard him often – and saw him. If I had not, how could I be telling you about him now?"

One day his friend was telling him again about Jesus when there came a long sighing. And the sighing changed to a rumble and grumble, and there was a sense of tossing as if Mother Earth was shaking herself. "Pray, Ivanovich," said the old man, and he thrust him down on his knees.

So, for the first time in his life he had prayed. He did not know what this praying was supposed to be like, so all he said was, "Good Jesus, good old Jesus."

He said it over a great many times, and after that he put his hands in his friend's and together they felt their way down to the other end of the pit where his mother had been working. All they found was a mountain of fresh earth, and underneath her boots sticking out. He had tried to get those boots. He had tugged and tugged, but the mine held them fast.

He had a playmate, a little boy like himself. One day they were playing at being miners, each with a pick of his own. Some way a stone became dislodged in the vault over them. It came crashing down, straight on top of the playmate, and that was the end of him. When Ivan was half grown he lost his old friend, too. He tripped on one of the ladders and came tumbling down the shaft. They buried him above ground in the churchyard. He was the only one of all Ivan knew who had been buried above ground.

Ivan grew up and became a miner. His eyes were all now for his pick and the bright masses of ore he struck. He saw Jesus no longer and forgot how his garments sounded rustling through the long galleries. Long ago they had left the old mine, deserted it. The new mine held no memories.

Down went the bucket – down went Ivan. All around him now sounded rushing water. "There is too much water," he said to himself. "If Jesus comes into the new mine he will see it is not safe, that shaft. If he pays no attention to it, it will go quickly one day."

The bucket scraped on the bottom. The old miner got out and shouldered his pickax. He tottered forward, mumbling, "Earth – water – darkness – they are all in God's hands."

He passed other miners, who spoke to him kindly but with humor: "See who comes here!" . . . "Good day, Father." . . . "Here's better walking." He answered them all alike – with a doffing of his old cap. He never spoke.

The gallery where he worked was high. He felt at home here. Sometimes when a terrible feeling of loneliness came over him he would sleep here all night. The comfortable security of the dark – that was the way he felt about it. The sun frightened him: it was too big and blazing. The stars he liked: they were small and friendly. He liked flowers. Sometimes he brought down clumps of sod with daisies growing in them. The water kept them alive for days; they gleamed like stars in the flicker of his lamp.

He began to work. Then he rested – he was tired. He looked out for rock that was not so hard to break. When he had a pile he broke the metal out and put it on the wheelbarrow, to wheel into the main gallery. This was hard work. He stumbled and fell many times. It was exhaustion that felled him. When he passed his fellow workers, one stopped him. "Here, wait a minute, I'll help you."

But another laughed. "What, do you think now that anyone is allowed to help old Father Ivan? He is the proud, ancient one."

Ivan brushed away angrily the one who had come to help. He lifted his shoulders, he straightened his tottering legs, he pushed on with his barrow.

The others watched him go, wagging their heads with approval. "He is as proud as Croesus," laughed one. "He is the ancient child," said another, and tapped his forehead meaningly.

And then someone cried out: "God! What was that!"

A few paces ahead Ivan dropped his barrow and stood huddled over it. No one stirred. It began with a sound of deep breathing, not human but the earth's. It was as if the mountain over them was taking great gusts of air into its lungs. Far off at first, then closer and closer. A rush of wind came upon them and blew out all their lights; water started gushing down on them from everywhere. Miners came running from other galleries like sheep in a pen. Only Ivan stood quite still.

The overseer came hurrying up – he had a lighted torch. They stumbled after him toward the shaft. There they came upon nothing but a mountain of fresh damp earth, and half of the bucket that had lowered Ivan into the mine. Under the earth one could see a face with eyelids set, and far from that a hand still clutching a slice of bread with salt on it. At the bottom of the pile the earth was changing fast to mud. At that rate, Ivan said to himself, it wouldn't take long to flood the mine.

"We are lost!" shouted one miner.

"Caught like rats in a trap!" screamed another.

Panic took them. They dug their nails into the rock that penned them in. They trod on each other; they clawed each other's faces. They cursed like madmen.

"Stop!" The overseer kept shouting at them. "It will not save your skins to kill your neighbors. Come! On to the long gallery – there may be a way out!"

The overseer led. They followed, quieted a little. But in the long gallery it was no better. Air was growing thin; water rushed at their heels. "Half an hour and we'll all be choking," groaned one. "If we knew the way into the old mine!" said another. And another answered, crying out with hope, "Always as a boy I was told there was a way from the new into the old mine."

Hope was killed the next moment. "What of it? No one knows the way. Better die here where we know where we are than go wandering, lost, into strange parts."

Behind them came another sound of shifting earth, soft, caressing. Then a crash: earth, rocks, driving water. Then a tumbling at their very backs. "We can't go back" . . . "We're shut off" . . . "God have mercy on our souls!"

A worse panic took them. They dug like beasts at the mass that shut them in until their nails hung torn and bleeding. They beat at one another with fists as hard as rock. They would have gone quite mad if something had not happened. Ivan took the torch from the overseer and spoke. It was the first time in ten years he had spoken, and the men in their amazement forgot their terror and stopped to listen.

"Hush," he was saying, "keep quiet, you men." His voice was strong, his eyes blazed. "How will we hear the rustle of His garments if you make such noise?"

"Look at him – he has gone mad," whispered one. But they kept listening to him just the same.

He was cocking his ear now, his eyes were searching the dark, narrow passage ahead. He kept sucking his lips in and out in a hushing sound. At last a look of foolish delight swept his face. "Ah, what did I tell you? Look! There He goes, the light about His head, just as I remember seeing it as a child. It is seventy years since I have seen Him."

He swung the torch above his head, beckoning. Then he stepped his way into the passage, crying: "I come, Lord, I come!"

"Stop!" cried the overseer. "What in the name of saints and devils do you see?"

Ivan turned. "See? What you yourself see. Come. It is Jesus. He will lead us safely out." He turned away and started along the passage again, repeating his cry: "I come, Lord, I come!"

Holding their breath, not daring to speak, they followed, to a man. At the end of the passage they came upon a blank wall. No way dismayed, Ivan pointed to the loose earth at the bottom and bade the men dig. "See" – he pointed – "His shining footsteps. He marches through the darkness like the sun."

Amazed, doubting, the men plied their picks. The rock crumbled. In no time there was an aperture. Gusts of fresh air rushed through. The men crowded about the diggers, pulling bits of rock away with their bare hands. Ivan slipped through the opening; the others followed. He led them along winding galleries; he led them through fissures and around yawning chasms where they could hear water rushing forty feet below; along narrow ledges with sheer walls on one side and horrible precipices on the other, where they had to crawl on hands and knees; and always Ivan leading with his cry: "I come, Lord, I come!"

He was sobbing with eagerness now, like a child. In and out, through this gallery and that, he wound. The floor of rock under them now was dry. Water no longer dripped from roof and walls. Suddenly he stopped, stock-still, and looked above his head. The men crowded and looked. They saw a small gray eye. They had reached the shaft of the deserted mine.

A hoarse shout went up, but it died as quickly as it had been born.

"The ladders are rotten as dead fish."

"A man might as well try to climb to heaven on cobwebs."

"What good is it to us to see daylight if we cannot reach it!"

"Let one of us try the ladders," said the overseer. "If one can get to the top, he can fetch ropes for the rest."

They turned, one to another, appraising, comparing. Who was the lightest, the most agile? Who had courage to try? No one noticed Ivan. He was following the rise of the ladders, as if watching for a signal. Suddenly he placed his old tottering legs on the first rung. He was thirty feet up the shaft before the others saw him.

"Merciful God."

"He will fall in a second and come down like a bag of stones."

"Look you," said the overseer. "Ivan is climbing on faith. While his faith lasts, the ladders may hold."

They climbed after him. Quickly, breathlessly; so close they went, it was as if each man mounted on the next man's shoulders. Up and up – they could hear Ivan's panting breath. At last they were above ground; strong Mother Earth was under their feet. Ivan scanned the blazing blue sky over him for an instant. He looked frightened, bewildered. Then he smiled suddenly, his face alight with the radiance of his Lord whom he had followed. Down he went like a tottering old tree. Only the overseer caught his last cry: "I come, Lord, I come!"

The Student

Anton Chekhov

Translated by Constance Garnett

AT FIRST the weather was fine and still. The thrushes were calling, and in the swamps close by some living creature droned plaintively, with a sound like blowing into an empty bottle. A snipe flew by, and the shot aimed at it echoed cheerfully in the spring air. But when it began to get dark in the forest, an unwelcome, penetrating wind blew up from the east, and everything sank into silence. Needles of ice stretched across the pools, and it felt cheerless, remote, and lonely in the forest. There was a whiff of winter.

Ivan Velikopolsky, the son of a sacristan, and a student of the clerical academy, was returning home along the path across the water meadows after a shooting expedition. His fingers were numb and his face burned in the wind. It seemed to him that this sudden onset of cold had destroyed the order and harmony of things, that nature itself felt ill at ease, and that was why the evening shadows thickened more rapidly than usual. All around it was deserted and somehow peculiarly gloomy. The only light was one gleaming in the widows' vegetable plots near the river; the village, over three miles away, and everything in the distance all round was plunged in the cold evening mists. The student remembered that, as he had left the house, his mother was sitting barefoot on the floor in the entryway cleaning the samovar, while his father lay on the stove coughing. As it was Good Friday nothing had been cooked, and the student was terribly hungry. And now, shrinking from the cold, he thought of similar winds blowing in the time of Rurik, Ivan the Terrible, and Peter the Great – during their reigns there had been just the same desperate poverty and hunger, the same thatched roofs with holes in them, ignorance, misery, the same desolation around, the same darkness, the same feeling of oppression – all these had existed, did exist, and would exist, and the lapse of a thousand years would make life no better. And he did not want to go home.

The vegetable plots were called "widows'" because they were kept by two widows, mother and daughter. A campfire was burning brightly with a crackling sound, throwing out light far around on the plowed earth. The widow Vasilisa, a tall, fat old woman in a man's sheepskin coat, was standing by and gazing pensively into the fire; her daughter Lukerya, a little pockmarked woman with a stupid-looking face, was sitting on the ground, washing a cauldron and spoons. Apparently they had just had supper. There was a sound of men's voices; it was the laborers watering their horses at the river.

"So winter's back again," said the student, going up to the campfire. "Good evening."

Vasilisa started, but at once recognized him and smiled cordially.

"Heavens, I didn't know it was you," she said. "That means you'll be a rich man one day."

They talked. Vasilisa, a woman of the world who had been in service with the gentry – first as a wet-nurse, afterwards as a nanny – expressed herself with refinement, and a soft, sedate smile never left her face; her daughter Lukerya, a village peasant woman who had been beaten by her husband, simply screwed up her eyes at the student and said nothing. She had a strange expression, as if she were a deaf-mute.

"It was on a cold night like this that the Apostle Peter warmed himself by a fire," said the student, stretching out his hands towards the flames. "That is to say, it must have been cold then, too. Ah, what a terrible night it must have been, granny! A dreadfully sad, never-ending night!"

He peered into the surrounding darkness, shook his head abruptly, and asked, "I suppose you were at the Twelve Readings from the Gospels yesterday?"

"Yes," Vasilisa replied.

If you remember, at the Last Supper Peter said to Jesus, "I am ready to go with thee into darkness and unto death."

And our Lord answered him thus: "I say unto thee, Peter, before the cock croweth thou wilt have denied me thrice."

After the supper, Jesus went through the agony of death in the garden and prayed, and poor Peter was weary in spirit and faint, his eyelids were heavy, and he couldn't fight off sleep; he fell asleep. Then as you know, Judas the same night kissed Jesus and betrayed him to the torturers. They took him bound to the high priest and beat him, while Peter, exhausted and troubled by anguish and alarm – he didn't have enough sleep, you understand – and feeling that something awful was going to happen on earth at any moment, followed behind. He loved Jesus passionately, to distraction, and now he saw from far off how they beat him.

Lukerya put down the spoons and fixed an immovable stare upon the student.

"They came to the high priest's," he went on.

They began to question Jesus, and meantime the laborers made a fire in the yard as it was cold, and warmed themselves. Peter, too, stood with them near the fire and warmed himself, as I am now. A woman, seeing him, said, "This man was with Jesus, too" – that is as much as to say that he, too, should be taken to be questioned.

And all the laborers that were standing near the fire must have looked at him suspiciously and sternly, as he was taken aback and said, "I know him not."

A little while after, again someone recognized him as one of Jesus' disciples and said, "Thou, too, art one of them," but again he denied it.

And for the third time someone turned to him: "Why, did I not see thee with him in the garden today?" For the third time he denied it. And immediately after that a cock crowed, and Peter, looking from afar at Jesus, remembered the words He had spoken to him at supper. He remembered, he came to himself, went out of the yard and wept bitterly – bitterly. In the Gospel it is written: "He went out and wept bitterly." I can imagine that quiet, terribly dark garden, those dull sobs, barely audible in the silence . . .

THE STUDENT SIGHED and sank into thought. Still smiling, Vasilisa suddenly broke into sobs and large, copious tears flowed freely down her cheeks. She shielded her face from the fire with her sleeve, as though ashamed of her tears, while Lukerya stared at the student and flushed crimson. Her expression became strained and heavy, like that of someone stifling a dreadful pain.

The laborers came back from the river, and one of them riding a horse was quite near, and the light from the fire quivered upon him. The student said goodnight to the widows and went on. And again the darkness was about him and his fingers began to be numb. A cruel wind was blowing – winter had really returned with a vengeance, and it did not seem as if Easter Sunday was only the day after tomorrow.

Now the student thought of Vasilisa: since she had shed tears, all that had happened to Peter the night before the crucifixion must have had some special significance for her.

He glanced back. The solitary fire flickered calmly in the darkness, and no figures could be seen near it now. Once again the student reflected that, since Vasilisa had wept and her daughter had been deeply touched, then obviously what he had just been telling them about events centuries ago had some significance for the present, for both women, for this village, for himself, and for all people. The old woman had wept, not because he could tell the story touchingly, but because Peter was close to her and because her whole being was concerned with what was passing in Peter's soul.

His heart suddenly thrilled with joy, and he even stopped for a minute to catch his breath. "The past," he thought, "is linked to the present by an unbroken chain of events, each flowing from another." And it seemed to him that he had just witnessed both ends of this chain; when he touched one end, the other started shaking.

After crossing the river by the ferry and climbing the hill, he looked at his native village and towards the West, where a narrow strip of cold crimson sunset was glimmering. And he reflected how truth and beauty, which had guided human life there in the garden and in the yard of the high priest's palace and had continued unbroken to the present, were the most important parts of the life of man, and of the whole of terrestrial life. A feeling of youthfulness, health, vigor – he was only twenty-two – and an inexpressibly sweet expectation of happiness, of a mysterious unfamiliar happiness, took possession of him. And life seemed entrancing, wonderful, and endowed with sublime meaning.

A Dust Rag for Easter Eggs

Claire Huchet Bishop

T HERE WERE FIVE CHILDREN talking things over
at the corner of the street of The-Cat-Who-Goes-
Fishing and the Boulevard Saint-Michel in Paris. They
called themselves The Gang of The-Cat-Who-Goes-
Fishing. They had spent countless nights in the same air
raid shelter during the five years of occupation and even
had managed, though they were only children, to play
tricks on the Germans. And now they went to school
together, came back together, and played together on free
days. At this time they were all surrounding ten-year-old
Charles. Remi, who was twelve and the oldest, with his
twin sister Louise, said, "What did the doctor say?"

"He said," answered Charles, "that it was all because
she has not had the proper food for five years – not since
she was born."

Louise said, "It's tough. Your father died a year after he
came back as a prisoner from Germany. And poor Zezette
not knowing him. I remember."

"I remember too," said Remi. "It was the time of the first British air raid."

"No use speaking about that," said nine-year-old Jules. "It's what to do for Zezette now."

"Sure," said Remi. "It makes me sick. I wish we could give Zezette a beautiful Easter. When I think of all the festivals we used to have – Christmas, the New Year, King's Day, Mardi Gras, and chocolate Easter eggs . . ."

"Oh, don't," said Jules sharply. "You and Louise are always talking of Before."

"Well," said Louise hotly, "please yourself. But it's true about oranges on the Christmas tree, and the cake of the kings on Three King's Day, crepes for Mardi Gras, and chocolate eggs at Easter."

Paul, who was eight, said, "Chocolate Easter eggs! If only we would have just plain eggs."

"For Zezette," said Jules.

"That's it," said Charles. "For Easter."

There was a silence. The circle broke, and they all stepped back and leaned against the wall of the house. After a while Louise said, "You must have ration points to buy eggs."

"Yes," said Charles, "Zezette should have one egg a week, you know, being five years old. But you cannot find any. And the last one mother found, a month ago, she had to pay twenty-five cents for. She cannot afford it. She doesn't make enough at the factory."

Jules said, "There are eggs. In the country. If one can go there."

"Yes," said Charles. "That's what the doctor said. But he said you cannot buy in the country with money. You have to have things to exchange."

"Of course!" they all answered at once. They all knew about that. They were used to that Indian way of living – barter, barter for everything.

"And to buy from country people," Jules went on, "you have to have the real thing to offer, like shoes, a wool blanket, a sweater . . ."

"Sure," said Remi. "And nobody has any of those things anymore."

"Except the very rich people," said Paul.

"Come on," said Jules, "there's no use talking. Let's go to the Luxembourg Gardens."

"Goodbye," said Charles, shaking hands with the gang. "Have to get home. It's only four-thirty and mother doesn't come home from work before seven. Have to keep Zezette company."

They said goodbye a little sadly, but not too sadly, because, as Louise said, "Well, that's life." And Charles, wishing he were going to the garden with the gang instead of going up the old stairway alone to take care of Zezette, shrugged his small shoulders and muttered, "That's life."

Yes, they all knew. But on their way to the Luxembourg Garden, Paul, who was the youngest of the four, kept saying as he kicked a stray pebble in front of him, "Plain eggs for Zezette at Easter."

"Shush . . . say . . . ," went on Jules, stopping the others on the Boulevard Saint-Michel. "The Gang of The-Cat-Who-Goes-Fishing should do something about this!"

"Sure," hastened Paul, who was very fond of Zezette. "Zezette belongs to the gang too."

Remi turned to Louise. "You are so good at knitting, Louise. Couldn't you knit something and we would sell it, that is, barter it for eggs?"

"Knit with what?" asked Louise, her eyes blazing. "Are you crazy? There isn't any yarn anywhere," she added bitterly.

They went on walking in silence. No, there wasn't any yarn to be had anywhere. What, what could The Gang of The-Cat-Who-Goes-Fishing find to barter for eggs? And Easter was only a month off. What? What? thought Louise as she lay awake that night. She and Remi lived alone with their father. Her mother had caught a cold during the flight before the German army in 1940 and had died of pneumonia. Louise was the woman of the family now, just as Charles was the man of the family in his home.

Next day was Thursday. There was no school. It was cleaning house day for Louise. She washed, she swept, she ran the dust rag on the floor. She picked up the old wool rag to shake it outside and nearly dropped it in the street. The old dirty rag was a discarded sweater of her mother's, so worn out, so full of holes that Louise had not noticed it before, not really. Carefully Louise spread the rag out on the floor. No, she thought, it's hopeless. Even if I could wash it, it could not possibly be of any use. She sat there on the floor fingering the dirty old thing. Suddenly she picked up the piece, shook it out the window a long time, then brushed it, and set it to soak in a pan of water. She could not spare any soap.

The next day, before going to school, she changed the water which was very black, poured fresh water, and let the rag soak again. At night she changed the water once more and also the next day. On Saturday night, instead of using soap for her own bath, she used it on the rag. And the next day she rinsed and rinsed until the water came all clear. When Remi came around he did not ask any questions, but he said, "Let me wring it dry for you." And later he said, "My room has the afternoon sun. You can put it there to dry."

And Louise said, "That's a good idea. I won't put it right in the sun, but the room is warm." She did, and three days later the old wool rag was dry. It looked awful, but it was pretty clean.

Then Louise started to unravel the whole thing. It took her ages because it was all in pieces and she had to tie the yarn together all the time. But finally she had four big balls of yarn. The next day, when they had said goodbye to Charles after school, she showed the yarn to the rest of the gang. They touched it respectfully, caressed it, ran their cheeks against it, and weighed it in their cupped hands.

Louise said, "I'm going to make a sweater."

"Won't be a pretty color," said Paul.

"What of it?" challenged Remi, somewhat angrily.

"Sure," said Jules. "Take it easy. But Paul is right. That ugly color will make it hard to barter.

"He is right," said Louise. "It should be dyed. But I have no dye," she added sadly.

That evening as she was getting supper there was a knock at the door. It was Jules. He gave her an envelope. "Listen, here is the dye. I stood in line two hours to get matches for the woman who runs the notions store, and in exchange she gave me the dye. Dark blue. That's all she had. So long! All for the gang!" he shrieked, tumbling downstairs.

The yarn was dyed, and Louise began to knit. She was a fast knitter and it was not long before she was working on the last sleeve. It was on a Thursday afternoon, and she took her work with her to show it to the others. Zezette could not get up yet, so Charles would not be able to come to the gardens.

The gang was very excited. Remi was proud of his sister, and they started discussing how many eggs they might get for the sweater. Jules said sharply, "No use kidding ourselves. We won't get much. The wool is too thin in too many places."

Remi snatched the sweater and held it against the sunlight. It was only too true. Louise did not say anything. She felt like weeping. All that work!

Remi said, "Louise, couldn't you fill these thin places? Like embroidering something?"

"With what?" asked Louise bitterly. "There won't be any yarn left."

Paul jumped to his feet. "I know!" he shouted. "Mother has a bagful of tiny pieces of yarn. All colors. She never throws anything away."

"Wonderful," said Louise, brightening up. "I could embroider all the thin places with colored yarn. Oh, Paul! Do you think your mother will let you have it?"

"I am going right home," said Paul, "to work it out. See you tomorrow."

That evening Paul set the table, wiped the dishes, took the garbage downstairs, all without being asked, and to top it all he went to bed without being told twice. When his mother came to say goodnight she said, "What's on your mind?" Paul threw his arms around her neck and said, "How did you know?" and he asked her about the colored pieces of yarn. His mother said, "Those pieces of yarn are very precious nowadays, Paul. You cannot have them to play with."

"I know," said Paul emphatically. "But it's for our gang, you know, The Gang of The-Cat-Who-Goes-Fishing. And we are making something. Something to buy a present for Zezette, who is sick."

"So," said his mother, smiling, "you are trying to barter setting the table, wiping the dishes, taking the garbage down, and going to bed at once, for my little pieces of colored yarn?"

"That's it," said Paul brightly. And as his mother remained silent, he added thoughtfully, "Perhaps that's not enough. You do have to offer a lot to get a little. If you wish, I can do it tomorrow too and the day after, and the rest of the week, and the whole month and . . . and always. Forever."

Mother stroked Paul's hair gently. "Zezette is a nice girl, isn't she? The gang is doing a good thing. You may have the pieces, only a little at a time every day as long as needed, provided that during that time you keep helping me. Is that a bargain?"

"Yes," said Paul, putting his hand in his mother's. Leaning back sleepily on his pillow, he yawned. "Mama, do you think it will take Louise an awfully long time to do the embroidery?"

AND NOW IT WAS HOLY WEEK, and the sweater was finished. It was all dotted here and there with brightly colored flowers and birds. It was unique. Pretty. Beautiful. Remi had been appointed by the gang to go to the country and barter it for eggs. Remi was a Scout, and he had a bicycle. It was Thursday afternoon of Holy Week, and Remi was standing by his bicycle ready to start, and his father was saying, "Rather strange, this outing. And where are you supposed to sleep tonight, Remi?"

Remi said mildly, "On a farm, Papa."

"Look here," said Remi's father, "no matter if you are a Scout, I don't like your riding around alone on country roads at night. You are too young."

"But, Papa, don't you remember last year? I sneaked out alone at night to bring a message to the Resistance."

Louise said, "Please, Papa, let him go. He will be all right. We are not like children of Before."

Remi was riding down the road, his bike bumping continuously through holes. He had gotten out of Paris easily. There was practically no traffic at all, and now he was alone in the middle of the Montmorency Forest. Trees, trees, trees. No houses, no cars except an occasional jeep. As the sun went down, Remi felt his heart thumping more heavily. The sun disappeared before he was out of the forest. In order to save fuel, he would not light up his lantern. He rolled along alone in the quiet twilight. An owl hooted mournfully. A deer leaped across the road. A bat brushed past his hair. Remi gripped the handlebars and went on. He would make it. He would. At last the forest was behind him. Remi stopped and lit his lantern, then continued rolling along the slightly hilly road bordered with poplar trees. By ten o'clock, he decided he had better sleep somewhere. It was still too damp to sleep in the open, but half a mile or so from the road he saw a faint light. He turned onto a side lane and went toward it. He nearly broke his lantern when he bumped suddenly into a pile of rubbish. The farm had been bombed. Remi knocked at the heavy door, and a man's voice asked gruffly, "Who's there?"

"I'm looking for a place to sleep, please," shouted Remi.

The door opened a crack and a storm lantern flashed in Remi's face. "A kid!" said the man. "Come in."

Remi went into a room crowded with all the stuff which had been saved from the bombing. He said, *"Bonsoir, M'sieur, Dame."*

"Bonsoir," said the man. "Park your bike there against the wall. You can sleep on the bench if you want to. There is nothing else." He made a circular motion with his arm. "We have been bombed."

"Yes, I see," said Remi gravely. He looked at the man and the woman standing there. They were young people. They were sad.

Remi said, "It's better if I say now that I can't pay."

"Pay for what?" asked the man.

"For sleeping here tonight."

The man answered, "My idea is that you should not be running along the roads at night alone. But nowadays, children . . . it's not like Before."

"No, it's not like Before," echoed Remi quietly.

The woman went to the cupboard, took a piece of dark bread and a pitcher of milk, and set it on the table.

"Sit down," she said. "And eat. As much as you want."

"But," said Remi, "the money . . ."

"Eat," ordered the man. "The wife told you."

Remi came toward the table. "My name is Remi Rennault," he said.

The man replied, "Ours is Bonnet." They shook hands and the three of them sat down. Remi ate and ate. He was very hungry. He ate the whole hunk of dark bread and drank the whole pitcher of milk. The man and the woman sat looking at him. The man asked how things were in Paris, and if there was enough food. "We cannot send anything to the city. No trucks. No trains. Nothing. Rich people manage to get something from the country. Some farmers are making a lot of money. I don't mean us. We have been bombed. We have just one cow left and a few chickens . . . and," he whispered, "our sorrow."

"Have you a little sister?" asked the woman abruptly of Remi.

"No," said Remi, "but there is Zezette. And it's because of her that I am on the road. I am not on the road for any rich people. I know how it is. But I am here for Zezette."

And he told them the whole story. Zezette's sickness. The doctor's advice. The Gang of The-Cat-Who-Goes-Fishing. The dust rag. The dye. The colored pieces of yarn. The sweater – the eggs. They listened quietly, with a funny expression in their eyes, as if they were about to weep.

"Let us see the sweater," they said. Remi showed it to them.

"Never seen anything prettier," said the woman. "And to think that it all came out of an old dust rag!"

"If you go on a little farther north tomorrow morning," said the man, "there they have not been bombed, and you should be able to get a lot of food in exchange for this sweater." Remi's eyes sparkled.

"You're a good kid," said Madame Bonnet. "I dare say all of you in The Gang of The-Cat-Who-Goes-Fishing are good kids . . . like my little angel who is in heaven," she added softly.

"Stretch out on the bench, Remi," interrupted the man. "*Bonsoir, mon gars.*" He snuffed out the lamp.

WHEN REMI AWOKE the next morning, he saw there was milk again on the table and another piece of dark bread. The sweater was spread on the table and next to it were two dozen eggs.

"*Bonjour,*" said Madame Bonnet. "Come and eat before you go."

"Here are two dozen eggs for Zezette," said Monsieur Bonnet.

"So do you like the sweater?" cried Remi.

"*Mon petit gars,*" said Monsieur Bonnet, "the sweater is worth much more than that. We cannot afford to barter for that sweater. We have been bombed. But here are two dozen eggs for Zezette."

"But," said Remi, "what can I give . . . I don't understand."

"The eggs, we give them to you. No money." And seeing Remi's puzzled expression, Monsieur Bonnet added, "We sort of would like to be honorary members of The Gang of The-Cat-Who-Goes-Fishing, see?"

"Listen, Remi," broke in Madame Bonnet gently. "We had a Zezette too. Only her name was Chlotilde. She would be five years old now. Just like Zezette. She died in the war . . ."

Remi said quietly, "Ah, poor Monsieur and Madame Bonnet. It's very sad. Zezette's father died, my mother, and your little Chlotilde also. It is very sad." They were silent.

"I guess I had better be going," said Remi. He arranged the eggs carefully in the wire basket on his bike, wrapping them in newspapers he had brought with him. They stepped outside. The ruins of the farm looked sadder in the bright morning light.

Monsieur Bonnet said, "Turn left on the main road and go as far as the big crossroad. That's about twenty miles from here. Then turn right and you will see a big prosperous farm. They have not been bombed out. You can barter the sweater, and be sure you get plenty for it."

"Yes," said Madame Bonnet. "Such a lovely thing, well knitted and all those lovely birds and flowers. Now watch that you don't break the eggs . . . It will be two or three weeks before we have another dozen, won't it?" she turned to her husband.

Monsieur Bonnet squared his shoulders and said, "Look here, Remi, I have not asked my wife, but I would like to let you have another two dozen in two or three weeks, for Zezette, if you can manage to come back."

"Do what my husband says, Remi," said Madame Bonnet evenly. "He is the boss."

"I'll come back. I'll manage it." He shook hands with them. "*Au revoir, au revoir,* Monsieur, *au revoir,* Madame." He swung on his bike, turned around, and shouted, "And may the good God bless you and send you another child."

Remi found the way just as Monsieur Bonnet had told him. And at the prosperous farm he bartered the sweater and got in exchange:

5 pounds of new potatoes
a heap of cornfield salad
some apples
1 pound of honey
2 pounds of butter
1 big fat chicken

Remi had a hard time cycling back to Paris. The basket was heavy, and he was holding the bag of apples and potatoes in his left hand, so he had only his right hand to direct the bike and steady himself over the bumps. He reached home after sundown on Good Friday, just as his father was coming in. Then, of course, everything had to be explained. Papa looked very suspicious, then very upset, then very happy. And he said, "Come and kiss me, and you too, Louise. Your mother would be proud of you."

"But Papa," said Louise, "It is not Remi and I only. It's the gang, The Gang of The-Cat-Who-Goes-Fishing. I made the sweater from the dust rag; Jules got the dye; Paul got the colored pieces of yarn to embroider over the thin spots; and Remi bartered the sweater."

"And what did Charles do?" asked Papa.

"He kept Zezette going," said Louise.

"Yes, he did," said Remi. "Kept her company every day. That was the hardest of all."

"Well, well, well," mused Papa. "And now there is all that food. What about having the whole gang here to eat it on Easter Sunday, Louise?"

And they did. The whole Gang of The-Cat-Who-Goes-Fishing was there – Louise, Remi, Paul, Charles, and Zezette, who got up especially for it. What an Easter it was! How they ate! Just like Before. Zezette was presented with the two dozen eggs from Monsieur and Madame Bonnet, and Remi had to say over and over again, "They said so. I can go back and get some more."

Ah yes! It was a beautiful Easter last year.

And now another Easter is coming. Louise, Remi, Jules, Paul, Charles, and Zezette, who is well now, thanks to the eggs of Monsieur and Madame Bonnet: They are all sitting in the Luxembourg Gardens and looking at a piece of paper, a letter which is addressed to Remi and says:

To The Gang of The-Cat-Who-Goes-Fishing:

Monsieur and Madame Bonnet have the joy
of announcing the birth of their daughter,
CHLOTILDE-ZEZETTE-CHARLOTTE-LOUISE-MIMI-
JULIA-PAULETTE BONNET

The Barge-Master's Easter

J. W. Ooms

I KNEW THE MASTER of *Gezina II* well. His boat was a sixty-ton canal barge, with its painted prow and steel frame. It had lovely lines, that inland-water boat. Some years before the war, when I was trying to find out more about the life and sailing of the canal barges, I was able to go on more than one trip with the *Gezina II.*

The master was an incredibly hard worker. He hardly allowed himself time to eat. I still remember once when we were sailing along above Zwolle on the Zwarte Water, the master said to his crewman and me: "Boys, the potatoes are done. I'll pour the water off over the port side and then I'll bring them down into the cabin. You go on down and get grace said."

The crewman and I went down into the tiny cabin, and the master poured off the potatoes. But what happened was that the lid slipped off the pot, and all the steaming contents fell out. Then he called down, "Just say thanks for the meal, boys, the potatoes have gone overboard!" Yes, that was just like him, the burly but honest skipper of the *Gezina II.*

IT WAS IN 1944, some weeks before Easter, that he received rather unusual orders. It was still wartime and the Occupation Authorities commandeered him through the freight office to ship a cargo to Lobith, where it was to be loaded onto a bigger boat. What was unusual was that it was a cargo of twenty-eight large bells taken from various church towers. But the master of the *Gezina II* did not like the sound of the job.

"Trina," he said to his wife, "I won't have anything to do with that cargo! The number of times we have lain moored on a Sunday at some place or other and listened to the church bells ringing! Then we say to each other, 'That's God's voice calling,' and off we go to church. Have I now got to take God's voice out of the country? That I cannot do, Trina. I can't and I won't."

His wife agreed that he was right and nodded her approval. But what would they say? In the war years you had to dance to the tune of the enemy. If you refused you could land up in prison. It was choosing or collaborating. And the captain chose.

"Will I carry away the bells? Never, never! They're going to melt the bells down to make guns and bullets. I'll have no part in that."

So the master wrote to the freight office that he had enough cargo and that he could not take on the freight. A fortnight passed and he heard nothing more about it, so he thought that he had got shot of the thing. He had indeed more than enough freight. There was sugar-beet and grain to be carried. Freight charges were high enough, too, as it was dangerous to sail, with fighter aircraft some-times shooting up inland-water boats. The dangers of war threatened everywhere, on land as on water.

The master thought he had got rid of the problem. But shortly before Easter he received an angry letter. He was ordered to load on the twenty-eight church bells at the Dude Hoofd in Rotterdam within four days, and to ship them to Lobith.

The master of the *Gezina II* took it calmly. He tore the letter into shreds and threw them overboard. "They'll have to order me harder than that," he said.

But four days later – and it was then two days before Easter – the cat was in among the pigeons. The *Gezina II* was lying berthed at the sugar factory in Puttershoek, when two fellows came on board. Actually there were three, but the third stayed on the wharf by the gangway with his rifle on his shoulder.

Now there was no way out of it. If the barger did not take the bells right away to Lobith, it would be regarded as hostile and punished accordingly. His boat, *Gezina II*, would be confiscated. "So, get on with it."

The master spent a good half day with his head bent, pacing up and down the deck. It had cost him much sweat and trouble to become owner of the *Gezina II*. For nine-teen years he had toiled from morning till night to pay off the loan on the boat. Now he had nearly reached the point where he could go to the lawyer Meijer in the Maaskade and say, "Here's the last installment on my loan."

The skipper thought to himself: "What is a boatman without a boat?" At last he said gloomily to his wife, "I'll have to do it after all, Trina. We can't get out of it."

Deep in her heart the woman was glad that her husband had given in, for she too loved the *Gezina II*. Their whole life was tied up with the graceful canal barge.

That same evening he sailed to Rotterdam, and the next day he loaded the bells on at the Dude Hoofd. It was fearfully hard work, even though he had a powerful winch. But church bells are unwieldy things. With those twenty-eight church bells, the *Gezina II* was laden right down below her plimsoll line. An old man had been standing silently on the wharf, watching the loading. When at last the *Gezina II* cast off and was gathering way the old man called out grimly, "Bell-skipper, bell-skipper, watch what you're doing."

They did not make much progress, because during the day the air was quite clear, with hardly any haze over the water, and many British planes were flying about. Every so often, air-raid sirens sounded on land, and that fearsome sound, carried over the waters, reached the ears of the skipper and his wife aboard the *Gezina II*. The skipper pretended to be deaf and dumb. He did not say anything, but his weather-beaten face was strained. Something was going on inside him. He was doing something he did not approve of, something against his conscience. He was carrying bells out of his country, eight and twenty church bells from which the enemy would make guns and bullets.

The barge had reached the neighborhood of Culemborg when British airmen caught sight of it. They first circled it quite high up, then they came diving down, like falcons plunging onto a robin.

The skipper was standing at the tiller. He saw them coming and called, "Trina, take cover, we're being attacked!"

Less than two seconds later, the aircraft's guns started firing. The noise was indescribable: bullets started hitting the bells, ringing them loudly. The whole boat sounded like a peal of bells. It was a truly remarkable sound, with the bronze voices sounding the same deep, imploring tone which had once rung out from belfries all over the countryside. Twice they received the full broadside. Amazingly, the skipper and his wife escaped unscathed. Once the aircraft had flown off to the west, the skipper stood again by the wheel. But his face was incredibly pale and his eyes seemed glazed. The bells were still echoing with a strangely beautiful, and at the same time melancholy, sound.

"D'you hear it now?" called the skipper. "D'you hear it, Trina? It is the voice of God, the same voice that used to call from the church spires on Sundays."

It was too much for the skipper. He collapsed like a sandbag by the tiller. Then Trina saw that they were taking in water. She rushed to the tiller, steered straight for the bank, and threw the grapple onto the land. Then she lowered a pail on a rope into the water and pulled up a pailful. She poured water on the skipper's cheeks and dashed some onto his forehead.

By good fortune the skipper soon came to. But Trina had got the *Gezina II* stuck on the mud bank of a narrow dyke. That was dire necessity, for the water was already gushing in below the waterline.

People came rushing up from all directions, for they had seen the planes attacking and heard the remarkable sound of bullets on bells ringing over the water.

Suddenly Germans appeared out of the air-raid shelter in the neighborhood of the waterway. They soon cleared the onlookers, and then they saw that the boat was making water and would have to be repaired before it could continue on its way. The soldiers were kind to the skipper and his wife.

"Come with us into the shelter," they said. "We shall tell the Kommandant about your rotten luck. Boat-repairers will have to come. But just come on into the shelter. We're celebrating Easter, come and join us!"

What else could the skipper and Trina do? The Germans were friendly, of course, because the skipper had a cargo for their homeland, a contribution to their war machine.

There the skipper and Trina sat, among the German soldiers in the shelter. There were candles set on a rough wooden table. The candle flames flickered restlessly, and just as restlessly a fire was burning in the skipper's heart. He realized he should have said "No!" He should have refused that cargo. He ought never to have given in, never shipped the voice of God out of the country.

But now it had been done, and he could not undo it. His *Gezina II* lay broken against the summer dyke of a waterway, and now he would have to do whatever the Germans commanded him to do. If he refused, they would take *Gezina II* away from him. Confiscated, that's what they had called it. But he could not survive without his boat; *Gezina II* had become part of his life. And now here he was, sitting in an air-raid shelter, right in the midst of the enemy. They offered him schnapps and made it clear to him that he and his wife were to celebrate Easter with them.

There was nothing else to be done. He would have to go along with it because he did not want to risk them taking his boat from him.

A corporal began to read a story. It was an Easter legend.

"I won't listen to it," thought the skipper. "I won't listen to a legend – and certainly not to a legend read by an enemy."

The skipper had often sailed into Germany before: iron ore from Ruhrort, coal from Mannheim. He and Trina understood German very well. No, the skipper did not want to listen. All the same he did listen. Even though there was sometimes a babble of voices, the corporal read on steadily. The story was about one of the soldiers who had to keep watch over the grave where Jesus had been buried. The soldier came from Bethlehem. His father had been a carpenter, and at that time he had received the order to make a crib for the stable of the inn "Good Hope."

The soldier remembered that something special had happened with that crib. When his father had finished the piece, it was discovered that in the wood there was a wonderful marking in the shape of a cross. The father was a pious man, looking for the redemption promised by the prophets. The soldier remembered his father saying to him, "This cross is the sign of a king. One day in this crib the promised king and redeemer will lie as a defenseless human child, but the cross will be a sign of his triumph and his power."

And all at once the soldier at the grave was certain that he was keeping watch over the grave of the promised king. That king had been condemned to the death of the cross and had died on the wood of shame, but would rise again in glory. Then the soldier threw away his arms and he deserted, calling to his companions, "He shall rise again, he shall rise again, it is Easter!"

The skipper and his wife listened to the corporal reading. When he had finished – most of the soldiers had been giving more attention to their drink than to the Easter story – the skipper said to Trina in a subdued voice, "I did not believe in God's promise that he would make everything all right. I let myself carry his voice out of the country. Trina, I did not put my trust in him, I did not believe in Easter. I put my boat above everything else."

Suddenly he turned to the Germans and said, "Even if you take everything from me, I won't take the church bells any further on my ship, Easter bells for you to make into guns. I won't do it; I won't carry the bells a mile further."

The Germans in the shelter did not understand what the skipper was getting at. Had he drunk too much schnapps?

What could the skipper do now? The twenty-eight bells could not be removed and hidden. Not even ten skippers could move a single bell from the hold of the barge without a strong winch. The skipper walked out of the shelter. Trina followed him, tears streaming down her face.

When they were alone together – meantime dusk had fallen over the land – the skipper said, "If I just do nothing, the Germans will bring another boat, and the bells will be loaded onto it and taken to Germany."

Trina sighed. "What can we do? We can do nothing."

They walked along the dyke, the skipper and his wife. They walked back and forth, just as he had used to pace up and down on the deck of his boat. Darkness fell. The two had been walking for hours on the dyke. But when high tide came about midnight, the skipper said, "Trina, I'm hoping to get her moving. We must try to get the *Gezina* off the mud bank at high water. Then I'll pull her over into the middle of the river."

That is what they did, the two of them. They took their most precious belongings from the cabin and put them into the rowing boat. And when the lovely barge lay in the middle of the river, man and wife stepped into the rowing boat. And they had to hurry. They could see how the *Gezina* was already lying deeper and deeper. There was a gurgling sound of water gushing into the hold. Suddenly quite quickly she slipped away, the lovely *Gezina II.* Down she went, and soon there was nothing more to be seen of her.

The skipper and Trina rowed slowly away. They did not get far. Even before they had reached the former towpath, where there is a sharp bend in the Lek, Germans in a patrol boat came upon them. They were taken once more to the air-raid shelter.

"You were ordered to take the bells to Germany, weren't you?" the soldiers accused them harshly. "You are guilty of sabotage."

The skipper kept calm. He pointed to the corporal, who was now sitting with a glass in his hand and appeared to be drunk.

"I did have an order, I did," answered the skipper. "That man read us a story. He gave me the order to believe in the Risen King. And the King said, 'Not through might or power, but through my spirit, shall it happen.'"

"What do you mean?"

"I don't know," said the skipper softly. "All I know is that it is Easter and that Christ has overcome. Easter bells must not become guns. That was a beautiful story, the story of the soldier at the grave. He understood what Easter was all about."

THE PEOPLE IN THE NEIGHBORHOOD no doubt still remember that, a few days after that Easter of 1944, by order of the Occupation, a sunken barge had to be raised because it was blocking the channel in the waterway. Hauled up by three winches from a derrick, the heavy barge was finally raised to the surface. But the bells fell out of the hold and sank again to the muddy bottom.

The skipper lost his *Gezina II.* His boat was confiscated, but he still felt at peace with himself. At least he had stopped them taking away the voice of God, the voice of the bells that every year proclaimed Easter over the land with their metal tongues.

The Ragman

Walter Wangerin Jr.

E VEN BEFORE THE DAWN one Friday morning I
noticed a young man, handsome and strong, walking
the alleys of our City. He was pulling an old cart filled with
clothes both bright and new, and he was calling in a clear,
tenor voice: "Rags!" Ah, the air was foul and the first light
filthy to be crossed by such sweet music.

"Rags! New rags for old! I take your tired rags! Rags!"

"Now, this is a wonder," I thought to myself, for the
man stood six-feet-four, and his arms were like tree limbs,
hard and muscular, and his eyes flashed intelligence.
Could he find no better job than this, to be a ragman in
the inner city?

I followed him. My curiosity drove me. And I wasn't
disappointed.

Soon the Ragman saw a woman sitting on her back
porch. She was sobbing into a handkerchief, sighing, and
shedding a thousand tears. Her knees and elbows made a
sad X. Her shoulders shook. Her heart was breaking.

The Ragman stopped his cart. Quietly, he walked to the woman, stepping round tin cans, dead toys, and Pampers.

"Give me your rag," he said so gently, "and I'll give you another."

He slipped the handkerchief from her eyes. She looked up, and he laid across her palm a linen cloth so clean and new that it shined. She blinked from the gift to the giver.

Then, as he began to pull his cart again, the Ragman did a strange thing: he put her stained handkerchief to his own face; and then he began to weep, to sob as grievously as she had done, his shoulders shaking. Yet she left without a tear.

"This is a wonder," I breathed to myself, and I followed the sobbing Ragman like a child who cannot turn away from mystery.

"Rags! Rags! New rags for old!"

In a little while, when the sky showed grey behind the rooftops and I could see the shredded curtains hanging out black windows, the Ragman came upon a girl whose head was wrapped in a bandage, whose eyes were empty. Blood soaked her bandage. A single line of blood ran down her cheek.

Now the tall Ragman looked upon this child with pity, and he drew a lovely yellow bonnet from his cart.

"Give me your rag," he said, tracing his own line on her cheek, "and I'll give you mine."

The child could only gaze at him while he loosened the bandage, removed it, and tied it to his own head. The bonnet he set on hers. And I gasped at what I saw: for with the bandage went the wound! Against his own brow it ran a darker, more substantial blood – his own!

"Rags! Rags! I take old rags!" cried the sobbing, bleeding, strong, intelligent Ragman.

The sun hurt both the sky, now, and my eyes; the Ragman seemed more and more to hurry.

"Are you going to work?" he asked a man who leaned against a telephone pole. The man shook his head.

The Ragman pressed him: "Do you have a job?"

"Are you crazy?" sneered the other. He pulled away from the pole, revealing the right sleeve of his jacket – flat, the cuff stuffed into the pocket. He had no arm.

"So," said the Ragman. "Give me your jacket, and I'll give you mine."

Such quiet authority in his voice!

The one-armed man took off his jacket. So did the Ragman – and I trembled at what I saw: for the Ragman's arm stayed in its sleeve, and when the other put it on he had two good arms, thick as tree limbs; but the Ragman had only one.

"Go to work," he said.

After that he found a drunk lying unconscious beneath an army blanket, an old man, hunched, wizened, and sick. He took that blanket and wrapped it round himself, but for the drunk he left new clothes.

And now I had to run to keep up with the Ragman. Though he was weeping uncontrollably, and bleeding freely at the forehead, pulling his cart with one arm, stumbling for drunkenness, falling again and again, exhausted, old, and sick, yet he went with terrible speed. On spider's legs he skittered through the alleys of the City, this mile and the next, until he came to its limits, and then he rushed beyond. I wept to see the change in this man. I hurt to see his sorrow. And yet I needed to see where he was going in such haste, perhaps to know what drove him so.

The little old Ragman – he came to a landfill. He came to the garbage pits. And then I wanted to help him in what he did, but I hung back, hiding. He climbed a hill. With tormented labor he cleared a little space on that hill. Then he sighed. He lay down. He pillowed his head on a handkerchief and a jacket. He covered his bones with an army blanket. And he died.

Oh, how I cried to witness that death! I slumped in a junk car and wailed and mourned as one who has no hope – because I had come to love the Ragman. Every other face had faded in the wonder of this man, and I cherished him; but he died. I sobbed myself to sleep.

I did not know – how could I know? – that I slept through Friday night and Saturday and its night, too.

But then, on Sunday morning, I was wakened by a violence.

Light – pure, hard, demanding light – slammed against my sour face, and I blinked, and I looked, and I saw the last and the first wonder of all. There was the Ragman, folding the blanket most carefully, a scar on his forehead, but alive! And, besides that, healthy! There was no sign of sorrow nor of age, and all the rags that he had gathered shined for cleanliness.

Well, then I lowered my head and, trembling for all that I had seen, I myself walked up to the Ragman. I told him my name with shame, for I was a sorry figure next to him. Then I took off all my clothes in that place, and I said to him with dear yearning in my voice: "Dress me."

He dressed me. My Lord, he put new rags on me, and I am a wonder beside him. The Ragman, the Ragman, the Christ!

Easter Under a Park Bench

Kirk Wareham

L OOKS LIKE I'M always getting into trouble for something. Seems like maybe I get into more trouble than all the rest of the boys in Bigelow put together. Funny thing is, I try so hard not to, and the harder I try the worse it gets. Just can't make it out. Lucky for me Dad seems to understand this kind of thing pretty well; seems like maybe he wasn't exactly a cherub when he was a boy.

I'm sitting with Ben Chapman on the school bus, heading down Highway 15. Last day of school before Easter holidays. Can't hardly wait to put away the books; spring is ready to burst out all over and school's no place to be when that happens, as any boy knows.

We're just coming into town past the monastery and Mrs. Acres is driving like a madman as usual, flattening me against the window every time she takes a left turn. On the right turns I pretty near send Ben flying into the aisle, but he's a fast learner and hangs on for dear life.

We swing onto Main Street, a couple blocks from school, where there's this little park with a fountain and a wishing pool and a few benches. Mrs. Acres straightens out onto Main and Ben squashes me up against the window again. I poke him in the ribs and we laugh together.

Suddenly I look out again, back behind us now, at the pool we just went by. I'm drying the steam off the window with my shirt cuff and trying to get a better look. Under one of the benches there's something I didn't notice before, something that looks a lot like a pair of shoes. I stand up and wipe the window fast to get one last look, and then it's gone. I sit down, my mind spinning.

"Ben," I say, and my voice is suddenly dry. "I saw some guy lying under the bench back there. Newspaper covering him over, just his feet sticking out."

"Oh yeah?" says Ben. "Lemme see." He leans across me to get a look.

"Too late," I tell him. "Out of sight."

Ben sits down again. "Probably just some homeless guy up from the city. That's where they usually hang out, you know, in the parks and stuff."

I sink back into my seat, but my mind is going in circles. Why in the world would some guy sleep under a park bench? Why doesn't he go home? Well, maybe he doesn't have one. How come his relatives don't look after him then, take care of him? Maybe he doesn't have relatives, or if he does, maybe they don't care about him. It goes round and round in my head; every way I turn it, I can't figure it out.

All through the school day I'm haunted by that pair of shoes, just can't get it out of my mind. In history class Mrs. Pender is helping Christopher Columbus plan his cargo on the Santa Maria back in 1492. Don't forget his shoes, I'm thinking. In math class we're calculating average income per capita and I'm thinking of some guy with zero income. Can't shake the image of those shoes. Can't concentrate on schoolwork. Imagine, some guy spending Easter under a park bench!

And then I get this crazy idea. Mom's going to blow her stack. Dad? Well, like I said, he's got a way of snoring through an earthquake; probably won't bother him in the least. Dad always says he and Mom are not cut from the same cloth; still, they love each other and I guess that's what counts.

Bell rings after eighth period. I grab my backpack, but this time I don't take the usual ride with Mrs. Acres. I take the side door. Heading off up Darley Avenue the second-guessing begins. Maybe I should talk to Dad first and visit the guy tomorrow. No, can't do that, tomorrow's Good Friday. Maybe he'd be gone by then anyway.

It's only two blocks to the fountain, but I get nervous as I approach the park. What if he's mean, or worse still, dangerous? Will there be other people around? What if he doesn't want to talk?

I can see the spray from the fountain and other people walking by on the sidewalk, so I press on. At last I can see the area with the benches. On the far side there's some guy sitting, just sitting there. He looks up as I approach.

"Hi, boy." His long hair is tied back in a ponytail and his bushy beard is a tangle of white and black strands, mostly white it looks like. His eyes are wild and haunting, but I can't look away. It's like I can see miles through him. He coughs a couple times.

"Hello," I say, and stand there awkwardly. Then my tongue kicks into high gear. "This morning I was riding the school bus past here and I saw someone sleeping under the bench. It bothered me, couldn't get it out of my mind all through school. So I thought . . . maybe after school . . ." My thought kind of trails off into nowhere. Truth is, it never was really clear in my mind what I was coming here for.

He doesn't answer. Just sits and looks at me, seems to be thinking this over.

So I ask him right out. "Were you sleeping under that bench?"

"Yep," he says slowly. "I was sleeping under that bench. So it bothered you, huh? How come?"

"I'm not sure," I tell him. "Just seems like everybody should have a home, I guess."

This seems to please him some; his muscles relax a bit and he doesn't seem quite so suspicious. "Yep," he says, "I've been around a bit. I guess I haven't seen the inside of a house for quite awhile. But don't worry about it, boy, I get along." He coughs again, then shifts a little on the hard bench, sort of gathering himself together.

I'm quiet, thinking this over. I'm bothered all the more by what he says. Just doesn't make sense. He looks thin to me, so I ask him "Do you get enough to eat?"

Now he's quiet and this faraway look comes into those eyes again. He squints and looks hard at me. "Hunger's a relative thing, boy. Take yourself for example. If you're used to eating at five and you don't get home to dinner till nine tonight, you'll think yourself starving, right? Then there are the folk in third-world countries who think having a bowl of rice twice a day is a feast. It's all relative, you see."

I can't stop staring at this guy. I'm more used to three-piece suits and ties, meticulously trimmed mustaches, and matching cufflinks.

"Homelessness has been going on for centuries," he says to me. "Even back in Bible times. Jesus himself was a homeless man, no place to rest his head, it says."

That's a new thought to me. Most of what I've heard in church has Jesus sitting on a throne at the right hand of God, King of Kings and all that. But it makes sense what the guy says. Jesus was a wanderer, poor and despised.

Before I can ask another question he beats me to the punch.

"What day is it tomorrow, do you know?"

"It's Good Friday," I tell him.

"Ah, yes, Good Friday. And what was so good about it, my boy?"

Now that he puts it like that, it's a good question. It stumps me for a minute, and before I can respond he answers his own question.

"Tough question, huh? Well, I'll tell you what was good about it. Men turned away from God and from his ways for thousands of years, scorned his prophets and put them to death. But all was not lost, right? God had an ace up his sleeve. When all else fails, he figured, he'd send down his Son."

"So he sends Jesus to the earth, Christmas, you know. What a great event that was for the whole universe, a tremendous outpouring of love from the Father! And yet the people didn't recognize him. Rather, they were threatened and disturbed by him. So the only way left was for the Son to take on the suffering of the world. Without his suffering, Easter, the victory of life over death, of light over darkness, of good over evil, would have been impossible. That's why it's called Good Friday."

He pauses for a moment as a tall, regal woman walks quickly past, closely followed by a well-groomed poodle on a leash. Disgust darkens her features as she glances our way; it oozes out of her and washes over the two of us like a cold, damp mist. Her glance is aimed at my friend but it hurts me as well. My friend waits until she is well out of earshot.

"Yes, homelessness and suffering, they're two sides of the same knife. There are different kinds of suffering, you know. Some suffering is senseless and cruel and pointless, suffering that seems to have no purpose. This is the hardest to bear. Some suffering is redemptive, because we understand its meaning. Men can suffer incredible tragedy and pain if they can only understand the meaning behind it."

He pauses as a city bus roars by, mute faces staring blankly out of the dirty windows.

"The Bible says that men learn obedience through the school of suffering. Someone who has experienced suffering himself can often give comfort to another who suffers, because they have gone through the valley of darkness themselves. They are able to comfort and encourage, to weep, to laugh, and to sing together with the suffering soul."

I sit down next to him. Never heard anything like this in church.

"I know about this, my boy." He glances over his shoulder. "Look here." Out of the folds of his overcoat he brings a small wooden cigar box. He unhooks the clasp and opens the lid gently, almost reverently. There's this scarlet satin cloth inside and he lifts a fold to expose a photograph, faded but clear. It's a boy about my age. He's got this Pittsburgh Pirates cap on and he's pounding his fist into his glove, face beaming with excitement. It's a beautiful photo. I look at it long and then look up at the man, and I can see the boy grown old and worn and tired. There are tears forming in the corners of his eyes, and as I watch they gather and swell and brim over and trickle down into the matted beard and disappear. I can hear the honk of a car horn behind me and the shouts of children down the street, but here in the park it is absolutely quiet.

"One afternoon at the park I'm hitting him fly balls," he says at last in a whisper. "I take this picture, set the camera down, and hit a long fly ball. It slices into the street. He goes after it, totally forgetting where he is, his whole attention focused on the ball. I scream at him but he doesn't hear. A pickup hits him and keeps right on going. I sit in the street with his head in my lap until the ambulance comes. He looks at me through suffering eyes and whispers, "But Dad, you hit it," "But Dad, you hit it," over and over and over. It cuts deep into my heart, like a condemnation of my soul. I never have a chance to ask his forgiveness; he's gone before he reaches the hospital."

Another pause. "His mother, God bless her, never survived his coming. He was all I had in this world. So I take to the road, searching for a reason for this terrible accident, an answer, a meaning, anything. Haven't found it yet, the redemptive part I mean, the purpose, the meaning." Then he's crying, softly but painfully, and the weeping is mixed with coughing.

I can feel the pain, the terrible suffering that pours out of the man. I don't know what to do or say, so I do what comes naturally. I reach out and take his hand and bury my face in his coat. I cry for his suffering, for the suffering of the world. I can feel his arms close around me and I can feel the sobs come deep. They shake his whole body for a minute and then subside slowly, like the tide going out. I can feel the hurt draining away, and I understand how pain and suffering are lightened when shared with another.

He closes the lid of the box, puts it away, and swings his sleeve across his eyes. "I'm still looking, boy," he says.

It's only then I realize how late it is. "I want you to come and spend Easter with us," I tell him. "I'm going to tell my Dad and Mom and tomorrow we'll be down to pick you up. We have plenty of room. OK?"

I look deeply into his eyes, then turn and walk off.

Next morning, after the Good Friday service, my Dad and I arrive at the park to pick him up. There's a couple of police cars there and yellow tape enclosing the area around the fountain; the whole place is cordoned off.

"What's going on?" my Dad asks one of the officers, a big burly fellow with a crew cut and neatly pressed uniform.

"Not much, sir. Just a homeless fellow from the city, died in the night, apparently of starvation. Clear the area, please."

I think Easter will always be associated with suffering in my mind. Actually, maybe that's its true meaning, after all.

I won't forget him, my friend at the fountain.

The Death of the Lizard

C. S. Lewis

What is it like to be in heaven, or in hell? In C. S. Lewis's book The Great Divorce, *from which this story is taken, we start in a grey and dreary city representing hell (or perhaps purgatory). The narrator, having seen enough of the place to want to leave it, catches a bus leaving town; his fellow riders are a collection of other human souls, the Ghosts. The bus lets out its passengers at the border of a bright land representing heaven. There, kindly Angels meet the Ghosts and offer to help them find full redemption so that they too can enter the bright land. Here we observe one of these interviews.*

I SAW COMING TOWARDS US a Ghost who carried something on his shoulder. Like all the Ghosts, he was unsubstantial, but they differed from one another as smokes differ. Some had been whitish; this one was dark and oily. What sat on his shoulder was a little red lizard, and it was twitching its tail like a whip and whispering things in his ear. As we caught sight of him, he turned his head to the reptile with a snarl of impatience. "Shut up, I tell you!" he said. It wagged its tail and continued to whisper to him. He ceased snarling, and presently began to smile. Then he fumed and started to limp westward, away from the mountains.

"Off so soon?" said a voice.

The speaker was more or less human in shape but larger than a man, and so bright that I could hardly look at him. His presence smote on my eyes and on my body too (for there was heat coming from him as well as light) like the morning sun at the beginning of a tyrannous summer day.

"Yes. I'm off," said the Ghost. "Thanks for all your hospitality. But it's no good, you see. I told this little chap," (here he indicated the lizard), "that he'd have to be quiet if he came – which he insisted on doing. Of course his stuff won't do here: I realize that. But he won't stop. I shall just have to go home."

"Would you like me to make him quiet?" said the flaming Spirit – an Angel, as I now understood.

"Of course I would," said the Ghost.

"Then I will kill him," said the Angel, taking a step forward.

"Oh – ah – look out! You're burning me. Keep away," said the Ghost, retreating.

"Don't you want him killed?"

"You didn't say anything about killing him at first. I hardly meant to bother you with anything so drastic as that."

"It's the only way," said the Angel, whose burning hands were now very close to the lizard. "Shall I kill it?"

"Well, that's a further question. I'm quite open to consider it, but it's a new point, isn't it? I mean, for the moment I was only thinking about silencing it because up here – well, it's so damned embarrassing."

"May I kill it?"

"Well, there's time to discuss that later."

"There is no time. May I kill it?"

"Please, I never meant to be such a nuisance. Please – really – don't bother. Look! It's gone to sleep of its own accord. I'm sure it'll be all right now. Thanks ever so much."

"May I kill it?"

"Honestly, I don't think there's the slightest necessity for that. I'm sure I shall be able to keep it in order now. I think the gradual process would be far better than killing it."

"The gradual process is of no use at all."

"Don't you think so? Well, I'll think over what you've said very carefully. I honestly will. In fact I'd let you kill it now, but as a matter of fact I'm not feeling frightfully well today. It would be silly to do it now. I'd need to be in good health for the operation. Some other day, perhaps."

"There is no other day. All days are present now."

"Get back! You're burning me. How can I tell you to kill it? You'd kill me if you did."

"It is not so."

"Why, you're hurting me now."

"I never said it wouldn't hurt you. I said it wouldn't kill you."

"Oh, I know. You think I'm a coward. But it isn't that. Really it isn't. I say! Let me run back by tonight's bus and get an opinion from my own doctor. I'll come again the first moment I can."

"This moment contains all moments."

"Why are you torturing me? You are jeering at me. How can I let you tear me to pieces? If you wanted to help me, why didn't you kill the damned thing without asking me – before I knew? It would be all over by now if you had."

"I cannot kill it against your will. It is impossible. Have I your permission?"

The Angel's hands were almost closed on the lizard, but not quite. Then the lizard began chattering to the Ghost so loud that even I could hear what it was saying.

"Be careful," it said. "He can do what he says. He can kill me. One fatal word from you and he will! Then you'll be without me forever and ever. It's not natural. How could you live? You'd be only a sort of ghost, not a real man as you are now. He doesn't understand. He's only a cold, bloodless, abstract thing. It may be natural for him, but it isn't for us. Yes, yes. I know there are no real pleasures now, only dreams. But aren't they better than nothing? And I'll be so good. I admit I've sometimes gone too far in the past, but I promise I won't do it again. I'll give you nothing but really nice dreams – all sweet and fresh and almost innocent. You might say, quite innocent . . ."

"Have I your permission?" said the Angel to the Ghost.

"I know it will kill me."

"It won't. But supposing it did?"

"You're right. It would be better to be dead than to live with this creature."

"Then I may?"

"Damn and blast you! Go on, can't you? Get it over. Do what you like," bellowed the Ghost; but ended, whimpering, "God help me. God help me."

Next moment the Ghost gave a scream of agony such as I never heard on Earth. The Burning One closed his crimson grip on the reptile: twisted it, while it bit and writhed, and then flung it, broken-backed, on the turf.

"Ow! That's done for me," gasped the Ghost, reeling backwards.

For a moment I could make out nothing distinctly. Then I saw, between me and the nearest bush, unmistakably solid but growing every moment solider, the upper arm and the shoulder of a man. Then, brighter still and stronger, the legs and hands. The neck and golden head materialized while I watched, and if my attention had not wavered I should have seen the actual completing of a man – an immense man, naked, not much smaller than the Angel. What distracted me was the fact that at the same moment something seemed to be happening to the lizard. At first I thought the operation had failed. So far from dying, the creature was still struggling and even growing bigger as it struggled. And as it grew it changed. Its hinder parts grew rounder. The tail, still flickering, became a tail of hair that flickered between huge and glossy buttocks. Suddenly I started back, rubbing my eyes. What stood before me was the greatest stallion I have ever seen, silvery white but with mane and tail of gold. It was smooth and shining, rippled with swells of flesh and muscle, whinnying and stamping with its hoofs. At each stamp the land shook and the trees dwindled.

The new-made man turned and clapped the new horse's neck. It nosed his bright body. Horse and master breathed each into the other's nostrils. The man turned from it, flung himself at the feet of the Burning One, and embraced them. When he rose I thought his face shone with tears, but it may have been only the liquid love and brightness (one cannot distinguish them in that country)

333

which flowed from him. I had not long to think about it. In joyous haste the young man leaped upon the horse's back. Turning in his seat, he waved a farewell, then nudged the stallion with his heels. They were off before I well knew what was happening. There was riding if you like! I came out as quickly as I could from among the bushes to follow them with my eyes; but already they were only like a shooting star far off on the green plain, and soon among the foothills of the mountains. Then, still like a star, I saw them winding up, scaling what seemed impossible steeps, and quicker every moment, till near the dim brow of the landscape, so high that I must strain my neck to see them, they vanished, bright themselves, into the rose-brightness of that everlasting morning.

While I still watched, I noticed that the whole plain and forest were shaking with a sound which in our world would be too large to hear, but there I could take it with joy. I knew it was not the Solid People who were singing. It was the voice of that earth, those woods and those waters. A strange, archaic, inorganic noise, that came from all directions at once. The Nature or Arch-nature of that land rejoiced to have been once more ridden, and therefore consummated, in the person of the horse. It sang,

> The Master says to our master, "Come up. Share my rest and splendor till all natures that were your enemies become slaves to dance before you and backs for you to ride, and firmness for your feet to rest on.
>
> "From beyond all place and time, out of the very Place, authority will be given you: the strengths that once opposed your will shall be obedient fire in your blood and heavenly thunder in your voice.

"Overcome us that, so overcome, we may be ourselves: we desire the beginning of your reign as we desire dawn and dew, wetness at the birth of light.

"Master, your Master has appointed you forever: to be our king of justice and our High Priest."

"Do ye understand all this, my son?" said the Teacher.

"I don't know about all, sir," said I. "Am I right in thinking the lizard really turned into the horse?"

"Aye. But it was killed first. Ye'll not forget that part of the story?"

"I'll try not to, sir. But does it mean that everything – everything – that is in us can go on to the Mountains?"

"Nothing, not even the best and noblest, can go on as it now is. Nothing, not even what is lowest and most bestial, will not be raised again if it submits to death. It is sown a natural body, it is raised a spiritual body. Flesh and blood cannot come to the Mountains. Not because they are too rank, but because they are too weak. What is a lizard compared with a stallion? Lust is a poor, weak, whimpering, whispering thing compared with that richness and energy of desire which will arise when lust has been killed."

"But am I to tell them at home that this man's sensuality proved less of an obstacle than that poor woman's love for her son? For that was, at any rate, an excess of love."

"Ye'll tell them no such thing," he replied sternly. "Excess of love, did ye say? There was no excess, there was defect. She loved her son too little, not too much. If she had loved him more there'd be no difficulty. I do not know how her affair will end. But it may well be that at this moment she's demanding to have him down with her in Hell. That kind is sometimes perfectly ready to plunge the soul they say they love in endless misery, if only they can still in some fashion possess it. No, no. Ye must draw another lesson. Ye must ask, if the risen body even of appetite is as grand a horse as ye saw, what would the risen body of maternal love or friendship be?"

Mary's Child

The Brothers Grimm

Translated by D. L. Ashliman

NEAR A GREAT FOREST dwelt a woodcutter and his wife with their only child, a little girl three years old. They were so poor that they had no daily bread, and did not know how to get food for her.

One morning the woodcutter sorrowfully went out to his work in the forest. While he was chopping wood, suddenly there stood before him a beautiful, tall woman with a crown of shining stars on her head. She said to him, "I am the Virgin Mary, mother of the child Jesus. You are poor and needy. Bring your child to me, and I will take her with me and be her mother and care for her."

The woodcutter obeyed, fetched his child, and turned her over to the Virgin Mary, who took her up into heaven. There the child fared well: she ate sugar cakes and drank fresh milk, her clothes were of gold, and all the little angels played with her.

When she was fourteen years of age, the Virgin Mary called her one day and said, "Dear child, I am about to make a long journey. Take into your keeping the keys of the thirteen doors of heaven. Twelve of these doors you may open and behold the glory which is within them; but the thirteenth, to which this little key belongs, is forbidden you. Take care not to open it, or you will be unhappy."

The girl promised to be obedient, and when the Virgin Mary was gone, she began to examine the dwellings of the kingdom of heaven. Each day she opened one of the doors, until she had made the round of the twelve. In each of them sat one of the apostles in the midst of great light and splendor. She rejoiced in the magnificence and beauty, and the little angels who always accompanied her rejoiced with her.

Now only the forbidden door remained, and she felt a great desire to know what could be hidden behind it. She said to the angels, "I will not open it all the way, nor will I go inside, but I will unlock it so that we can see just a little through the crack."

"Oh, no," said the little angels, "that would be a sin. The Virgin Mary has forbidden it, and it might easily lead to unhappiness for you."

To that she said nothing, but the desire in her heart was not stilled. On the contrary, it gnawed away, tormenting her, and would give her no rest.

Then one day when the angels had all gone out, she thought, "Now I am quite alone, and I could peep in. If I do, no one will ever know."

She sought out the key, and as soon as she had it in her hand, she put it into the lock and turned it. The door sprang open, and there she saw the Trinity sitting in fire and brilliance. She stayed there a while, looking at everything in amazement. Then she touched the light a little with her finger, and her finger became quite golden. Immediately a great fear fell upon her. She slammed the door shut and ran away.

But her terror would not leave her, do what she might. Her heart pounded furiously and would not become still. The gold, too, remained on her finger and would not go away, no matter how much she washed and rubbed.

It was not long before the Virgin Mary came back from her journey. She summoned the girl and asked her to return the keys of heaven. When the maiden gave her the keys, the Virgin looked into her eyes and asked, "Have you not opened the thirteenth door as well?"

"No!" she replied.

Then the Virgin Mary laid her hand on the girl's heart and felt how it pounded, and saw well that she had disobeyed her order and had opened the door. Then she said once again, "Have you not done it?"

"No," said the girl for the second time.

Then the Virgin Mary noticed the finger which had turned golden from touching the heavenly fire and knew that the child had sinned, and she asked for the third time, "Have you not done it?"

"No," said the girl a third time.

Then the Virgin Mary said, "You have not obeyed me, and you have lied as well. You are no longer worthy to be in heaven."

Then the girl sank into a deep sleep, and when she awoke she lay on the earth in the midst of a wilderness. She wanted to cry out but she could bring forth no sound. She sprang up and wanted to run away, but wherever she turned she was held back by thick hedges of thorns, through which she could not break. In the wilderness where she was imprisoned there stood an old hollow tree, and this had to serve as her dwelling place. She crept into this tree when night came. Here she slept and found a shelter from storm and rain, but it was a miserable life, and bitterly did she weep when she remembered how beautiful it had been in heaven and how the angels had played with her.

Roots and wild berries were her only food, and for these she sought as far as she could go. In the autumn she picked up the fallen leaves and nuts and carried them into the hole in the tree. The nuts were her food in winter, and when snow and ice came, she crept among the leaves like a poor little animal, that she might not freeze. Before long her clothes were ripped to shreds, and one bit after another fell off her.

When the sun shone warmly again, she went out and sat in front of the tree, and her long hair covered her on all sides like a mantle. Thus she sat year after year, feeling the world's pain and misery.

One day, when the trees were once again clothed in fresh green, the king of the country was hunting in the forest. Following a roe deer as it fled into a thicket, he dismounted, tore the bushes asunder, and cut himself a path with his sword. When he had at last forced his way through, he saw a wonderfully beautiful maiden sitting under the tree, covered down to her very feet with her golden hair.

Filled with amazement, he stood still and looked at her. Then he spoke to her and said, "Who are you? Why are you sitting here in this wilderness?"

But she gave no answer, for she could not speak.

The king continued, "Will you go with me to my castle?"

To this she just nodded her head a little. The king took her in his arms, lifted her onto his horse, and rode home with her. When he reached the royal castle, he had her dressed in beautiful garments and gave her all things in abundance. Although she could not speak, she was so beautiful and charming that he fell wholeheartedly in love with her, and it was not long before he married her.

After a year had passed, the queen brought a son into the world. Then the Virgin Mary appeared to her in the night when she lay in bed alone, and said, "If you will tell the truth and confess that you unlocked the forbidden door, I will open your mouth and give you back your speech. But if you persevere in sin and stubbornly deny it, I will take your newborn child away with me."

Then the queen was permitted to answer, but she remained obstinate and said, "No, I did not open the forbidden door." And the Virgin Mary took the newborn child from her arms and vanished with it.

Next morning, when the child was not to be found, it was whispered among the people that the queen was a witch and had put her own child to death. She heard all this and could say nothing to the contrary. But the king would not believe it, for he loved her very much.

When another year had gone by the queen again bore a son, and in the night the Virgin Mary again came to her and said, "If you will confess that you opened the forbidden door, I will give you your child back and release your tongue, but if you continue in sin and deny it, I will take away with me this child also."

Then the queen said again, "No, I did not open the forbidden door," and the Virgin took the child out of her arms and took him away with her to heaven.

Next morning, when it was found that this child also had disappeared, the people declared loudly that the queen had devoured it, and the king's councilors demanded that she be brought to justice. The king, however, loved her so dearly that he would not believe it, and commanded the councilors, under pain of death, not to say anything more about it.

The following year the queen gave birth to a beautiful little daughter, and for a third time the Virgin Mary appeared to her in the night. She took the queen by the hand and led her to heaven, and showed her there her two oldest children, who were playing with the ball of the world. They looked up and smiled at her.

When the queen rejoiced at this, the Virgin Mary said, "Is your heart not yet softened? If you will confess that you opened the forbidden door, I will give you back your two little sons."

But for a third time the queen answered, "No, I did not open the forbidden door." Then the Virgin let her sink down to earth again and took away her third child as well.

Next morning when the loss was reported abroad, all the people cried loudly, "The queen is a witch, for she has devoured her own children – she must be judged!" And the king was no longer able to restrain his councilors.

A trial was held, and since she could not answer and defend herself, she was condemned to be burned at the stake. The wood was collected and piled around her. When she was bound fast to the stake and the fire began to burn round about her, the hard ice of pride melted. Her heart was moved by regret and she thought, "If I could only confess before my death that I opened the door."

Then her voice came back to her, and she cried out loudly, "Yes, Mary, I did it!"

Immediately rain fell from the sky and extinguished the fiery flames. A light broke forth above her, and the Virgin Mary descended with the two little sons by her side, and the newborn daughter on her arm. She spoke kindly to her and said, "Whoever repents a sin and confesses it will be forgiven." Then she gave her the three children, untied her tongue, and granted her happiness for the rest of her life.

The King and Death

Ger Koopman

O NCE UPON A TIME there was a king. His name was Sigmund. He reigned over a large kingdom and was very rich. He fought continually against the countries around his kingdom, and in every war he was victorious. Although he was still young, he was a real fighter. His soldiers loved him. He was always the first in the battle and the strongest on his large, strong white horse, in his purple coat, with his mighty sword in his hand.

Now he was preparing for another battle against one of the countries which he had not yet conquered. Once this country had been conquered, he would be the most high, most mighty king in the world. That was his aim! He was not married. There were princesses enough who would like to marry this young, mighty, and famous king, but he did not think about marrying. All he thought of was the new war for which he was preparing.

And then, suddenly, he became ill, seriously ill. His own doctor, and later many other doctors, came to him to try to help him and to cure him, but nothing helped. He lay on his bed, weak and very angry. But it was useless to be angry; it helped him little. He was nearly the mightiest king of the world, yet all the doctors could not help him. He grew worse and worse. The doctors stood around his bed and looked very serious. They whispered to each other that nothing could help the king.

At that moment, the king saw another person standing at the end of his bed, who had not been there before. "It is Death," the king said quietly, but nobody heard him, and none of the doctors could see Death.

"It is time," Death said softly. "Your time has come, King Sigmund."

"No, no," said Sigmund, "I cannot go with you. There is still so much to be done. I am not married, I have no children; who shall be king when I am not here?"

"Your time has come," Death said again. "There are men enough who would like to be king; do not worry about that."

"But they need me. Everyone can tell you that. Ask my ministers, ask my soldiers, ask everyone. They will all tell you that they need me. They always tell me that if I was not king, everything would go wrong."

Death came a step closer to the king, "I have no more time, King Sigmund; come!"

But the king cried, "I shall give you all my money, all my gold, my diamonds, everything you ask for, if you will let me free."

Death smiled. "What shall I do with gold? I want no money. I only want your life. Why are you so afraid, King Sigmund? You were always so brave."

"I am not afraid, but my people need me!"

Then Death said, "Do you really think so? Well, you can give it a try. I will give you seven days to find out. If you can find someone in those seven days who will die instead of you, you shall be free. It may be an old or a young man, a woman or a girl, a rich man or a poor man – it is all the same to me; but I can give you only seven days, and they must do it free willingly."

When he had said that, he disappeared suddenly. At the same moment, the king felt his strength coming back to him. How the doctors wondered, when they saw the king jumping out of bed! He told them what Death had said to him.

"Oh, that is good," they all said, "that is very easy. We think the prime minister is the man you need!"

"Call him," the king said.

When the prime minister had come, he said, "Oh, that is very easy. We must ask one of your ministers. I cannot do that. You need me!" They called all the ministers. And all the ministers told the king that it was fine, and that he must ask his soldiers, but they themselves would not do it. Did not the king know that they were very important, and that the country needed them?

In the six days that followed, the king raced through his whole kingdom, from south to north and from east to west. He grew more and more angry. There was nobody, really nobody, who would die instead of him. And because Death had told him that they must do it free willingly, he could not force the people. The soldiers would not; the poor people would not, nor the rich people; and even the princesses who had always told him that they so very much wanted to marry him would not die for him.

On the afternoon of the sixth day, he was riding on his horse through a wood, accompanied by many soldiers and high officers. The king stopped suddenly and said to his officers, "Go on. I will stay here for a time. I will follow you soon." He wanted to be alone; he had so much to think about. He thought thus: "All that my people have ever told me is nonsense. They were not interested in the death of their king, only in their own life." He had given his whole life to make the kingdom the mightiest in the world, and now they were not grateful. No one said, "It is worthwhile to die for such a king." No, they all sent him to another. And, as a fool, he had crossed his whole kingdom to beg them to die in his place. He had still another day, but why should he wait any longer? It made no sense. He could call Death now. And rising in his saddle he called loudly, "Come now, Death, come now!"

At the same moment he saw Death coming on a horse, a black horse. Death stopped and said quietly, "You have still another day, O king."

The king bent his head, "I have lost, Death; it is of no use to try any longer. Take me with you!"

Death answered, "You have learned your first lesson. But there is more to learn. Go and follow this path. At the end you will see a little village. But before you come into the village, there is a little house. Stop there and ask for a drink."

"Why?" asked King Sigmund.

"There is no 'why' when you speak with me," Death answered, and disappeared at the same moment.

The king hesitated awhile, but at last he followed the path. Ten minutes later he reached the end of the forest and saw the little house. A woman was sitting outside the house on a bench. She had a baby on her lap. "It is better that they do not know that I am the king," he thought. He stopped his horse, took his purple coat off, bound his horse to a tree, and walked to the house. "Good afternoon," he said to the woman. "Can you give me a drink?"

"Well, stranger," the woman said and stood up, "come in. It is just teatime. We will make a cup of tea. But you must make the fire, because I have to watch the baby." She went into the house, and the king followed her. In the room was an old woman sitting in a chair.

"Who is that?" the old woman asked when she saw the king.

"A soldier, I think, a soldier of the king. He will make a fire for us, Mother, and then we will have a nice cup of tea. Come, stranger, there is the wood. Chop it first!"

The king tried to handle the axe. He had never before lit a fire or chopped wood. While he was busy, the woman talked. "Are you one of the soldiers of the king?"

"Yes," the king said.

"Well then, you can tell me more about him. They told me that he is seriously ill and that he will soon die. Do you think he will?"

"I think so," the king said quietly.

"There is only one thing I hope, and that is, that whoever becomes king in his place will not be such a fighter as King Sigmund. And what use were they, all these wars? My husband was a soldier. He was forced to be a soldier! He was killed in one of the wars. Now I am alone with my mother and my baby. The boy will never have a father. We are poor. I have to work to earn money. My mother takes care of my boy, but she is old. When she dies, what happens then with my boy? And there are thousands of widows in our kingdom! And for what? When he dies, I will not be sad, and I think not many people in the country will be, either!" The king said nothing.

"Uh-oh, stranger," she said, "you handle the axe as though it were a sword. We will never have tea at this rate. Come on, let me do it. Here, you take the baby." She gave the baby to the king. It was a boy, about one year old, a very lively boy. The king was rather anxious, as men are who have never before had a baby in their arms. He was afraid that he would drop him or hurt him. But the little boy laughed at him and pulled at his beard and spoke words which nobody could understand. But it pleased his mother. "He will never play on the knee of his father," she sighed. "I often think how useless all these wars are. Do you like fighting?" she asked suddenly, and looked straight into the eyes of the king.

He bent his head over the boy. "I thought I did, but, well, I do not know," he answered.

"When I was a young girl, my father took me once to the capital, and there we saw the old king, the father of King Sigmund. My father said then, 'That is a good king, my girl. History will never speak about him, because he never fought a war, but the people bless him for that, and that is more important than a name in history.'"

The king said nothing. Tea was ready, and the woman took her baby back. He drank his tea. "I must go," he said finally, and stood up. "Well," he said to himself, when he was riding again through the forest. "That was a lesson. But why must I hear that now, while I have only one day to live? And is the woman right? My ministers never told me that my father was a better king than I. They always agreed with my wars. Where is the right answer?" He sighed.

Suddenly he stopped his horse. Through the trees, he had seen something moving very quickly. He saw that it was Death on his black horse, riding very fast. "Where is he going?" the king asked himself, astonished. He followed him. Death rode faster and faster. The king had the best horse in the kingdom, and now he drove him as fast as he could. He drew nearer and nearer. And then he saw where Death was going. Before him, the king saw high rocks. Between the cliffs, deep down, was a river. A young girl had been picking flowers on the other side of the canyon. She had come too near to the edge, slipped, and fallen. In falling she had caught a branch of a tree, and now she was hanging there on the branch above the deep canyon. When the king saw this, something sprung up in his heart. Here was a fight, a fight against Death. The canyon was wide, and therefore Death chose another way, where it was easier to reach the other side. The king knew that the canyon was too wide to jump over with his horse. "It is the only way," he said. He clamped his teeth together and gave his horse the spurs. His horse flew forward, like an arrow from a bow, and sprung. It was like a miracle, but he reached the other side. The king flew from his horse. "Hold on!" he cried to the girl. The girl looked up. Hope came again into her eyes when she saw him. He descended carefully and reached her. He lifted her up, then took her in his arms in front of him on his horse.

Then he saw Death standing before him. "That was a dangerous thing to do, King Sigmund. But it was a fine sight to see. I will give you another week." Before the king could give an answer, Death had disappeared.

The king brought the young girl to her home. She did not seem to be very shocked, but wanted to know who he was. "I have never seen such a beautiful purple coat before. You look like a king," she said. "And your horse! Did he really jump over the wide canyon? I cannot believe it. It must be the best horse there ever was! Come into my home, then my mother can see you and thank you. I could not have held on any longer; if you had not come – but no, I will not think of it."

The king, however, would not come into her house. He went on alone. There was a strange light in his eyes. "Another week," he said. "A week can be long, if you use it well. First I must see the woman with the baby. I gave her nothing for the tea she offered me."

HE DROVE HIS HORSE quickly to reach the village, and once again, when he came near, he saw Death on his black horse. He raised his eyebrows. "Wherever Death is, there must be a fight," he said to himself, and went faster. But what he saw gave him a shock, worse than any he had ever had before. The little house where he had had his tea, where he had held the boy on his knee, and where the mother, without knowing it, had given him a strange lesson – that little house was on fire. He saw a crowd of people gathered around it. Yet nobody could help. There were flames everywhere. He saw the mother crying, and a few men held her to prevent her running into the house. "Oh, God," he cried, "the little boy must be in the house; Death is going for him!" In his mind, he saw the boy again, pulling his beard and laughing at him. Death hastened on. He flew like the wind on his black horse. But, if ever a horse ran swiftly, it was King Sigmund's white horse at that moment. It went like a whirlwind. The king saw Death reaching the house, climbing off his horse, and going to the window. He did not wait for his horse to stop; he jumped off, and the moment Death was about to enter the house through the window, the king was at his side, pushed him away, and jumped through the window.

The little room was completely filled with flames and smoke. "The boy must still be alive! I am in front of Death," was all the king could think. And then he saw that, like a miracle, a piece of the ceiling had fallen over the cradle in which the baby was sleeping and prevented it from burning. Swiftly he took the little boy in his arms and ran to the window. It was high time. The moment he came out and had given the boy to his mother, he fell down unconscious. A man took his burning coat off and others threw water over him.

Then they heard a loud noise. A band of soldiers came up and cried, "It is the king! The king!" Among the high officers was a doctor; he knelt by the king.

"What has happened?" one of the officers asked.

"Happened?" said one of the crowd. "The mother was out; she works in the village. The boy was sleeping. The old woman was outside on the bench sleeping too. When she awoke, the house was burning. She called us. We could not do anything. The mother came. She wanted to go into the house. We could not allow that. It was too dangerous. And then – oh, I never saw anything like it before – this man came. You say it is the king? Well, I must believe you. They often told me that he was a fighter. He is! How he knew that the boy was in the house, I do not know, but he knew. He came out of the forest like – like a whirlwind, flew off his horse, through the window, and brought the boy out. They told us that the king was ill, that he would die. Well, that was a lie. And it is a lie, too, that our king only thinks of himself. This is a king we can be proud of!"

The people stood in a circle around the king. The woman with the baby in her arms was weeping. "He saved my boy," she said, "and I told him horrible things. I told him that he was a bad king!" At that moment, the people saw the king awake and sit up. It was horrible to see him. His clothes were burned, but the worst thing was his face. He must have been in great pain. It was as though he was looking at someone, but there was nobody in front of him. They saw how he moved his lips, as if to speak. Then they saw how he smiled; he smiled as though he were very happy in spite of his pain! The people looked at each other. What was happening with the king? How could he laugh? Had he gone mad?

WHEN THE KING AWOKE, he saw Death standing before him. He looked serious and said: "We cannot go on like this, King Sigmund! So far you have been my friend. I had only to follow you when you went out for wars, to gather the dead. And now? I cannot move, but you are there before me!"

That was when the king had smiled! He said: "This is what I found out after I had helped the young girl. I was born to be a fighter! I always thought war to be a good thing. But now I know that there is a better fight. The fight against you, Death; but also against all your helpers: illness, poverty, famine. And, oh, if only I had time to live, I would show you how I would fight this war!"

Death answered: "I like a fight. I shall give you another year, and perhaps more. But you must know that you will not see me again, and that I am a fighter, too! Watch out for what is coming your way; if you could see your face, you would stop this fight at once. And this is only the beginning!"

At this the king laughed loudly. "Even when I cannot see you, I know where to find you, and I will be there." He received no answer. Death had disappeared.

They brought the king home. On the journey there, his officers and soldiers wondered how it could be that a man could be in so much pain and still be so cheerful; he always had a smile on his burned face. But in the years that followed – for the king lived a long life – they gradually came to understand why he was so happy. It was the joy of battle: the battle against Death.

The Selfish Giant

Oscar Wilde

EVERY AFTERNOON as they were coming from school, the children used to go and play in the Giant's garden.

It was a large, lovely garden, with soft green grass. Here and there over the grass stood beautiful flowers like stars, and there were twelve peach trees that in the springtime broke out into delicate blossoms of pink and pearl and in the autumn bore rich fruit. The birds sat on the trees and sang so sweetly that the children used to stop their games in order to listen to them. "How happy we are here!" they cried to each other.

One day the Giant came back. He had been to visit his friend the Cornish Ogre, and had stayed with him for seven years. After the seven years were over and he had said all that he had to say, for his conversation was limited, he determined to return to his own castle. When he arrived, he saw the children playing in the garden.

"What are you doing there?" he cried in a very gruff voice, and the children ran away.

"My own garden is my own garden," said the Giant. "Anyone can understand that, and I will allow nobody to play in it but myself."

So he built a high wall all round it, and put up a notice-board which said:

TRESPASSERS WILL BE PROSECUTED

He was a very selfish giant.

The poor children had now nowhere to play. They tried to play on the road, but the road was very dusty and full of hard stones and they did not like it. They used to wander round the high wall when their lessons were over and talk about the beautiful garden inside.

"How happy we were there," they said to each other.

Then the Spring came, and all over the country there were little blossoms and little birds. Only in the garden of the Selfish Giant it was still winter. The birds did not care to sing in it, as there were no children, and the trees forgot to blossom. Once a beautiful flower put its head out from the grass, but when it saw the noticeboard it was so sorry for the children that it slipped back into the ground again and went off to sleep. The only people who were pleased were the Snow and the Frost.

"Spring has forgotten this garden," they cried, "so we will live here all the year round."

The Snow covered up the grass with her great white cloak, and the Frost painted all the trees silver. Then they invited the North Wind to stay with them, and he came. He was wrapped in furs, and he roared all day about the garden, and blew the chimney-pots down.

"This is a delightful spot," he said. "We must ask the Hail on a visit." So the Hail came. Every day for three hours he rattled on the roof of the castle till he broke most of the slates, and then he ran round and round the garden as fast as he could go. He was dressed in gray and his breath was like ice.

"I cannot understand why the Spring is so late in coming," said the Selfish Giant as he sat at the window and looked at his cold white garden. "I hope there will be a change in the weather."

But Spring never came, nor the Summer. The Autumn gave gold fruit to every garden, but to the Giant's garden she gave none.

"He is too selfish," she said.

So it was always winter there, and the North Wind, and the Hail, and the Frost, and the Snow danced about through the trees.

One morning the Giant was lying awake in bed when he heard some lovely music. It sounded so sweet to his ears that he thought it must be the king's musicians passing by. It was really only a little linnet singing outside his window, but it was so long since he had heard a bird in his garden that it seemed to him to be the most beautiful music in the world. Then the Hail stopped dancing over his head, and the North Wind ceased roaring, and a delicious perfume came to him through the open casement.

"I believe the Spring has come at last," said the Giant, and he jumped out of bed and looked out.

What did he see?

He saw a most wonderful sight. Through a little hole in the wall the children had crept in, and they were sitting in the branches of the trees. In every tree that he could see there was a little child. And the trees were so glad to have the children back again that they had covered themselves with blossoms and were waving their arms gently above the children's heads. The birds were flying about and twittering with delight, and the flowers were looking up through the green grass and laughing. It was a lovely scene; only in one corner it was still winter. It was the farthest corner of the garden, and in it was standing a small boy. He was so small that he could not reach up to the branches of the tree, and he was wandering all round it crying bitterly. The poor tree was still quite covered with frost and snow, and the North Wind was blowing and roaring above it.

"Climb up, little boy!" said the tree, and it bent down its branches as low as it could; but the boy was too tiny.

And the Giant's heart melted as he looked out. "How selfish I have been!" he said. "Now I know why Spring would not come here. I will put that poor little boy on the top of the tree, and then I will knock down the wall, and my garden shall be the children's playground forever and ever."

He was really very sorry for what he had done. So he crept downstairs and opened the front door quite softly and went out into the garden. But when the children saw him they were so frightened that they all ran away, and the garden became winter again. Only the little boy did not run, for his eyes were so full of tears that he did not see the Giant coming. And the Giant strode up behind him and took him gently in his hand and put him up into the tree.

And the tree broke at once into blossom, and the birds came and sang on it, and the little boy stretched out his two arms and flung them round the Giant's neck and kissed him.

And the other children, when they saw that the Giant was not wicked any longer, came running back, and with them came the Spring.

"It is your garden now, little children," said the Giant, and he took a great axe and knocked down the wall. And when the people were going to market at twelve o'clock they found the Giant playing with the children in the most beautiful garden they had ever seen.

All day long they played, and in the evening they came to the Giant and bid him goodbye.

"But where is your little companion," he said, "the boy I put into the tree?"

The Giant loved him the best because he had kissed him.

"We don't know," answered the children. "He has gone away."

"You must tell him to be sure and come here tomorrow," said the Giant. But the children said that they did not know where he lived and had never seen him before. And the Giant was very sad.

Every afternoon when school was over, the children came and played with the Giant. But the little boy whom the Giant loved was never seen again. The Giant was very kind to all the children, yet he longed for his first little friend and often spoke of him.

"How I would like to see him!" he used to say.

Years went by and the Giant grew very old and feeble. He could not play about anymore, so he sat in a huge armchair and watched the children at their games and admired his garden.

"I have many beautiful flowers," he said, "but the children are the most beautiful flowers of all."

One winter morning he looked out of the window as he was dressing. He did not hate the Winter now, for he knew that it was merely Spring asleep, and that the flowers were resting.

Suddenly he rubbed his eyes in wonder, and looked and looked. It certainly was a marvelous sight. In the farthest corner of the garden was a tree covered with lovely white blossoms. Its branches were quite golden, and silver fruit hung down from them, and underneath stood the little boy he had loved.

Downstairs ran the Giant in great joy, and out into the garden. He hastened across and came near to the child. And when he came quite close his face grew red with anger, and he said, "Who hath dared to wound Thee?" For on the palms of the Child's hands were the prints of two nails, and the prints of two nails were on the little feet.

"Who hath dared to wound Thee?" cried the Giant. "Tell me, that I may take my big sword and slay him."

"Nay!" answered the Child. "But these are the wounds of Love."

"Who art Thou?" said the Giant, and a strange awe fell on him, and he knelt before the little Child.

And the Child smiled on the Giant, and said to him: "You let me play once in your garden; today you shall come with me to my garden, which is paradise."

And when the children ran into the garden to play that afternoon, they found the Giant lying dead under the tree, all covered with white blossoms.

From The Everlasting Mercy

John Masefield

I DID NOT THINK, I did not strive,
The deep peace burnt my me alive;
The bolted door had broken in,
I knew that I had done with sin.
I knew that Christ had given me birth
To brother all the souls on earth,
And every bird and every beast
Should share the crumbs broke at the feast.

O glory of the lighted mind.
How dead I'd been, how dumb, how blind.
The station brook, to my new eyes,
Was babbling out of Paradise;
The waters rushing from the rain
Were singing Christ has risen again.
I thought all earthly creatures knelt
From rapture of the joy I felt.
The narrow station-wall's brick ledge,
The wild hop withering in the hedge,
The lights in huntsman's upper story
Were parts of an eternal glory,
Were God's eternal garden flowers.
I stood in bliss at this for hours.

O glory of the lighted soul.
The dawn came up on Bradlow Knoll,
The dawn with glittering on the grasses,
The dawn which pass and never passes.

"It's dawn," I said, "and chimney's smoking,
And all the blessed fields are soaking.
It's dawn, and there's an engine shunting;
And hounds, for huntsman's going hunting.
It's dawn, and I must wander north
Along the road Christ led me forth."

So up the road I wander slow
Past where the snowdrops used to grow
With celandines in early springs,
When rainbows were triumphant things
And dew so bright and flowers so glad,
Eternal joy to lass and lad.
And past the lovely brook I paced,
The brook whose source I never traced,
The brook, the one of two which rise
In my green dream in Paradise,
In wells where heavenly buckets clink
To give God's wandering thirsty drink
By those clean cots of carven stone
Where the clear water sings alone.
Then down, past that white-blossomed pond,
And past the chestnut trees beyond,
And past the bridge the fishers knew,
Where yellow flag flowers once grew,
Where we'd go gathering cops of clover,
In sunny June times long since over.
O clover-cops half white, half red,
O beauty from beyond the dead.

O blossom, key to earth and heaven,
O souls that Christ has new forgiven.

Then down the hill to gipsies' pitch
By where the brook clucks in the ditch.
A gipsy's camp was in the copse,
Three felted tents, with beehive tops,
And round black marks where fires had been,
And one old wagon painted green,
And three ribbed horses wrenching grass,
And three wild boys to watch me pass,
And one old woman by the fire
Hulking a rabbit warm from wire.
I loved to see the horses bait.
I felt I walked at Heaven's gate,
That Heaven's gate was opened wide
Yet still the gipsies camped outside.
The waste souls will prefer the wild,
Long after life is meek and mild.
Perhaps when man has entered in
His perfect city free from sin,
The campers will come past the walls
With old lame horses full of galls,
And wagons hung about with withies,
And burning coke in tinkers' stithies,
And see the golden town, and choose,
And think the wild too good to lose.
And camp outside, as these camped then
With wonder at the entering men.
So past, and past the stone-heap white
That dewberry trailers hid from sight,
And down the field so full of springs,
Where mewing peewits clap their wings,
And past the trap made for the mill

Into the field below the hill.
There was a mist along the stream,
A wet mist, dim, like in a dream;
I heard the heavy breath of cows
And waterdrops from th'alder boughs;
And eels, or snakes, in dripping grass
Whipping aside to let me pass.
The gate was backed against the ryme
To pass the cows at milking time.
And by the gate as I went out
A moldwarp rooted earth wi's snout.
A few steps up the Callows' Lane
Brought me above the mist again;
The two great fields arose like death
Above the mists of human breath.

All earthly things that blessed morning
Were everlasting joy and warning.
The gate was Jesus' way made plain,
The mole was Satan foiled again,
Black blinded Satan snouting way
Along the red of Adam's clay;
The mist was error and damnation,
The lane the road unto salvation,
Out of the mist into the light;
O blessed gift of inner sight.
The past was faded like a dream;
There come the jingling of a team,
A ploughman's voice, a clink of chain,
Slow hoofs, and harness under strain.
Up the slow slope a team came bowing,
Old Callow at his autumn ploughing,
Old Callow, stooped above the hales,
Ploughing the stubble into wales;

The Everlasting Mercy

His grave eyes looking straight ahead,
Shearing a long straight furrow red;
His plough-foot high to give it earth
To bring new food for men to birth.

O wet red swathe of earth laid bare,
O truth, O strength, O gleaming share,
O patient eyes that watch the goal,
O ploughman of the sinner's soul.
O Jesus, drive the coulter deep
To plough my living man from sleep.

Slow up the hill the plough team plod,
Old Callow at the task of God,
Helped by man's wit, helped by the brute
Turning a stubborn clay to fruit,
His eyes forever on some sign
To help him plough a perfect line.
At top of rise the plough team stopped,
The fore-horse bent his head and cropped
Then the chains chack, the brasses jingle,
The lean reins gather through the cringle,
The figures move against the sky,
The clay wave breaks as they go by.
I kneeled there in the muddy fallow,
I knew that Christ was there with Callow,
That Christ was standing there with me,
That Christ had taught me what to be,
That I should plough, and as I ploughed
My Savior Christ would sing aloud,
And as I drove the clods apart
Christ would be ploughing in my heart,
Through rest-harrow and bitter roots,
Through all my bad life's rotten fruits.

O Christ who holds the open gate,
O Christ who drives the furrow straight,
O Christ, the plough, O Christ, the laughter
Of holy white birds flying after,
Lo, all my heart's field red and torn,
And Thou wilt bring the young green corn,
The young green corn divinely springing,
The young green corn forever singing;
And when the field is fresh and fair
Thy blessed feet shall glitter there.
And we will walk the weeded field,
And tell the golden harvest's yield,
The corn that makes the holy bread
By which the soul of man is fed,
The holy bread, the food unpriced,
Thy everlasting mercy, Christ.

Sources

THE PUBLISHER HAS MADE EVERY EFFORT to identify the owner of each story in this book, and to obtain permission from the author, publisher, or agent in question. In the event of inadvertent errors, please notify us so that we can correct the next printing.

THE WHITE LILY is an adaptation by Jane Tyson Clement of Frances Jenkins Olcott's story "The Beauty of the Lily" in *The Wonder Garden: Nature Myths and Tales from All the World Over* (Boston: Houghton Mifflin, 1919). Copyright © 2015 by Plough Publishing House.

THE COMING OF THE KING is taken from Laura E. Richards, *The Golden Windows: A Book of Fables for Young and Old* (Boston: Little Brown, 1903).

HOW DONKEYS GOT THE SPIRIT OF CONTRADICTION is taken from André Trocmé, *Angels and Donkeys: Tales for Christmas and Other Times,* trans. Nelly Trocmé Hewett (Intercourse, PA: Good Books, 1998). Reprinted by permission of Nelly Trocmé Hewett and the Swarthmore College Peace Collection.

THE CHURCH OF THE WASHING OF THE FEET is an excerpt from Alan Paton, *Ah, but Your Land Is Beautiful* (New York: Scribner's, 1982). Reprinted with the permission of Scribner Publishing Group, a division of Simon & Schuster. Copyright © 1981 by Alan Paton. All rights reserved.

STORIES FROM THE COTTON PATCH GOSPEL is an excerpt from Clarence Jordan, *The Cotton Patch Gospel: Luke and Acts* (Macon, GA: Smyth & Helwys, 2013). Used by permission of the publisher.

SAINT VERONICA'S KERCHIEF is from Selma Lagerlöf, *Christ Legends,* trans. Velma Swanston Howard (New York: Henry Holt, 1908).

THE WAY TO THE CROSS is an abridged excerpt from Lew Wallace, *Ben Hur* (New York: Grosset and Dunlap, 1880).

ROBIN REDBREAST is from Selma Lagerlöf, *Christ Legends,* trans. Velma Swanston Howard (New York: Henry Holt, 1908).

THE ATONEMENT is an excerpt translated from Ludwig von Gerdtell, *Ist das Dogma von dem stellvertretenden Sühnopfer Christi noch haltbar?* (Stuttgart: M. Kielman, 1905). Translation by Hela Ehrlich and Nicoline Maas. Copyright © 2015 by Plough Publishing House.

THE FLAMING HEART OF DANKO is an abridged excerpt from Maxim Gorky, *Heartache and the Old Woman Izergil,* trans. A. S. Rappoport (London: Maclaren, 1905).

Sources

JOHN is taken from Elizabeth Goudge, *The Lost Angel: Stories* (New York: Coward, McCann & Geoghegan, 1971). Used by permission of Harold Ober Associates. Copyright © 1971 by Elizabeth Goudge.

THE LEGEND OF CHRISTOPHORUS by Hans Thoma is taken from *Legenden: Alte Erzählungen in der Dichtung unserer Zeit,* ed. Fritz Schloss (Sannerz: Neuwerk Verlag, 1920). The version included in this book is adapted from a translation by Francis and Sylvia Beels, copyright © 2015 by Plough Publishing House.

ROBERT OF SICILY is taken from Sara Cone Bryant, *Stories to Tell to Children: Fifty-One Stories with Some Suggestions for Telling* (Boston: Houghton Mifflin, 1907).

TWO OLD MEN is taken from Leo Tolstoy, *Twenty-Three Tales,* trans. Louise and Aylmer Maude (Oxford: Oxford University Press, 1928).

THE GOLDEN EGG by Ivy Bolton is taken from *Easter Chimes: Stories for Easter and the Spring Season,* ed. Wilhelmina Harper (New York: E. P. Dutton, 1942). Used by permission of the Community of Saint Mary.

THE CASE OF RACHOFF is adapted from Eileen Robertshaw's translation of the story "Der Fall Rachoff" by Karl Josef Friedrich in *Die arme Schwester der Kaiserin und andere Gottesfreundgeschichten* (Berlin: Furche Verlag, 1919). Copyright © 2015 by Plough Publishing House.

THE DESERTED MINE is taken from Ruth Sawyer, *The Way of the Storyteller* (New York: The Viking Press, 1942; Penguin Books, 1976). Copyright © 1942, 1962 by Ruth Sawyer; copyright renewed 1970 by the author and 1990 by David Durand and Margaret D. McCloskey. All rights reserved.

THE STUDENT is taken from Anton Chekhov, *The Lady with the Dog: And Other Stories,* trans. Constance Garnett (New York: Macmillan, 1917). The English has been modernized.

A DUST RAG FOR EASTER EGGS by Claire Huchet Bishop is taken from *More Favorite Stories Old and New,* ed. Sidonie M. Gruenberg (New York: Doubleday, 1948).

THE BARGE-MASTER'S EASTER by J. W. Ooms is taken from *The Easter Storybook,* ed. Ineke Verschuren (Edinburgh: Floris Books, 2001). Reprinted by permission of Floris Books, Edinburgh.

THE RAGMAN is taken from Walter Wangerin Jr., *Ragman: And Other Cries of Faith* (San Francisco: HarperSanFrancisco, 1994), 3–6. Copyright © 1984 by Walter Wangerin Jr. Used by permission of HarperCollins Publishers.

Recommended Titles

Bread and Wine
Readings for Lent and Easter

An unparalleled anthology of reflections for Lent and Easter from approximately fifty classic and contemporary Christian writers, including Wendell Berry, G. K. Chesterton, Blaise Pascal, Dorothy Sayers, John Updike, Oscar Wilde.

Home for Christmas
Stories for Young and Old

This companion to *Easter Stories* includes nineteen time-tested favorites by some of the world's most beloved children's authors – Selma Lagerlöf, Ruth Sawyer, Elizabeth Goudge, and Pearl Buck – as well as little-known European stories appearing in English for the first time.

The Secret Flower
and Other Stories

Jane Tyson Clement

A collection of perennial favorites for adults and children alike. "Clement writes with simplicity and directness, probing insistence, and conviction" *(Friends Journal)*.

available at *www.plough.com*
PO Box 398, Walden, NY 12586, USA
Brightling Rd, Robertsbridge, East Sussex TN32 5DR, UK
4188 Gwydir Highway, Elsmore, NSW 2360, Australia